I0690189

LESSER KNOWN MIGRATIONS

by

Sam Red

WIND PUBLISHING
ST. JOHNSBURY

Library of Congress Cataloging-in-Publication Data
Red, Sam

ISBN 9781936711222

1. Fiction

Jacket design by Susanna V. Walden and Nat Elf

Cover paintings by Emil Nolde (1867-1956), from his Caribbean collection. Cover: Island Girl
Back Cover title unknown

First Edition 2012

Published in the United States by
Wind Publishing
394 Railroad Street, Suite 2
St. Johnsbury, Vermont 05819

For Jennifer

Chapter 1

Nicholas Pope
June 22, 2001

The unofficial French possession of Saint Sulpice is one of forty-nine islands to call itself The Jewel of the Caribbean but it is one of only eight to say so in French. Twenty-three towns claim to be that same *bijou* and of these the port of Saint Sulpice is the second largest. It might be first if it would stoop to high-rise condos on the beach and oil slicks in the harbor. As it has been trying without success to stoop to such things for three or four generations, its preservation as a living museum of early colonial splendor is now seen as an unambiguous reflection of God's will and is a matter of much local pride. Late colonial improvements include a power plant that almost always works, tolerable drinking water for a third of its people, and a *quartier* where a little hard currency still confers distinctions that feudalism might have envied. There is also a banking system based on certain well-known features of the Swiss model and for this reason a number of absurdly comfortable exiles pine their lives away on seventeenth-century verandas, eighteenth-century balconies and pre-Cambrian beaches, gazing off to sea and dreaming of home. Home would be where you can eat duck with a little fat on it, take a tram somewhere, see a stranger in galoshes. Home, too, is where they'll send you straight to prison if someone doesn't shoot you first, so let's elevate our conception of this pining above the merely nostalgic and add to it a refined, ironic air of tragic injustice stoically borne.

In 1976, the man named Nicholas Petraki left Chicago for the first time in his life and eventually turned up in Saint Sulpice on the seaplane from Saint Croix. He carried with him a copy of Burton's *Anatomy of Melancholy*, a ridiculously expensive Louis Vuitton bag that he'd bought on a whim in Miami, three rather good suits that he'd had made in Kingston, some shirts, four ties, an extra pair of socks, as many blue jeans as he'd ever owned at one time and a pair of beat-up Florsheim shoes. He wore the shoes for three days while he looked for something more suitable, gave it up, and moved into sandals for life. He wore the blue jeans for years, then paid three hundred dollars a pair for replacements. He could afford them but, still, his suits had only cost two hundred apiece. About once a year, usually early in January, he'd pick up the Burton and resolve to finish it. By 1990 he was up to page seventy-six.

In 2001, on his fiftieth birthday, he took a seaplane back to Saint Croix and bought two pairs of shoes and a ticket to Orlando. He carried with him Burton's *Anatomy of Melancholy*, an interminable English paraphrase of the *Guerre et Paix* of Léon Tolstoï and three Simenons he must have read before but couldn't remember; for the outer man he took six shirts, six pairs of socks and underwear, four pairs of perfectly broken-in blue jeans, a black nylon carry-on bag made in Taiwan and a Canadian passport in the name of Nicholas Pope that had cost him exactly ninety thousand dollars and was good everywhere but Canada. In theory it was good there too but he had been sternly warned that the closer one gets to a hometown one has never seen, the sooner things can start to unravel. It was not a warning that bothered him much. Canada was not Chicago. He and Canada owed each other nothing.

On Saint Croix, Mr. Pope rented a room but his nerves were

playing up a little and instead of sleeping he tried to read his *War and Peace*, as the thing was called. At first he tried to read it silently, then aloud, and then aloud while pacing, but the thing was so ploddingly inferior to the original French that nothing he did could rouse it. In ten long hours it barely managed to kill off Pierre's old man, and that only by faking a prim Edwardian parody of old Bezoukhoff's flamboyant departure. Toward dawn, almost time to board his plane to Orlando, he finally accepted that France and Russia were never going to get around to fighting this time, so he waited until no one was watching and stashed it behind a stack of Zane Greys at the back of the lobby. Then he walked onto the airport shuttle feeling just a little bit silly, which did serve for a while to take his mind off what he was up to.

He had booked a window seat but sat between two thirty-ish French sisters because one had to have the window and the other liked the aisle. Flirting should have been the last thing on his mind but he was still a little nervous and over the years a certain amount of the jive called *galanterie Française* had rubbed off on him, mostly third-hand. But everything he thought to say he imagined them repeating in the customs line, and he bit it off. By means of these cryptic evasions in fluent but oddly-accented French, he unwittingly made himself something of a romantic mystery. He let them hear his French because he'd grown afraid of where his English might land him, and was putting off the moment he'd have to use it. The man called Johnny told him it was fine but, for the soundest of reasons, Johnny had never passed much time in Chicago, so what could he know? Finally Johnny picked eastern Canada for his home just to make him comfortable. Johnny told him to say *oot* a lot and leave the *eh* alone: say *I'm going oot for dinner.* Nick figured that the first time he said anything like that six vacationing Mounties would corner him. Johnny rolled his eyes. "Then you tell them you just spent eight years in LA, and by the way, fuck off." The closer the plane got to Orlando, the smarter Johnny seemed. By the time they were halfway there the sisters were debating whether he was from Interpol or the *Guides Michelin.*

Nick Pope said his goodbyes from the aisle while the women wrestled with too many carry-ons. He didn't wait for any replies, made himself think of Humphrey Bogart and Jean Valjean. That was a bust: he walked off his plane like a shy kid on the first day of school. Jesus, he thought, I'm flashing guilt in neon. Johnny had said, "Of all the Federal employees you need to worry about, and I mean FBI, Treasury, everybody, the best every time, no shit, is the next rank and file customs agent you see. Say you got some hashish in your shoe. You get to the head of the line, one customs guy asks his buddy, 'Hey Frank, you want the old lady with the Belgian lace or the guy with the hash in his shoe?'" Nick picked out a grinning blond fat man and turned him into a tourist on Saint Sulpice. He made the man say, "Damn, they sure do like their dirt, don't they?" He had him shout, "Hey, buddy, anywhere you can get some real food here?" He saw old Sophie Artois try to sell him her tarted up conch shells and watched him twitch in distaste and just a little fear. Nick rebuked him silently. "I'm a proud Canadian citizen and I don't have to put up with your kind." He found that it gave him just enough edge. When he handed over his card and his passport he was feeling quite plausible. He confessed to a liter of Martel and two hundred Caporals because Johnny insisted you should always have something to declare. He said, "Tourism. But if they want me for Mayor of New Orleans I'm taking it." He wasn't even alarmed to be asked to open his bag. Up came *Maigret et l'Homme du Banc.*

"Speak French, Mr. Pope?"

"*Un peu.* Not as much as they'd like in Montreal." Thank you, fatty.

"Us, it's Spanish," agreed the man, in spite of which his badge said he was a Diaz. Then he zipped the bag up and made a mark in chalk on the side.

Six feet past the gate stood a slim young man in black livery, holding a sign that read "Mr. N. Pope." He saw Nick see it and reached out for his bag.

"Sal Ruiz, Mr. Pope. From Johnny."

Nick scarcely heard him. He was gawking. "They all look like tourists," he said.

"They *are* tourists, Mr. Pope. This is Orlando." And flipped open a cell phone and told it, "We're moving."

"Where?"

"You need to rent a car, sir," leaving Nick to wonder why a chauffeur would think so, and then to gaze at all the streamlined bustle, and then just to keep up. But soon they came to an abrupt halt behind a heavyset man struggling to replace some scattered bags onto a cart. Suddenly Ruiz was born again. "We got time sir, right?" he demanded. "So we help the gentleman, right?" Intensely, like, maybe you demure and then I rip out your eyelids. But Nick *did* agree, so this was excessive. And the gentleman needed help because one hand held one of the ubiquitous cell phones, into which he muttered at a fool named Maud who still didn't seem to grasp that her call had made his cart tip over.

Trying to balance a floppy garment bag on a set of golf clubs had Ruiz muttering too. "Well? You going to share it with us?"

The heavyset man had never stopped muttering but now what he muttered was, "Clean. Nobody yet." As Nick mimed wishing for a bungee cord, he realized that the man was now telling Maud, "We need some more tan but the hair's okay. Jeans, medium fade, like new Calvins. Medium brown loafers, no socks, no shirt, sky-blue V-neck pullover, I would say lamb's wool, sleeves pushed halfway up, not rolled, no belt showing, square gold watch with gold mesh band."

"Cashmere, actually," Nick said. He whispered it but even so it didn't come off as he'd intended and he winced as he heard himself.

This had the man, who was kind of shaped like Ernest Borgnine in a corset, sneering openly at poor Maud. "That so, Maudie? The rest okay with you?" Turning red, Nick only nodded. "Man says the sweater's cashmere." Then, a crescendo building, "Thanks for the help gents. I can *manage* the rest, nobody else wants to *catch up* on my freaking *day*."

Ooo, Maudie was going to get it, so they didn't hang around. But nobody seemed to notice and indeed Nick could see that he and young Ruiz were behaving *comme il faut*, that in Orlando and possibly other places, tourists do not *always* stop to explore their mutual amazement at encountering others of their kind.

Approaching a rank of counters, Ruiz stopped. "I'll wait here, sir. I went with you it would look wrong. You got the license, okay? Johnny says use the MasterCard. One way reservation, you turn it in next Friday in Lexington. Insurance and a tank of gas, you did that on the phone. Have both cards out and just give them to her. You're in a hurry, sir. You're important and she's not even a face to you."

Nicholas Pope had a New Brunswick driver's license that had cost thirty thousand and was spotless except for an illegal left turn in 1989. He had a dim curiosity about how it was obtained but the man called Johnny was reassuringly blank. To atone for it he told Nick all about the three credit cards (eight thousand each) – *Someone gets an address they can use, gives themselves a name and opens a checking account. In a month they have eight or ten offers. Helps, you open a couple of store charges. Anyone can do it, go in and pay four hundred down on something that costs six, you'll always get credit on the rest. Then the first thing the store does is they sell your name. You get cards from a few small banks, buy all they'll let you, pay it off fast. You do that on the phone or the Internet, that way you show no ID. This gets the big banks after you. You transfer your balances and they think they just took you. Then when you tell them, now I want a twelve grand limit or I dump you, they believe it 'cause now you got a* profile. *See, there's overhead, and you're doing good to get back eighty percent on what you buy. You got to work it on a certain scale, which we do. You understand, Mr. P, you need to call in and pay the balance when it's due. You forget, we'll cover it but if you don't like their interest, you sure as hell won't like ours.* Nick also had forty thousand in a checking account in Saint John (price, fifty-five) and got a lecture from Johnny on how to top it up. He listened, too, even though he was sure nobody on earth knew more than he did about wiring money and how not to do it. He listened because a little ignorance here on Johnny's part could jail him in an hour, and he was relieved and mortified to learn five or six things he'd never heard before.

Ruiz, too, seemed to be right about everything. The only time the woman saw him was when he took the papers and said, "You've been very kind." Then she looked like she'd been slapped and Nick swore that from then on he'd do just as he was told. He turned away as Ruiz swept past him, telling his phone, "Outside, sir, please," and Nick followed him out the door.

It was a mild day but only after Saint Sulpice. Chubby tourists were melting right and left and it seemed that most of the tourists were chubby, if not worse. Nick and Ruiz stayed back in the doorway, next to a young and emphatically not chubby Hispanic woman in a tight pink suit. "Hi, honey," Ruiz said "In your dreams," she said, grinning. "Give her the folder and your MasterCard," Ruiz said. "You get them back tomorrow night." The woman stepped out, looked both ways, stepped back and said, "Go." They went.

The limousine was immense. Ruiz said, "Please sit with me, Mr. Pope. It's easier to talk." Even the front seat was huge. "Please read this," Ruiz said, and handed him an envelope. "We're driving," Ruiz told his phone. The car crept out of the airport and suddenly shot off at an amazing speed that Ruiz didn't seem to notice. Nick pulled out an itinerary in the names of Mr. and Mrs. Billy Markham, Jacksonville to Nashville. The Markhams took off in five hours.

"I think," Nick said, "that it's time for you to explain what we're up to."

"Soon as I talk to my Auntie Monica. She scolds me for not calling sooner, we're fine. Uncle Raul comes on, we got a change of plans."

Nick watches the trees, the signs, the buildings but mostly the highway. Nicholas Pope has a driver's license that cost thirty thousand US but he's forgotten how to drive a car – not how to make it go but what to do in all this traffic. He's driven a motor scooter for twenty-five years. For the last twenty he's had one that he still thinks of as new. After Jean Pierre changes its spark plug they sit outside over a little rum and discuss the world as men of affairs. On his scooter he winds through ungovernable mobs of people, goats, dogs and chickens, whips around carts and nuns and hasn't worried about hitting one for decades. Driving straight at half the speed of sound, then knowing where to stop or turn – has he really done this before? Ruiz does it all with one hand, singing away in Spanish into his phone.

"Things all right at home?" Nick asks as Ruiz snaps his phone shut.

"I'm a worthless nephew but everything else is fine. Okay. First thing was get you out of the airport, which we just did, okay? Anybody's interested in us, then renting the car makes no sense 'cause why would you when you got a driver? But anybody was interested in us, I'd be heading to the tank for drunk and disorderly, three different guys would fake coronaries and you'd be on your way to Miami in the back of a cargo van. So what the hell, right? It didn't happen. By now

Mr. Pope and his cashmere sweater are on the interstate heading the other way, then on through Georgia up to Nashville. He'll make Atlanta easy by tonight and he'll stay in a nice place where they got hours to bust him, or wire his car, or set up a tag, which means follow him. They don't bust him, he drives the rest of the way tomorrow, except a lot of people watch him and he stops for a while and somebody looks over his car. Understand, they won't find nothing. They don't know about you 'cause if they did, the airport was the place to do it. But you got to be sure and this way you are."

Well that's all right then, Nick thinks. At last I'm finally sure. But maybe Ruiz isn't quite as sure as Nick because just then he cuts through three lanes of honking, squealing traffic and up a ramp. Glancing serenely in his mirror and seeing nothing but the mess he's made, he takes one hand off the wheel so he can wave away any doubts that Nick, against all reason, might still be holding onto.

"So now you're Mr. Billy Markham" – and another wave – "and you're going to pull up at JAX, that's Jacksonville International, in a limo just like a hundred other fine people with expense accounts, except most of them dress better than you going to be dressed by then. But that won't be no problem, 'cause you going to meet Mrs. Markham and fly to Nashville and wait for Mr. Pope to catch up to you. Mrs. Markham, she'll explain the rest. Now we got a extra hour in case we needed it back there. We can get a hamburger up here or there's a place further on, about an hour or so, they got some real nice gator tail or shrimp. You like conch fritters? Got them too."

Somewhat after noon they pulled up to an unpromising roadside bar. Nick had some amazing frogs' legs and a tasteless beer. There was a ball game on and he laughed at himself for expecting to recognize the players. Then he stopped laughing when he realized he'd never heard of either team. In the parking lot Ruiz got out his bag and a rag and wiped off the customs man's chalk mark. He unbuckled the ID tag and put a new one on. "You take this off in Nashville, right?" Then he pulled a couple of boxes out of the back and gave the smallest one to Nick. "Please find one that fits, sir. Ring finger of the left hand, please."

Nick opened it and found half a dozen identical and ostentatious wedding bands.

"Not you, huh?" Ruiz grinned.

"Not really."

"See, that's the point. Nice watch, sir, but please put it in your bag. Take this one."

"Are you really giving me a Rolex?"

Ruiz grinned again. "You're lucky, sir, she'll still be ticking when you land. Sure stands out though, don't it? Now these glasses, please sir."

Aviator style, yellow lenses, no prescription. "I can bend the frame sir, they don't fit." But they did.

"Now sir, you got room in your bag for the shoes you got on? 'Cause if you don't I got this other little bag, you get two carry-ons."

"White sweat socks?"

"What guys like Markham wear with their Nikes. This is five hundred, little money, mostly twenties. Don't use any cards as long as you're Markham, okay? Or Mrs. Markham can pay – one look, everybody'll know you give her your paycheck."

Ruiz gave him a maroon sweatshirt with a hooked green bass jumping right off it. "You maybe want to pack your good sweater sir, it's a little hot for two of them. But get used to this look. You keep your hat on all the time now sir, they told me to tell you. I know, my old man's got a problem with that too."

The hat was silver mesh, like a baseball cap but with another leaping fish.

"Do people really look like this?"

"My advice, sir, is there's a little mirror on your shade. Check yourself out a while, get used to it. Might help a little when you get a look at your wife though, my opinion, nothing could."

Trailer parks and golf courses, mile after mile of pines and half of them burnt. Not just ordinary golf courses but golf palaces, estates, duchies given over to the worship of golf. Were trucks always this big?

"What's a gated community?"

"Oh, man. You really been away, ain't you?"

Nick slept. One minute he thought he was fascinated by everything and the next he was asleep. Waking up, he watched a few more miles go by. Ruiz drove with one finger, nodding slightly to very faint Latin music. Outside, the road seemed unchanged: cars he didn't know, endless trucks, burnt trees, billboards claiming that beautiful places were just down the road. Unspeakably beautiful places, incredibly exclusive and also cheap as dirt.

"Why am I going to Nashville? I mean, why is Markham?"

"Listen to that pure white trash music, sir, why else?"

"There used to be a man named Cash."

"I think there still is sir. I don't see them except when they're selling trucks on TV."

"We sell trucks on TV?"

"Little trucks like everybody drives now sir. You see, there, and over there. Say some redneck gets famous for his singing, they put him in a cowboy hat and make him tell people, since I got so rich and famous I ain't even got to tell you who I am, all I want to do is drive this truck. Don't want to screw, don't want to sing, don't even want to get drunk. Just want to drive my truck in the mud. See, that's what you looking like now sir, one of the people buy into that. That's what makes you safe. Nobody going to expect nothing from you at all."

"And you're not going to tell me anything about my wife."

"Well shit, sir, what kind of woman could you get?"

"You like your work, don't you, Sal?"

"For a simple second generation dude with no ambition, it's about the best you can do. You see that, sir? Outlet mall? You know what they are?"

"I've never seen any of this before."

"Outlet mall, that's what you came here for. Somebody asks where you and Mrs. Markham been, you say Jacksonville, man, they got this great outlet mall. All the conversation you need."

Over a couple of bridges, a river he couldn't name, briefly through a city of brand new skyscrapers that somehow looked like the airport in Orlando, then pulling off with a solid lane of traffic onto a road leading nowhere but with another airport promised in just a mile or two.

"What we do now sir is I pull up at the terminal and let you out. You let me give you your bag, give me a dollar like you think you just put my kids through college and walk on through the door. You was really in character, you could say, 'Take care, Jose' but it's okay to skip that. Inside there's a bar on your left, right inside. You walk in and your honey'll find you. Now you didn't get out of no limo, you came back from the john or something, okay? 'Cause you already checked your big bags and everything and picked up your boarding passes."

"I did? We know that?"

"It's all cool or Uncle Raul would have called about the barbecue. Now you don't need to do no acting, except dumb. You only been gone five minutes, so no 'Hi, sugar, I missed you so much,' which might be kind of hard anyway, you'll see. What you want is a drink and that would be a light beer, or six of them really, 'cause that funky beer's about all you do anymore. Ask what kind of light they got and name one, then drink it like you been waiting your whole life, see, it's a part nobody can overdo. Other than that just follow her lead — with what you both been showing, everybody'll expect that. Only there's two words. You say one, then she says one. Not right off, you work them in. The first word is DiMaggio, that's yours. Her word is Vince."

"What is that about?"

"Hocus pocus, sir, part of the package. For your comfort level, no extra charge."

"*Comfort* level?"

"Some guys, sir, they ain't got the stones for this. They get on that plane and it hits them, hey, how do I know she ain't ATF or something? Not you, sir. You doing fine but we got to keep to the script."

Out of the car, Nick wondered briefly if this was really a different airport, if they hadn't driven in circles for four hours, and he decided to pay attention to his comfort level (and to stop wondering if that was a phrase Ruiz had made up). Putting himself in mind of any buffoon in a Hawaiian shirt handing a dime to a carriage driver in Saint Sulpice, he gave Ruiz a hundred and walked away (he had three thousand in his wallet which maybe he shouldn't have been carrying, oh well). Inside he felt again that he was back where he'd landed. He'd had this feeling several times already – here, on the road, which, had he consulted a map, he'd have been surprised to learn was really several roads – but he hadn't yet recognized this sense of sameness for what it would become quite soon. It hadn't yet challenged his conviction that there was still a country, a country he knew, on the other sides of airports and highways.

In this he was fortunate; at this early point in his homecoming he might not have dealt with it very well.

Chapter 2

Roddy John Hall
1943 – 1972
Nicholas Petraki-Petrov, Anne Marie Marceau, Johnny W.
Spring, 2001

Nick is telling Johnny about Roddy John Hall and his incongruous role in their lives. First he tells him on Anne Marie's balcony, then over a latish lunch back inside, later still while walking around the square, and finally over a bottle of red at the café. Anne Marie drifts in and out, sometimes disappearing for half an hour or more. The story bores and outrages her by turns and with Johnny present she can interrupt no more than the curate's wife might think proper – and that odious constraint she can only protest by scarcely interrupting at all. Intolerably, Nick and Johnny will take this for deference, politeness, even respect. And Johnny wants it told in French, which he's trying (by some people's definition, anyway) to learn although he's left it way too late in life, and dear Nicky is trying to get his English back and probably wondering if he can, so first it's one, then the other and you could go mad waiting for them to switch again. But she is there at the start and so we begin with a dose of the amiable Francophone *Docteur* Neek, arch and languid high table *philosophe*, saucing his facts with a weak and lumpy gruel of wit before passing them out with unctuous care.

Anyone (says *Docteur* Neek) who has spent some time observing games of chance will have noticed prolonged runs of luck that last far longer than the overly informed would think possible. Perhaps it's not luck in the sense that somebody wins or loses continuously. Perhaps nineteen red cards are dealt in a row, and later someone who has never played explains how that's so unlikely as to be practically impossible. But it isn't. It happens all the time. It's always happening somewhere because the world never stops dealing. Roddy John Hall's life was such a run until his twenty-ninth year and as soon as that run stopped another one began that, God willing, is still going strong today.

As a small boy he had plump, ruddy cheeks that aunts and such couldn't help but pinch and remember at Christmas and birthdays. As he grew older he began to look like an athlete without doing anything to earn it. In fact his favorite pastime was eating, but girls were always asking what number he wore on this team or that and when that's the first thing girls think to ask you, it would be churlish not to adjust your ambitions to the market. But his teachers liked him too. He skated through classes on the strength of a good memory and a nonchalance that seemed like charm. Even the other boys liked him, because he was just one of those people good things go looking for, and unlike so many of them, Roddy John Hall never, ever rubbed it in.

So to the University of Illinois with no plans for a major, except he suspected that something in business would pay best. He moved toward his destiny with artless simplicity. When he found a class to his liking, he registered for the next in the series. By the end of his sophomore year this method had revealed that he was to be an accountant, a decision that pleased him because accounting courses were not only very easy but also vaguely interesting. This freed him for the serious business of being sociable and attractive, and as there were plenty of opportunities for both, his life continued very much as a great many people think life ought to do.

In his junior year, his grandmother, adored for her fat capons and roast potatoes and chopped liver, broke her hip, went to bed and died for five weeks – five ghastly weeks to hear of it but the thing was, he didn't hear: he was away at school, wasn't he, and what he heard came in timid, worried little phone calls that barely got through the excitement of this party or that game, and then she was dead: well, a sudden death at the end of a long and useful life: you can deal with that. She really was quite old (but those potatoes, long as any French fry and almost as thin, roasted in the fat of the bird!) There was a sadness, or a *tristesse* as one would say here, but Roddy felt it as a kind of coloration to everything else, a novel tint to his still expanding world that hung on for a while and slipped away the moment he began to tire of it.

Here Anne Marie interrupted to ask Johnny, "Has he ever told you about me? Perhaps that we were lovers once and I behaved this way or that?"

Johnny looked at Nick, who shrugged. "Sure he told me. Who wouldn't?"

"Oh, a few over-bred kinds of man, mostly extinct, such as in fact he now pretends to be. But what I really ask is did he speak of me – like this?"

"Of course not. Why would he?"

"I suppose that is a relief. Possibly all this is true then and even means something. I always hoped that he despised the man at least a little before he destroyed him."

"Anne Marie?" Nick said. "Sorry but I mostly liked Roddy.

Shallowness only being my idea of a flaw when I don't like the surface. Which I thought you'd have noticed by now. In fact, now that I–"

"Nick?" Johnny said. "Anne Marie? Here's my advice. Be like me. Only remember the good times. You broke up so you wouldn't get like this, remember? So why do it anyway?"

One day at the end of Roddy's senior year the recruiters were on campus and he was walking to the student union to stand in line for some interviews. An irritated and out of breath little man in a Madras sport coat and thick bifocals stopped him and asked his way to the same destination. Roddy said he could tell he was there to hire an accountant. The man forgot about being irritated and began to look a little scared. His name was Maloney and he was looking for a cost accountant for Bricker Thresher, world headquarters in downtown Chicago. So, Roddy asked, what's it pay? So, Maloney countered, what are your grades? Neither of them made it to the union and while Roddy's fellow students were hearing consoling words from the Dean about how the job market was bad all over that year, he was packing for a week off before he started his new job. He went to Las Vegas with a friend and won two thousand dollars at blackjack; his stake had been a twenty. He came home for a couple of days, then went up to the near north side to look for a place – but, first, refreshment. At the counter in a pancake house he said hello to a nice old lady and she asked if he knew a quiet, reliable tenant who'd take over that bastard's lease and not leave in the middle of the night. It turned out to be the nicest flat of any of Bricker Thresher's young accountants, and they all loved to come over and have nice, quiet times together.

He then had the good fortune to fall hopelessly in love, and win the girl, and marry her, and learn very soon to take her for granted – so thoroughly for granted that, later, relatively old acquaintances would be quite surprised to learn that he was married. Yes, he would allow, and I'm still hopelessly in love, and then he would change the subject.

Bricker Thresher was into every kind of business you could imagine so long as it had some tenuous connection to farm machinery or agriculture. Roddy found it fascinating. Whenever he felt boredom coming on he was abruptly transferred to something else. He was little more than a gopher, the undermost of underlings, but they handled him well and he felt like a trusted troubleshooter, like the promising rookie brought in to learn the really tough assignments. One day he found a small announcement on the department bulletin board. The company was establishing an inactive joint venture with a West German partner and needed a volunteer to keep its books in addition to his or her regular duties. The job could take up to five hours a week and came with no extra pay. Should the venture go active, which would not happen for at least a year and possibly never, the volunteer could expect serious consideration for a high position in its accounting department. There was a signup sheet next to the note. At the time Roddy was thirty-third on the department's seniority list. He signed.

A week later an amusing old man named Dunphy sat him down and explained it. A large West German agricultural combine called Himmelskirch AG was looking to make its first post-war foray into North America and needed a partner. They had a couple of broadband herbicides – Metamort and Orthotox – which could be expected to do reasonably well in the western US and Canada, but the impetus for the venture was a fiendish worm-killer called Nematodt, which they were looking into renaming Nematotal for the linguistically-constrained US market. Nematodt was effective against *Pratylenchus coffeae* on tobacco, the Columbia lance nematode on soybeans, cotton and alfalfa, and even against *Meloidogyne incognita* on cotton. (Anne Marie's eyebrows are through the roof.) Until recently a nematicide called Slithyban had dominated those markets but, alas, upon mandatory re-registration of the product, the white mice got sick – the real bad kind of sick. Nematodt had no such problems. Nematodt killed any man, woman, worm or mouse straight out, two ways, which had earned it two special, nasty labels. First, Nematodt got a big skull and crossbones for being about as lethal as nerve gas – when you inhaled a single droplet you got maybe a spasm and six twitches before you stayed down for good. Then it got a small skull and crossbones for being an explosive almost as powerful as TNT, though a little less stable. Anything that deadly is incapable of causing cancer in anything and the scant predecessors of the EPA were favorably disposed. Of course there were risks – in Morocco, some fool had tried to remove the top of an empty drum with a cutting torch and afterwards they'd been unable to locate his head – but the great advantage of Nematodt was that, once applied and exposed to oxygen, it did its work in seconds and then decomposed into common, lazy organic compounds. It was approved in seventeen countries and the USDA liked it a lot. What the USDA didn't like was turning over the safety of several strategic crops to a German company, especially one located in Berlin. Hence the need for a joint venture with a US partner, one who'd remain safely at home with all the formulas and the right to use them in the event of whatever, overseas. Bricker was to set the company up; if it did get off the ground, Bricker was to supply the initial staffing. Perhaps nothing would come of it. Perhaps it would be big.

Dunphy liked Roddy and when Dunphy liked you, your life changed in interesting ways. He considered himself a very bad man because he'd studied for the priesthood and quit it. To protect others from themselves he preemptively did every evil thing that seemed to him inevitable – and by the time Roddy met him he had acquired a considerable store of pessimism about what was inevitable at Bricker Thresher. As far as he was concerned, the deadlier the product, the more likely it was to be indispensable to someone and hence the more urgent that he make it his own. This especially applied to what he called the Himmelskirch Thanacopoeia. This was wicked stuff that was sure to get someone in the worst kind of trouble someday, and Dunphy was determined to be at the wrong end of the pointing finger when that happened.

A year passed. Dunphy protected Roddy John Hall by taking him to regular lunches in a delightful throwback of a downtown restaurant. There men of Dunphy's generation subsisted amid gleaming brass and woodwork on cigars, Guinness, and turtle soup, and over prodigious quantities of these essentials Dunphy laid out the new company. Dunphy's plans were straightforward, even elegant. He described the distribution pipeline: farmers buy in the end but on credit. They buy from local distributors and grain elevators; the smaller of these buy from bigger distributors, who in turn buy from the company itself. At some point the crops begin to emerge, the banks cut some cash loose, and over a period of weeks this climbs back uphill. Now describe for me what our salesmen are doing all this time. What are our marketing efforts, and how do we manage them? Also notice that we work all year but mostly get paid on July first. What are the consequences of this?

This means, sir, that we live for eleven months of the year with a seriously negative cash flow.

Note that he does not say, *It means we'll have to pile up plenty of money, always available for my friends to steal.*

The cash flow will be especially negative in the fall, when all the product is made. The product is made from an active ingredient formulated in Germany, which is mixed upon arrival with many catalysts and inert ingredients to get it to semi-finished state. Then, depending on the orders one expects to fill, it is packaged in various sizes and even under various names, because there is no reason not to let competitors sell it under their own label – competition, sometimes, is such a pain in the ass. But about this very simple manufacturing process: anybody who has an air mill can do it, and the south in particular is full of companies that do. The liabilities of mixing one's own are enormous and the overheads are not justified by three weeks' worth of production. Therefore the keynote will be subcontract manufacture – describe, please, a framework for managing that.

Again, there is no record of Roddy mentioning that routine payments in the millions might be susceptible to hijacking. In spite of his omissions the company slowly took shape on napkins and tablecloths.

The licenses one needs to strew poisonous explosives over the landscape are not trivial. In these matters the public interest is best protected by moving mountains of paper at glacial speed. Another year passed while this selfless work bogged ahead "impersonally," as a great man has said, "in the manner of planets or vegetables."

"That doesn't bother everyone, you know," Johnny said. "Governments being like that. When they're thinking of indicting you, you don't mind at all how long they take. Later on you mind it even less, they haven't got around to tying you to the gurney like they're supposed to."

Anne Marie went for another walk.

Nick waited until she was out the door and said, "Why is it okay when you do it?"

Half of Roddy's boyhood friends were drafted and went to Viet Nam. He never heard a word from his draft board. The kids in Accounting went to the track and had a contest to see who could make the silliest bet. Roddy won the contest, then won three hundred on the ticket. The next morning he was walking to the El, heard a noise, looked up and caught a two-year-old who'd fallen from a third floor window.

"No," Johnny said. "He didn't."

"Truth," Nick protested. "I saw the article. He kept it out of sight, but sooner or later we all got a peek."

The joint venture was approved. It got a name, Infratox North America. It got a Director of Marketing, a good, solid man Dunphy didn't entirely despise. It got a Director of Research, a nematode specialist hired away from a Very Big Company. The Germans heard his name and almost fainted with delight.

Anne Marie was back with curried fish and yellow rice from a sidewalk vendor and white wine that, being already cold, had to come from the hotel. The food was ambiguous but the wine was either a bribe or a peace offering.

Johnny smirked as soon as Anne Marie looked away.

Nick appealed silently to heaven before she could get the wine open and turn around again.

Everyone got a glass. The fish and rice went onto the stove to heat.

Infratox got a President, too, and Roddy was assigned to shadow him three hours a day. The President was a fearless ex-scientist named Petersen, summoned up from Bricker Thresher's Research Department and presented to the Germans like a Christmas pony. He was both lazy and exceptionally incompetent. Many people are called that but Petersen's incompetence as a scientist really was exceptional.

You could work around him and for him and even with him for years and never suspect that it was there. There was only one infallible way to detect it and that was to have him work for *you*. Then you began to see how, no matter what you told him to do, something ever so interesting but just a little different got done instead.

Similarly, his laziness was like that of preachers, judges and safely tenured academics: so wrapped up in august, dignified reticence that one felt churlish for suspecting it. Only when you needed work from him and got a double dose of dignity instead did you begin to regret how well it had impressed you.

"When did *you* suspect it, Nicky?" Anne Marie asked. "Did so much dignity impress *you* for a very long time?"

Johnny said, "Good *point*, Anne Marie. You're saying this part of the story's what somebody must've *told* Nick here. You're saying it's not one of his famous first hand observations that we know we can always bank on."

"Did I say it was?" Nick said. "If I did, I'm sorry. But I promise you it's what Roddy thinks or at least it's what he thought back then."

Johnny looked at Anne Marie and sighed. Anne Marie shook her head and turned back to the fish. Nick said, "All right. I promise you it's what Roddy *said* he thought."

"*Enfin!*" Anne Marie said, and downed half a glass to celebrate.

"There," Johnny said. "Was that so hard?"

Men like Petersen are given companies to run only in unusual circumstances, and he owed his position to two of these. The first was his Ph.D. and the peculiar blindness that the word *Doktor* induces in Germans. Indeed, this blindness is one of the least-known failings of the German character and ought to receive far more attention than it does. At least among the men of Himmelskirch AG, *Doktor* could not be spoken without summoning a deep spell of worthiness, such that the phrase, *Herr Doktor Petersen is an idiot*, for example, for a most apt and germane example at that, was to them impossibly paradoxical and hence not worth a serious man's time. That explains why the Germans accepted Petersen but not why his former colleagues inflicted him on them. After all, there was supposed to be a partnership, trust, fair dealing – why betrayal at such an early date, and in a matter so important?

Alas, no minutes survive and nobody who might remember is talking anymore but, really, it's not so hard to imagine. Suppose that, for years, you've helped to run a highly technical department doing difficult and hard-to-appraise work that demands intense concentration and professional discipline. Suppose, then, that you find yourself cursed with a fraud, a man who to all appearances belongs exactly where he is, a man who ingratiates himself in the corporate world in ways you wouldn't think of doing or know how to do if you tried: a man who cannot be driven out and must be given trivial work to do if serious work is not to be contaminated. A man, most of all, who insists on his spurious status and needs his trivial work to come wrapped in ever-larger shares of scarce budget and scarcer assistants. Now suppose that one day from high up in the stupefying outer world of business comes a summons, seemingly from Heaven's own church as it were, an order to select one of one's very best for sacrifice to the gods of commerce. Is it really so wicked to imagine that such opportunities are to be seized? To read words like "must get on well with people in both formal and informal settings… interpersonal skills that inspire trust… adept in questions of administration… sound appreciation of business strategy…" To read all these synonyms for politician and think, *science will never see the man I choose again*. Of course Petersen was as much a fraud in business as he was in biochemistry but that is not an idea a real scientist can understand as we do. To a real scientist everything but science is incomprehensibly bogus, the distinctions (if one bothers with them at all) being between the innocently bogus and the corruptly bogus, and these not mattering much even to those who make them. It's only a hypothesis but there certainly are precedents. In any case – they gave him up, the Germans took him and there we are.

There Roddy was, anyway, and he understood the man in a flash. The environs of Roddy's ears were still quite damp and there were many approaches his future boss could have taken that might have preserved his innocence for some time to come. The approach he chose instead was one Roddy couldn't fail to see through. Roddy was given copies of memoranda addressed to Petersen and requiring replies. He was told to offer his thoughts, in writing. He then saw his own words incorporated verbatim in new memoranda and, most damning, he rarely saw a word of Petersen's that hadn't first been his. Petersen couched his demands in the time-honored and unconvincing *let's-see-if-you-agree-with-me-about-this* subterfuge. If this had been confined to accounting issues and if Petersen had been more forthright about what he was up to, Roddy could have accepted it, even welcomed it for what it portended. But after Roddy composed and Petersen published a five-thousand-word essay on marketing policy, he ran to Dunphy.

Nicky becomes animated at this point in his tale, concerned with conveying some especially delicate point of nuance. He begins to quote dialogue as if he'd been there and remembers every word. Anne Marie and Johnny glance at each other warily, both alert for the coming punch line.

Nicky makes Dunphy say, "Let's go eat."

He makes Roddy say, for once, "No, I've got a real problem here."

He tells how Dunphy had listened quietly for half an hour. At the end of this time he recalls Dunphy saying, "What you seem to be telling me is that Petersen is a moron. He is. I follow that. What I don't follow is your idea that this is not the best thing that could ever happen to a young man in your position."

Next Nicky mimes desperation, because now Roddy is desperate. Dunphy has never been the least bit slow before and now he can't find the starting gate. It's all melting away and Roddy can't think of a single thing to say. "He wants a plan," Roddy says but then he and Nicky stop. It's hopeless and Nicky grimaces horribly to show what hopelessness is like.

But Dunphy isn't through, no, not Dunphy. "Plans are necessary," agreeable, oblivious Dunphy says. "I thought we made a good one. What's wrong with it?"

This is worse than hopeless. Nicky and Roddy are almost crying. "It's all in notes, or in my head. I haven't begun to write it out and I don't know how to, not so that idiot could follow it."

"Well then," Dunphy says, triumphant at last, "I suppose he'll just have to take your head, won't he?"

Nicky paused to make sure everybody got it. Well past primed, Anne Marie wasn't having any: she just looked on attentively, as though surely the *dénouement* must come soon, *ne c'est pas?* After a moment Johnny sighed and said, "Gee, Mr. P., that sure was a good one. Think we can move on now, maybe?"

Roddy was twenty-five years old and suddenly Treasurer of a corporation that would do a hundred million dollars in its first year, and thereafter Petersen was the Moron to him.

After the company became real it moved to a remodeled warehouse on the south edge of the Loop. Roddy arranged the lease and the floor plan and in doing so met and charmed the other officers and department heads. The research man liked him at once; accountants can be poison to R & D – basically, their attitude is *why do it?* – but Roddy seemed like a man you could live with if your estimates footed and you got your expense reports in on time. The marketing man may not have liked him quite as much (accountants, after all, almost never understand that marketing is the soul of business and accounting is a tumor no one knows how to excise), but Roddy liked *him:* he presided over the nightly forays for beer and he had no problem telling Roddy what he was doing so long as Roddy didn't complain about the cost. Since what he was doing was implementing the Moron's plans that Roddy had compiled himself from Dunphy's lessons, Roddy had no complaints at all.

He met other people too and some of them were memorable. In particular, and we'll get back to this pretty soon, he met a man named Diego Fuentes. Though Fuentes did not draw a paycheck, he was the company's man in Mexico – and Mexico is a place where a company like Infratox most definitely needs a man. Doing business in Mexico presents special challenges to the uptight foreigner but not to a man like Diego Fuentes. He tells you how many new TV sets he needs, you send them, and the customs people regain their sense of fair play. Of course you know he cheats you but would you want an amateur who didn't? Because Mexico is a more important market than many people suppose.

Roddy imagines advance men sprinkling little Latin worms among the crops. There is Hoplolaimus columbia in the coffee, Pratylenchus coffeae in the tobacco – and there appears to be more tobacco in Mexico than one realizes at first. Beyond the patches one readily finds on official maps, there are the important offshore crops, whence the famous, ah, *Mexican* cigars the world so eagerly covets. The less said about these, thank you, the better, and though Diego is a man of endless words about almost everything else, about world-famous cigars and the little worms that threaten them his discretion is absolute, worth every penny it costs. But *isn't* he a bandit, though – strolling out of customs at O'Hare with his smile, his perfect teeth, his dancer's walk under his jaunty black fedora, and four bent golf clubs in a rotting canvas bag... Dumping these in the nearest trash can, he hugs Roddy and demands the schedule for the evening's club crawling; after disappearing the next morning with the Moron for a two hour schmooze, it's back to the airport with Roddy, but now with a shiny new set of Ben Hogans to go with his customs declaration. These meetings with the Moron drive Roddy to the brink of despair. "He's going to try to borrow money," Roddy warns the Moron urgently. "Don't do it, we'll never see it again." And the Moron taking Roddy aside later to say, "You were right. He took it pretty well though when I turned him down." As well he might, for it soon comes out that *turning him down* means offering ninety-day terms on all future shipments...

Things like this were not all that disheartening; things like this made life interesting.

Roddy went hunting in Colorado and on his first morning shot the biggest elk taken that season. Four men had to drag it through the aspen.

He hired an old friend's wife, Darlene, to be his secretary. Darlene ran Accounting, freeing him for serious work. Darlene also did the hiring and firing though nobody knew this but them. If you applied for work and she didn't like your looks, you didn't get an interview. If you already worked there but weren't pulling your weight, it was amazing how quickly Roddy found out about it. The staff shaped up nicely. The Germans – they were called "The Germans" – imposed amazingly complex and irrational reporting requirements on their subsidiaries. The worst of these took half of every year to get right and was called The Master Plan. This is not a joke: the Germans actually called it The Master Plan. When completed, it consisted of hundreds of pages of schedules predicting the performance of every corner of the company right down to the pfennig. Thereafter every actual result had to be compared to the Master Plan and every variance explained in excruciating and convincing detail. Sister companies in Europe had a dozen or more accountants working on it full time. The Moron allowed Roddy exactly none for the job but the plan was always delivered on time, though his staff – accountants, clerks and secretaries – sometimes worked until midnight in the days before the deadline. In Berlin his Master Plans invariably drew the highest praise. The Germans told the Moron how lucky he was to have Roddy. They also said things like, "Herr Hall tells us Montana will be unprofitable for three years. Explain please therefore the fall campaign in Helena." The Moron had a cabin just outside Helena but that wasn't the kind of explanation The Germans were looking for. It just didn't occur to them that their man was cowishly crooked.

"Cowishly?" From Johnny, as Anne Marie guffawed.

"Yes. *Vachement.* I'm sure I used to say cowishly all the time."

Now, it befitted a man of such sleazy indifference to have as his secretary a treacherous suck-up like one Mona, who heard what Darlene and Roddy's other women called her boss. The Moron took the news badly. He tired easily and always had; also he was a man of whims. He banished Accounting to the remotest wing of the building. From now on Roddy's people would sit at beat-up steel desks and walk up and down on bedraggled gray carpets, while Marketing or Administration or Research or Operations was redecorated every few months. Roddy composed outraged memos and Darlene made sure everyone in Accounting got a peek. The group's exile bound them together in defiant contempt of the Moron and his creatures. Some of the Moron's creatures sat at teak desks on upholstered rockers that they picked for themselves from the very front of the catalog. The lowliest accounting clerk would work until seven and sneer while the Moron's women got bonuses for almost always showing up or, if they couldn't manage that, for being personable and having well prepared excuses. In public Roddy deplored these injustices but privately he found them mildly satisfying in ways he'd have found difficult to explain, had he ever bothered to try. But on Secretaries Day in 1972 the Moron went too far. He took every woman in the company to lunch – every woman but Roddy's. Roddy's were instructed to cover the phones. They covered the phones until three in the afternoon, when a few of the more sober partiers straggled back in. From the minute Roddy got the Moron's call – I'm taking my girls out, have yours cover for them, okay? – he and Darlene fumed with zeal. Throughout the afternoon they tracked down husbands and boyfriends. That evening no one was permitted to work late and when his women left the office at five o'clock they were hustled into cabs, which delivered them to a trendy steakhouse in Roddy's neighborhood. Most of their men were already waiting in the bar but a great deal of merriment was transacted before the stragglers showed up. The party left at midnight, with instructions not to appear the next morning before ten. It was Roddy's finest hour but it was also the approximate hour of his doom. He walked home in a mood to discuss his latest triumph of leadership and found his wife in a strangely parallel mood of her own. He detected no unpleasantness in their conversation. The only unsettling point was her need to be absolutely clear on why he had taken thirty people out for a drunken midweek dinner without first speaking to her. But he explained it clearly, several times in fact, and later he was quite bewildered to hear that she accounted it his intolerable final insult. But it must have been true: several people said she mentioned it and her lawyer put it first on the list of his transgressions. What he couldn't figure out was why she never mentioned it herself, but then she never said anything at all about leaving him, period. She simply moved away while he was at work, and then the lawyers took over, and then for the longest time his feelings hurt him terribly.

The Moron was a man of whims but some of his whims lasted decades. On top of this, his stupidity now had driven away the woman upon whom Roddy's happiness was founded (for in retrospect that much was clear). The gloves came off. Suddenly accounts of all the Moron's handiwork found their way into the public domain and no one ever doubted how they got there. It is not clear what Roddy hoped to accomplish; it was probably unclear to him. He may have imagined that you could work for Infratox and not know what the Moron was; if so, he was wrong. He must have imagined that something would come of his disclosures. All that came was the utter destruction of his status among his peers. Every one of them knew that he was right, and a fool for letting it be seen. His fellow managers knew all about the Moron, and also knew who could promote or fire them, and long ago had made the decision real management material makes in those circumstances.

Of course there are no good times for one's luck to vanish but soon it became clear that this one was as bad as could be. So many projects depended on Roddy alone. That should not have been but time after time it turned out that no one else could be trusted. Always he began by imagining that other managers could participate as subordinates but each time it became apparent that only he was unwilling to settle for mediocrity. To protect the company from itself he assumed greater and greater responsibilities. Desperate for help, he pushed through a new computer system and mercilessly ran through a series of bewildered technicians to get it running just so. That others were willing to lend Roddy their authority says much about them and little about him. That he was so clearly right about his peers' shortcomings and the quality of their work may have been a source of comfort for him; it certainly wasn't for anyone else.

Above all, what had seemed like Roddy's charm evaporated. It had never been more than gracious acceptance of life's favors and now that it had no basis it was simply gone. But Roddy had no equivalent experience in fortitude or stoicism to prop him up. If there had been one word for him before, it would have been *attractive.* Suddenly people used many words, amounting, always, to one tepid sneer or another.

All of which he noticed and all of which began to chafe. *That Hall — he needs to get over it, get on with it, deal with it or how about just forget it.* Which, in turn, he heard (because he was meant to) and then he knew his doom was public. *If only,* he thought – on the basis of almost nothing, just a sense, no more, that he was suddenly seeing life for what it is – *if only it was not too late.* But it was too late. It was too late because it's always too late when we finally get around to thinking that one, but the trouble is that so few people have the decency to agree with us even then. Thus it all began to stall, and turn around, and recede the other way, and then keep on receding for every year to come. If people could have read his mind, they would have said, they would have whispered in wonder: *all this agony for nothing*! All for a mere *presentment,* for a feeling not worthy of a *name.* An orphaned, nameless feeling, yes, a touch of sullenness, such as maybe prompted Job to question God: a mere twinge like that, the itch preceding a premonition, never quite as intense as a moderately bad hangover: why couldn't he just put it aside? But people couldn't read his mind, so they didn't know that's all it was. As time dragged on they noticed that it wasn't getting any better and they began to think it was something serious after all, and they kept mercifully quiet about it when, less and less often, his still awesome duties required him to come around and speak to them.

"How drunk was he when laid this shit on you?" Johnny said.

"He talked about it a lot, sometimes drinking, sometimes not. The story didn't change."

"He talked like that *a lot* but only to you," Anne Marie said.

"I don't know that, but I don't know who else it would have been."

"My God," Anne Marie said.

"What?" Nick said.

Johnny explained. "It's what she thinks it makes you. Being, you know, his only friend."

"Oh, if that's all…" Nick said.

"I forget sometimes. That's all," Anne Marie said.

Every year Roddy went back to Colorado for the hunting and didn't bag a thing. Every year he bought a new rifle and sighted it in expectantly. Once he saw a mule deer a few hundred yards away. Once he almost shot a horse or the idiot on its back. He bought a Cadillac that broke down constantly. He was on the phone with the dealer several times a week. In the end they refused to talk to him and gave him a number in Michigan. He hired a lawyer who listened to his story, took his money and then told him that the law didn't quite cover it but he'd write him one hell of a letter. Aside from car repairs and guns, he put his money into stocks that failed without warning. He bought a condo with a leaky roof. He hired a roofer and the other tenants sued him for moving the leak. He met another woman, married her and thought the jinx was off, but was single again in a matter of months. Thereafter on Sundays he watched football with the guys he grew up with and got a little drunk and complained about his car. After a while their wives stopped trying to fix him up, which shocked him into taking just a little stock of his life. He saw that while he wasn't looking, his parents had grown old and cranky and his sisters had had seven kids between them; holidays were now at their houses, watching football and drinking beer with brothers-in-law who looked up to his job and way, way down on him. Determined to work through it, he flew off to Cancun and got food poisoning. Scarcely able to walk, he flew back and hired Nick Petraki.

Once it became clear to Roddy that this Petraki would be the one to actually finish the computer system, the two became inseparable, first at work, then at lunch, then after work several times a week: all the time there was, in fact, except when Nick could sneak away, which to hear him tell it was never often enough.

"You poor man," Anne Marie said, "he drove you to it, didn't he?"

"Did I ever claim that? Once?"

"Of course not, Nicholas. But how often you have wished for this epiphany to burst upon me!"

Roddy's slowly-built isolation neared completion. Those who did not shun him because the Moron wanted them to shunned him because he was so far out of sight. By now he was bringing his lunch to work – cold meatball subs and crushed pastries in a second briefcase. Now he was always the one who was out of the room when it was time to start talking about somebody. Somehow as a consequence the vagaries of keeping books in two currencies seemed less tractable each year. He delivered lectures on the difference between the balance sheet rate and the P&L rate but every month he had to repeat most of it to someone. The rate that mattered most was the mean between the buying and selling price on the last day of the month, and to preserve this against future inquiry he kept a permanent stack of the *Wall Street Journal,* which he called, simply, The Journal. Among the morning rituals in Accounting was the delivery of his Journal. He said things like, "Where's my Journal? I need to see if my stocks are still listed." This was meant as an endearing joke and it must have been a good one because it got a fine response every day. One afternoon when Darlene was filling in for the A/R clerk she couldn't balance a deposit and brought it to him, frustrated almost to the point of tears. "Where's the journal?" he asked. She gawked and pointed to his newspaper. He gawked back. He'd meant the cash receipts journal. She was three months pregnant but he didn't know it. She appraised his countergawk and quit on the spot. After that her husband was always busy when Roddy wanted to take in a ballgame.

Anne Marie had made it through lunch and had finished washing up, but now that she had nothing to do but listen, her disgust at this maudlin potboiler, this *tres bon marché* irony-substitute finally began to pour down her face, indistinguishable from tears of softheaded feminine compassion. Nick and Johnny were concerned, or considered pretending to be. *"Merde!"* she stormed, and stomped away.

Chapter 3

Billy Markham
June 22-23, 2001

To Nick's left was a moat or lagoon of green light under a canopy, with tables set up and TVs on pedestals defining four corners. In the center was a bar and there were more TVs above it, so drinking people could sit or stand any way they liked and never have to turn unless they really wanted to. On some of the TVs a golfer was lining up a putt, on some of them stock cars were spinning out and crashing into each other but on most of them a sweaty, overweight pitcher was shaking off sign after sign. Instinct telling him to be really interested in that, Nick wandered in with his eyes fixed on one of the screens.

"You know, I was beg*in*ning to *think* you fell *in*."

From maybe twelve feet to his right and a little behind, not that loud but in a thoroughly penetrating contralto. The whine was only in the words; the tone was the most ominous deadpan imaginable. Above him, in the real world, the catcher had walked to the mound, jawboned, and was stalking back. His uniform said he was Rodriguez. The pitcher was mangling the rosin bag like it was the batter's heart but the grave sanity of baseball did not entirely penetrate the bar. Some of the grave sanity of baseball washed up against two or three islands of vibrating psychosis and evaporated like dew hitting a forge. From these places the synapses of a few disintegrating drunken folk buzzed and crackled. There was also just the faintest echo of a crazy jangling of fear, but it had bounced off far too many walls to be tracked back to its source. Nearby he sensed its counterpart, a heap or pool of hungry reptilian surliness that had only now devolved from speech and, in compensation, yearned to move suddenly in really dreadful ways. And soon, in spite of, or because of all this highly un-Caribbean lunacy, he would have to turn and look at her.

"Oh hi, sugar," he said, eyes glued to his ballgame. "I missed you so much."

"Your pal Ruiz teach you to say that?"

And then he looked, but by then he was almost ready. What he saw was his age, cheeks bubblegum pink on top of bottle tan, luminous brunette going this way and that in all kinds of flips and curls and with half the crayon box dyed into it, little piggy black eyes, what was once a cute little upturned nose, and a pouty mouth painted almost black. Nothing, that was nothing. Five-three and a hundred and forty, one more *ounce* and it would all explode but, amazingly, she was still shaped like many people's idea of a woman. And he knew exactly how she was shaped and so did everyone else in the airport. Satiny leopard-print pants so tight they shimmered when she breathed: nothing. Iridescent plastic sandals with five-inch heels in violet and green shot with gold flakes and showing matching toenails: still nothing, any of it, because the woman was standing there in a tight black mesh tee shirt with a black lace bra popping out of it. Only the very front of the shirt was solid anything and it was solid silver script announcing *If Mama Ain't Happy, Ain't Nobody Happy*. Oh my, he thought, and in the back of his mind behind any number of alarms and boggles sounded a most comforting idea: nothing can go wrong now because Johnny is a genius and this is how he proves it. No Nick

Pope could ever have landed in Orlando because in this crazy world there is only silly Billy Markham. Somehow this happy mama woman has been showing silly Billy Markham off for hours and a thousand hugely amused people will gladly swear to it.

Turning back to see the catcher block a curve ball in the dirt (hey, that was a curve ball), he said, "Sugar, I don't need Ruiz to tell me when I miss you." He felt an audience start to build around him and decided to stick with *sugar* because he'd almost said *cherie*.

"Oh yeah? You think you still got something left after last night?"

Chuckles and a hoot, so he said, "I *meant*, could you get me a beer while I watch DiMaggio strike out?"

More hoots, a great success. "Knew it *had* to be something like that—" a cacophony of hoots, she'd won, no question "—and get your own fucking beer, precious. That Pedro couldn't strike out Joe's brother Vince. And bring me another one."

They sat at a little table and drank the watered-down beer Ruiz had told him he lived for and just then that didn't seem like much of a leap. More proof of Johnny's genius (all genius today was due to Johnny) was a large, nipple-covering metal button that said "Hi! I'm Dolly!" and half-obscured the leftmost "Happy." Billy and Dolly, of course, with a hundred years between them. Dolly slapped his hand playfully and gave him a wink that meant, *you done fine*. The batter singled up the middle and two runs scored. One was named Gonzalez and Nick didn't see the other's name. The batter made the turn at first and Nick saw that he was Perez. And the catcher was Rodriguez and the pitcher was a Pedro. My, my.

"Look," Dolly said, "there's those nice people from in line. Wave, shithead."

Billy waved. An elderly couple in matching Stetsons looked a little startled, hurriedly waved back and hotfooted away.

"You already been to your gate?" a tall, thin man asked, mostly staring down at the right breast, which said "Don't Just Stare – Introduce Yourself!"

"Got number five and six for Nashville," Dolly said proudly and pulled two yellow cards out of her purse to prove it.

"Smart," the thin man said. "That way you get your pick." And Nick realized that he had not seen a string tie in a quarter of a century and had not missed them even once.

"I get mine, anyway," Dolly said. "He gets next to me, except today they's starting in Tampa so we'll be lucky to be together. Go get us one more, babe, 'cause they load in ten minutes."

Walking up to security Nick asked, "How much did the guy in line look like me?" and Dolly said, "The guy in line looked like a yellow-eyed largemouth bass in a hat, next to two big tits."

Walking to the gate Nick asked, "Did I talk to anybody?" and Dolly said, "Do I look like I let you get a word in edgewise?"

A little further on she whispered, "Speed it up just a little" and then they were walking straight through the gate and up to the tail end of a line just disappearing through the door. As the line halted a few feet down the tunnel, she pulled out an open magazine, stuck it in his face and said, "Here, read that, it's what I was telling you." And then, every few seconds, "You see? You with me yet?"

Nick read: Patti somebody and Mickey somebody might be breaking up but maybe they weren't. "It doesn't say one way or the other," he eventually protested.

With exasperated patience she told him, "They don't even *print* those stories if they don't already *know*. We don't see them this trip, we'll have to wait till they get back together and that could be five or ten *years*."

Getting into it, he asked, "And *how* much will it cost?" but she was ready with "About ten hours of that overtime you always *say* you're working."

She passed up several open seats and led him to the back of the plane. "Take the window, pull your hat down and sleep. At least pretend to. I have to write a letter."

"To whom?"

"You, darling."

Apparently he did sleep, because he woke up. His tray was down, an unopened can of the ersatz beer-fluid on it next to a small bag of peanuts. He looked out and saw densely-farmed green and brown squares through a few wispy clouds, some woods, a river, lakes, much more farmland, a town, more woods. He started to follow a railroad track and woke up again with a start. His peanuts were gone. He looked over at Dolly. She was reading. He bent down to look at her book and she held up the cover for him. It was called *Nurse Sultry's Dalliance*, with, sure enough, the top half of a stacked, redheaded nurse wearing little more than a stethoscope, and the corresponding half of a pompadoured young doctor. His left hand was ripping away her last button. His right hand was out of sight but her expression said that it wasn't really lost.

"Interesting?" he asked.

She sighed. "That don't half cover it. You know life don't never measure up but still, it gives you hope. Here, baby, this is for you." And handed him a few folded sheets of greenish steno paper covered with violet ink. He opened his can of placebo, took an acrid but otherwise tasteless sip and settled down for what he confidently expected would be an exercise in divination. Instead he read this:

Instructions and Observations Concerning Our Journey
Dolly's Airplane Talking Rule. You could look around and not see anybody close by. Then you might want to say something Billy wouldn't say to Dolly in public. Don't. First reason is, when Dolly's on an airplane and she isn't reading, she's listening to people. The best conversations are usually eight or nine rows away and Dolly's hearing is no better than average. Dolly has heard a man make a

date while his wife was in the head; that was from fifteen rows away. The second (and better) reason is, it's against Dolly's Airplane Talking Rule.

That was the end of the first sheet. Nick looked up. Dolly leered sweetly.

"You write well."

"Better than you read, shithead." And elbowed him hard in the ribs. "Finish it, sugar."

He turned the page.

Dolly's Taste in Reading. You have made a natural but nonetheless grievous mistake. Dolly is reading Schiller. Once you get past Die Lorelei *he can kind of sneak up on you. Do you read German? You may nod or shake. If you like, Dolly will read to you later.*

Nick shook twice.

"Figures," Dolly said.

"Peek?"

"Trusting fucker, ain't you? Maybe this is a recipe for pound cake."

He picked it up. The cover was taped over the book inside. If it wasn't Schiller, it was at least in verse.

"I got lots more just as good," Dolly said. "Read your own damn stuff."

The third page of the letter read,

What You Can Still Learn from Dolly's Taste in Reading. Dolly fooled you. Think about it. The world is full of people who'd love to do that. Ponder this.

"I haven't thought about much else for six months," Nick said.

"As usual that ain't what I meant. I put my face on, it ain't nothing no other woman can't do. But once you see stupid, your own brain quits. Stupid falls right off your radar. But it never was no big thing. Just thought you should know. Keep reading."

Dolly's No Talking after School Rule. Dolly doesn't know very much about you or what you're going to do next and you are not to try to tell her. This is for Dolly's protection, not yours. Dolly trusts you but only so far. For instance, Dolly does not trust that if the world becomes a sorrowful place after Dolly has left you, you will not imagine that she has been telling tales. For this reason you are forbidden to transfer information to Dolly unless she requests it, and you are to evaluate her requests most circumspectly. Be especially careful of asking questions that reveal anything you haven't heard Dolly confess that she knows – for example, 'What time do we rob the bank tomorrow?' or even 'When does Phoebe Darwinkle, the love of my life, arrive by shuttle from Nantucket?' Any violation of Dolly's No Talking after School Rule will be dealt with as a breach of contract. There will be no second warning.

"Fine with me," Nick said.

"No, it ain't. It never is, so it ain't for you, but remember to pretend real hard like you mean it. The big one's next."

What Will Not Happen when We Get where We're Going. Dolly doesn't mean to be insulting but she'll take the chance. We're not really married, you know. Dolly is strictly a delivery service.

Nick considered a reply to this one for quite a while. Once or twice he thought he had something but none of it got past Dolly's Airplane Talking Rule. Finally he contented himself with, "I'm not that easy myself," and stared fixedly ahead while she shrieked with laughter.

"You go back to sleep now baby," she said. "Nobody needs you for a while."

He woke when the wheels smacked the runway. Dolly said, "You tag along," and they walked away from the gate to buy breath mints at one kiosk and three fan magazines at another, paying all the cash a Saint Sulpice fisherman would see in a month. The airport was not *exactly* like the two in Florida. Nick wandered – was shooed – into a men's room and when he emerged Dolly was arguing with yet another cell phone. "Madge, we just *got* here, I get him out of the motel I'm doing good, all he wants to do today is sleep. Hey, can I help it if I'm irresistible? Shit, he's been that way long as we been together, wants his month's supply in one night and then hibernates. If we don't see them tonight we'll catch them tomorrow, okay? We *got* all weekend. Call you soon as we do." And folded it up and started walking.

"Aunt Madge," she explained.

"She okay?" Just maybe, there weren't quite as many fat people in Nashville.

"Nosy as ever, God bless her. Didn't think she'd ever let me go."

"Good thing Uncle Rufus didn't answer."

Dolly walked on a few steps and said quietly, "Fucking Ruiz and his fucking mouth."

"So what if—"

"Just shut up about it, okay? Something works for years and the ignorant little show off – never mind, sugar. Not your fault this time."

Alert for stupid now, Nick begins to see how she speeds up and slows down at random and mixes this in with darting little turns to see what's on the TV in that bar, what's the headline on that newspaper, are those tee shirts dumb enough for us? Especially she has to read every poster for every act, and the airport is papered with them. He can see how hard it would be to stay casually even with her but she doesn't seem to be looking for anyone. He thinks, *somebody else is looking.* Then he thinks, *she's just doing this because she always does.* Finally he thinks, *one thing's working: I'm not supposed to know and I don't.*

At baggage claim she veers toward a car rental line and confides discreetly. "Little bit of acting now. I talk, you make faces, anything but embarrassed will do, and you don't say nothing."

Nick grapples with *acting?* We're *trying* to *stand out?*

She demonstrates. "Can you just *stand* here and *watch* these bags and *not* that little girl's titties any more than you *have* to?"

On the one hand, she isn't really all that loud. On the other, twenty or thirty heads turn while she marches away and only one or two of them follow her. Nick freezes, mortified, a thought screaming up: *grin, you fool, Billy would*. And he finds that, just barely, he can grin, and stare more or less after her, and still see people think horrible things about Billy and Dolly. Thus he finds that with no effort at all he can see this Billy as they do. He realizes that he's seen this Billy type any number of times himself and always dismissed him as a person who might amuse or annoy but otherwise simply didn't matter. Didn't matter because he couldn't possibly matter, Q.E.D.

Back and with papers in hand, Dolly half shouts, "Come on, shithead," and, jaws aching, he follows her outside while half of Nashville snickers openly. In Part III, section iv, member 1, subsection 2 of *Anatomy of Melancholy*, Burton says, "If the world will be gulled, let it be gulled," and while Nick has always sensed the wisdom in these words, he feels at last that he has penetrated to their core. She leads him to a post by an ashtray, leans against it, digs in her purse for a cigarette, lights it, puts an arm around him and says, "Beautiful grin. You can turn it off now. Billy don't grin when Dolly hugs him. Dolly loves her Billy so much, and he's so handsome and all the girls see it and Dolly's getting old and fat and sometimes it all just goes to her head, you know? Then she says mean things and embarrasses them both and Billy has to grin and then Dolly has to hug him like this. But Billy don't grin when Dolly has to hug him 'cause deep down Billy loves his Dolly too, even if he does see every cute little butt there is and don't care who sees him looking. And Dolly don't even need to say she's sorry 'cause Billy knows she is, and that's why they been together so long and always will be, no matter what her mama said those times."

A cop was sauntering carefully up the sidewalk, saw them without seeming to and dived into a doorway. Dolly saw him do it and didn't even tense, so Nick thought he owed her a little last stand bravado of his own, but the best he could come up with was, "I didn't realize you smoked."

"Working I do one or two a day 'cause it gives you a reason to take time out like this. I do this two or three days straight, I got to stop or I'd start up for real."

The cop came out, leading two of his friends. They walked to a post thirty feet away and pretended to take a smoke break of their own. One of them watched the traffic while the other two sneered frankly at Billy and Dolly, but Dolly had ice water for blood and Nick decided that if she could stand it, he could too.

"What did we just do? Don't tell me it was the quietest way to get out of there."

"We were being different from you."

"Ah. Yes. As I'd say if you were French, a good quarter hour before his death, he was still alive – but you know, it really doesn't sound nasty enough in English."

"I guess it doesn't. You think you hear me but you don't. What we did, what we're doing right now, we're being different from you *in disguise.* Anybody looking for you knows how to ignore hats, beards, limps, wigs, any way you could fool the average person. In fact those are the things they'd look for. They'd be looking for a package with you inside it. Your build and all, I've seen half a dozen since we landed that I'd want to check out plus two more on the plane. But we give them something you can see clear through. Couple of monsters named Billy and Dolly."

"I see. I sneak through airports disguised as a monster." Stumbling a little on that because apparently he was angry now and it had started out as *déguisé comme monstre.*

"Hell no, Sugar. As a half a real one. See, Sugar, you ain't one whole anything anymore. You're half of something that's so big and so plain that nobody would think to look at the pieces. Now we'll just stand here a minute like monster families sometimes do. Then I got to call Madge 'cause I forgot to tell her something. Then we'll get our car and go check in. But before that, right now'd be good, you show the world why you're with me. You start pretending you're going to get laid like isn't going to happen. Like Billy'd take one finger and run it up Dolly's arm, right there where it's handy. Then if somebody noticed like say those gentlemen there, Billy'd stare them straight in the eye but not too hostile, like, See buddy, I got mine, why don't you go get yours? Billy does that, everybody in the world knows what's coming next. It's just about the least suspicious act on earth."

Possibly out of professional respect for the least suspicious act on earth, the cops ground out their butts and slipped back inside to summon the SWAT team. Dolly still failed to crumble and led Billy to the rental car just as if they were really going to make it. In the car Nick looked off at downtown Jacksonville and said, "So this is Nashville."

"Not quite yet but getting there."

"Amazing."

"What is?"

"Does comfort level mean anything to you? Is that something people say now?"

"Sure. Been around for years."

Nick peered into the mirror and saw no more than a thousand Feds behind them.

Dolly was still into her act, reaching over to thump him on the chest, saying, "You still with me?" Snapping her gum at him like he hadn't seen close up since high school.

"I'm not going to get a straight answer, am I?"

"Hell no. What about though?"

"About whether we were really looking for people following us."

"Yes we were really looking. No there weren't any and no we didn't expect any. How scared *are* you?"

Dolly showed some worry now for the very first time. Nick was not worried about Nick being *scared*, he was more concerned with a car coming up fast on their right, shiny and black and full of Feds.

"I think I'm fine. If I'm not I'll let you know. It's simply, ah, *salaud...*" The Feds cut in front, slowed down and took up convoy station. It was all Nick could do to not look back for the other car that would seal them off from behind.

"Put your head back, shut your eyes and hold your nose, *now. Shut them. Hold it, tight.* I'll tell you when to breathe and it'll be a while. Don't worry about suffocating yourself, they say it can be done but you're not the man to do it. That's better. Here, hold Dolly's hand. Wait just a little, you need to slow it down a little more. A little more. Now you can take one breath. One but keep your eyes closed. Okay. Say something."

"Jesus. What was that?"

"It's got lots of names. Basically it means you don't do this every day and I do and that's all it means."

They turned off the highway and onto a busy commercial strip. They drove a couple of blocks while Nick reminded himself, *the Feds are gone and these are called blocks.*

"What next?"

"Motel. Dinner. A movie, a bar, you name it, but we want to stay up a little late. Tomorrow we hang around the room till three or four, then Billy disappears and I drive what's left of you to your hotel. Bowling, how's that sound? Let's take that Motel 6."

"No reservations?"

"Billy and Dolly?"

"You mean, if you don't know what you're going to do, how would anyone else?"

"I mean, stay in character is all. Even when you don't need to like we don't need to now, because you always need to really."

"Ah, Dolly? I remember about after school but I want to ask a very careful question. Is that all right?"

"Probably not. You really need to?"

"I think so."

"Think some more. Then if you have to, you have to. Wait here, precious." And she was out of the car and swaggering toward the office while he thought about Johnny.

Because Johnny once told him, "When you need to be invisible, you either need to be alone or with other people who think they look like you."

Johnny, now: Johnny stuck out. There was never any question of Johnny turning invisible but for some reason that didn't keep Nick from believing him.

Johnny said, "In your case, you don't have someplace special to be, you stay in pretty good hotels near airports. You don't know these places, Mr. P, so you need to trust me. Last thing you remember you were a kid. Probably, things start taking you back like they will, you'll start thinking like you're still that kid. You need to realize nobody else will see you like that. For everybody there's a place people expect to see them and that's as invisible as it gets anymore. You, they see a fit older guy with a lot of casual Euro class and people in your average Hyatt, your Marriott, they can see themselves in you, no problem. I mean fat guys from Jersey in polyester, no problem."

And Nick could see that, somehow, fat guys from Jersey could never be a problem at the Hyatt, he could understand and agree with that. But now came the part that was giving him his current spasm of shivers, because Johnny went on to say, "Now you take that look to the Motel 6 and heads start turning and maids start talking." Especially, which Johnny didn't have to say, if you take your gorgeous, well-bred mug there with a… well, with a… well, with Dolly. Kind of a coincidence that he'd actually named the chain, wasn't it? "You take it to the streets where you used to fit right in and the first guy who checks you out is a cop. Not 'cause you ring any bells but 'cause you *don't*. Guy drives up and down all day, walks his turf all day, and all he's looking for is whatever don't fit in. And any place you used to hang, what don't fit anymore is you. Doesn't mean he'll bust you, doesn't mean he'll even talk to you but he will *see* you, Mr. P, and so will everybody else who really belongs there. But put you on the airport shuttle anywhere on earth and one hour later, nobody'll remember a thing."

Nick caught glimpses of Dolly through the motel office blinds. She was hopping around like a madwoman. No, she was doubled over from food poisoning. No, she *and* the woman behind the counter were hugging, holding each other up, about to pass out from laughter. He relaxed just a little and got back to Johnny.

Johnny told him, "There's just two things, Mr. P. Your credit card needs to be perfect, and I mean perfect. And any phone call you make is public record forever. That goes for anything else you buy but you got to understand about phones. There's guys, lots of them now, that can say, 'Get me anyone at any hotel in the US called one of these numbers this week and oh yeah throw in his travel plans,' they get their answers in two hours tops and most of that's red tape. And they don't have to break one fucking law that'll stick."

Johnny told him, "I can't prove it or at least I don't want to, but I know it's true. There's some scary shit in the world today, Mr. P. Somebody gets on any phone in the country and says 'Nicholas Petraki' three times, somebody's going to show up. First time it happens they might not come for two or three weeks. Next time it'll be half an hour, and I mean anywhere in the country. Only problem is they can't use it, so they got to fake a story – I mean, NSA's about as legal as we are, right? But don't worry, by the time you get arraigned some blind woman you were in the third grade with recognized you from six blocks away."

Johnny told him, "Mr. P, you don't want to believe this stuff, I know that but if you, you personally yourself I mean, ever send me an email, the first thing I do is run and the second is I find you and hurt you till I just can't hurt you anymore. That goes for Pope, Petraki, Petrov and double for Pluto the Pup."

Nick held his breath for several seconds and then he made himself actually think about all of this, not just slide through it in remembrance, and thus he learned that he could still think just a little. He reminded himself: *I'm a monster named Billy Markham.* He remembered that Johnny was talking to Pope, Petraki and Petrov. He decided that Dolly's phone calls were Dolly's business. He decided that he'd never emailed anyone yet and probably never would. When Dolly got back to the car he said, "I think I worked it out by myself," and she said, "See? I figured you could."

Right next door was a barbecue chain and Nick had a whole slab of ribs and two pieces of pecan pie and a salad (only so it could come with Thousand Island dressing, which was just like he remembered). Next door to that was a bar. About the time they walked in the fear let go of Nick for a while. They had one beer each but Nick couldn't stand the volume and suddenly he was way past tired, so they walked back to the motel. Dolly said, "Beautiful night, ain't it?"

Nick looked up and saw a third as many stars as he was used to. He almost choked on the exhaust fumes.

"It's swell," he said. "Do we still say swell?"

"Sure. You just did, didn't you?"

Dolly came out of the bathroom in a floor-length flannel nightgown and a towel wrapped around her head. Nick went in, turned on the shower and looked around for her wig. It wasn't there and he wondered when she'd slipped it into her suitcase and what kind of alarms would have gone off if he'd tried to open it. He came out wearing Billy's sweatshirt and a towel wrapped chastely around his waist. He kept it on as he got into his bed and under his covers. From her bed Dolly simpered delightedly and turned a page of a book called *One Nurse's Ecstasy*.

"As interesting as the last one?"

"Ever so."

"My book's more recondite than yours," he said and held up the Burton.

"Did you just say recondite?"

"I think so, yes. Why?"

"No reason."

"Burton's on to Billy and Dolly, you know."

"Is that so?"

"It is. *Erasmus vindicates fooles from this Melancholy Catalogue, because they have most part moist braines, and light hearts, they are free from ambition, envie, shame and feare, they are neither troubled in conscience, nor macerated with cares, to which our whole life is so much subject.'* He talks like that a lot. Recondite."

"I know who Burton is. I read that once when I was doing Ben Jonson off Broadway and I thought I'd immerse myself."

"You read it all?"

"Sure. Why?"

"No reason. So. Are you ever getting back into acting?"

When she had finally finished laughing she grinned for several seconds but didn't speak, as though afraid she might start up again. "You know," she finally said in a pleasant mezzo-soprano from somewhere northeast of Boston, "I think that could be the best review I've ever had."

In the morning Nick put on his sky blue sweater and pushed, not rolled, his sleeves halfway up his forearms. He bundled up Billy's clothes, watch and ring and Dolly packed them away. Then he taught her to play two handed belote and took her for a hundred and fifty-two pennies, which were mostly scratched out on the back of a Grand Ole Opry flier. Aunt Madge was bursting with curiosity and called four times, even though Dolly told her each time that Billy was still resting up from closing a place called The Prancing Filly and no, weren't nobody important playing except they was just too good to walk out on, you know? But tonight, yeah, soon as he gets up they'll eat and then they'll go down and see them. The fourth time Madge called she told Dolly that she'd better get Billy up now because if he slept any longer they'd miss it again. Dolly told Madge it was *their* goddamn vacation and if they wanted to spend it in bed then that's what they'd damn well do and she was hanging up now because cell phone batteries don't last forever and they might want to use it tonight if they did decide to go out which maybe they wouldn't now on account of some people thought mid-afternoon was already too late. Then she hung up and told Nick, "Well, you're here and ready to check in."

Nick examined himself in the mirror (yes, he was back) while Dolly issued the last of her instructions. She seemed to take a special pride in remaining Dolly, no matter how far she wandered from the things of any conceivable Dolly's world. She gave him a pager and showed him how to use it. "At night you turn on the sound but most of the time you leave it on vibrate, see? You want to get away from somebody or you're just not sure if you should, you look surprised, pull it out and say, 'Sorry, this'll only take a minute.' They tag along to the payphones, then you know. That happens, you call the number. You remember the number?"

Nick recited it.

"Good. You call that and say anything at all but try to work in exactly where you are or where you know you can get to. Then you stall. Otherwise, nothing like that happens, you just hang around for a few days till somebody tells you different. Go outside, go swimming if you want but check your pager every time you get out. Other than the pool stick to the hotel."

In the car Nick said, "Um…"

Dolly said, "Understand, there's different ways to tell you this. Ruiz'd say, have a blast, nothing's going to happen. He's probably right but I like my way better. You watch out."

Nick said, "Ah…"

Dolly said, "I'm supposed to tell you one more thing. When you check in and not before, there will be some calls made to get it started – whatever *it* is – and that will take as long as it takes. I hope that makes sense."

"It makes sense. It means they thought I'd get cold feet."

She pulled into the curb fifty yards short of a cab rank. "Don't look back, don't wave. Nicholas Pope can't explain no Dolly and sometimes car hikers remember. Check in and get the envelope for Mr. Pope. It'll have the claim check for the car, the keys, the rental papers and your credit card – nobody needs to see you open that, right? That's it. Maybe I'll see you on the way back."

"Maybe," he said, and got out and felt utterly alone and helpless for the better part of a second.

Chapter 4

Roddy John Hall
1972 – 1974
Nicholas Petraki-Petrov, Anne Marie Marceau, Johnny W.
Spring, 2001

Johnny told Nick to speed it up because he needed to get some sleep before dawn. Out of deference to Johnny and what he'd come to see as his own innate politeness, Nick slowed it down only a little.

Roddy's hair began to thin and he got a fungus on one toenail that wouldn't stay away.

No matter how much care he took getting dressed, his belt was always inside out when he finished.

One day, also, it was very tight. Suddenly he began to put on serious weight.

Ruined though he was, he was still the Treasurer of the Corporation, and he had a big office, and in one corner of it was the Telex machine. This was way before we had email, even before we had faxes (both of which Nick has heard of and Johnny has actually seen). In those days we had Telexes, or *twixes* as we called them, as though they were an especially tasty kind of children's cereal. That damn Telex machine provided all the grief even a lucky a man could handle and, oceans and time zones being what they are, always late at night or early in the morning. There was the time he got to work early to find a single, bland paragraph instructing him to refuse credit to the company's third largest US customer, on the overtly stated grounds that their parent company competed too well with Himmelskirch for the Egyptian market. All morning Roddy frantically groped for his half-remembered business law as he hammered out a two page rant about the US Government's attitude toward flagrant restraint of trade. Eventually the company's counsel had to draft a letter of protest; he recruited the West German consulate's commercial attaché as an expert witness. His victories were all like this: retarded defeats. Soon came the week of the convoluted two-page EXTRA PRIORITY HALL EYES ONLY SPECIAL monument of hysterical abreaction to one of Petraki's more innocent practical jokes. Apparently Berlin had asked how the staff would like to be listed in the corporate register. Apparently Petraki had thought it over and replied, Western Hemisphere Data Processing Manager. Now Herr Doktor Thus and Herr Doktor So MOST IMPORTANTLY AND STRENUOUSLY advised Roddy with ABSOLUTE DISCRETION AND TRUST IN HIS DELICATE JUDGEMENT to SUGGEST MORE APPROPRIATE RANK AND POSITION without IN LEAST WAY SEEMING TO DISPARAGE THIS VALUABLE COLLEAGUE OR HIS CONTRIBUTIONS.

"You see, asshole," he told Nick, "they're worried about the day they've got two hundred subsidiaries here and you think they made you manager of the hemisphere."

Nick protested. "But I *am* Himmelskirch's Data Processing Manager in this hemisphere."

"No, you are Data Processing Manager for Chicago Accounts Payable. It's a very responsible position that I just made up."

"Accounts Payable? I do a whole lot more than that. I do—"

"A lot more than they know you do. A lot more than they'd want you to do. And someday maybe you'd like to get paid for it, and wouldn't it be nice if you weren't already King of the World so I could promote you?"

"Oh. I see." Straight faced. As if, only now, he saw.

These were the routine, bothersome twixes. The really strange ones began a few months later. The first one came, for once, while Roddy was at his desk. The machine whirled and clattered, then shut up quickly. Roddy thought the call had been disconnected and waited for it to start again. When it didn't he walked over and tore it off.

FUR HALL. ZUCKERLAND IST FERTIG, ZURICH AUCH. ENDE.

Roddy went to his dictionary. Zurich might be a bank – they had a bank in Zurich, though no one who'd ever dealt with it could have doubted its readiness. Sugarland was a problem. Roddy looked on both the customer and vendor lists and found neither Sugarland nor Zuckerland. He called Sales and was told that there were no known proposals out to any such companies, but distributors, perhaps… Knowing the answer already, he called Marketing and was patronized with the assurance that nothing the company sold did sugar the least bit of good. He laid the twix on his credenza and went back to work.

The next day, though, he came in to find a translation, as though perhaps his illiteracy had prevented the correct reply to who knew where.

FOR HALL. SUGARLAND IS READY, ALSO ZURICH. PLEASE FORWARD. ENDS.

This time he showed it to Morris, the Accounting Manager. "See?" he said. "At least one extra word, so it's a young guy, doesn't think he's sending a telegram." Morris was as blank as Roddy but at least he'd asked someone. But forward?

A weekend passed.

FOR HALL. PLEASE FORWARD. WHY DO YOU DELAY? SUGARLAND IS DOUBTFUL.

Roddy called the Moron, who said it was probably a wrong number. Roddy bit. "A wrong number? A wrong number that happens to be a telex machine with a Hall sitting next to it?" But the Moron had a company to run and no suggestions for new ways Roddy might waste their time.

On Tuesday morning Roddy came in early but the twix was already there.

URGENT FOR HALL. PLEASE FORWARD IMMEDIATELY REGARDLESS COST OR DISTANCE. SUGARLAND PROTESTS INACTIVITY STRONGEST TERMS. ZURICH QUESTIONS COMPETENCE. FULL REPORT REQUIRED AT ONCE. IF UNABLE TO FORWARD, HALL REPLY PERSONALLY EXPLAINING CIRCUMSTANCES.

Roddy took the extraordinary step of calling the Zurich bank. It was almost closing time there and he only had one name, a Herr Doktor Fassler he'd spoken to once a year before. Himmelskirch's name got him to the phone but very little got through their lifelong mutual neglect of each other's language. It took Roddy ten minutes to get past *telex*. Roddy had had a telex (he'd had four). It came from Zurich but that was all he knew (he didn't even know that). He had no idea what it was about (by now he was almost sure). Could the bank have sent it? Because other than the bank he knew no one in Zurich.

"Neimand auf Zurich?" Fassler translated in horror.

"Right," Roddy said. "I know nobody in Zurich, except your bank."

But Fassler had to elaborately regret that, though they much looked forward to his future business, neither he nor the bank had seen fit to contact the good Herr Hall, and Roddy hung up to find Morris hanging just inside the door.

"Schrenk's here," Morris said. "New guy from Berlin?"

And with that Schrenk was indeed there, through the door and charging Roddy's desk, hand outthrust and barking, "Schrenk, Alois," followed by what might have been a sneeze but turned out to be *Beteiligungsverwaltung*, which Roddy eventually decided meant internal auditing. And there went Roddy's morning. Schrenk, it seemed, would be living with him for three years, and his first priority was showing that he was a hands on kind of guy. Younger even than Roddy and determined to not let anybody think that meant anything (mustache, pipe, Irish thornproof suit cut in England), he was deep into the Master Plan before Morris could get next door to his own office. Entirely prepared to resent it all mightily, Roddy found himself liking him quite soon. It's not hard to understand, is it? He grasped what he was told before Roddy could finish a sentence: about what Roddy did; about what everyone else did; about what some people didn't do; he got it all and everything he got would go straight back to Berlin.

About eleven-thirty Roddy called Nick Petraki in and introduced them.

"I thought we might go to lunch. You tell Mr. Schrenk what you're up to and if you manage to keep it slow, I get to eat."

Nick stuck out a hand and said, "Thought you were coming last Thursday, Mr. Schrenk." In every office there's somebody who always hears everything and in this one it was Nick Petraki.

"I was to have come then, yes. Settling my wife in Kentucky turned out to take some time."

But Roddy was looking at the little pile of curling yellow paper on his credenza and said, "Ah, Nick? Maybe we'd better wait a few minutes. I'll call you when we're ready."

Roddy followed him to the door and closed it, picked up the pile and handed it to Schrenk.

"If people thought you'd be here last week, maybe you know what these mean."

Schrenk read them quickly and looked ready to swear in irritation.

"Someone has been very childish. You should not have been bothered. May I make a call, please?"

He meant, would Roddy leave the room, and Roddy did. He walked around his desk and then straight to the door and he didn't exactly dawdle, but in that time Schrenk had an address book out and had dialed and, just as Roddy shut the door, he was asking someone for a Señor Diego Fuentes, *por favor.*

Johnny said, "I don't want to jump to conclusions but did two guys named Schrenk and Fuentes really know each other when I was in kindergarten? Am I really hearing this?"

And Anne Marie would appear to have returned, because she now said, "But how perceptive, Johnny, how unexpectedly acute! At last, a dog still has not barked in the nighttime!"

Chapter 5

Up in his room, the man now known as Nicholas Pope checked his creases, shined his new shoes and read the room service menu. High on his homecoming list was a very large rare steak and it looked like he'd have it tonight. There was a whole page of bizarrely named and quite expensive red wines that he supposed came from California, and he wondered briefly whether he'd take the risk or pay fifty dollars for a bottle of ordinary Beaujolais. Then it occurred to him that he was going down to the bar anyway and they'd sell him a glass of one or two of whatever he cared to learn. Two or three times he walked to the door and turned around, once to check that he'd folded everything away neatly in his dresser, once to make sure that he hadn't forgotten some vital article of clothing, finally to collapse on the bed in a fit of sobbing. He got up in a while, went to the window and looked down. He looked up and down the street several times before satisfying himself that he'd never seen this place before, never dreamt of it, and only a fool of a kind that he most definitely was not could mistake it for anything called home. Then he undressed and went back to bed. At one-thirty in the morning, fully dressed and shaved again, he ordered down for a rare New York strip and a bottle of somebody's Cabernet. The steak was superb and the wine held its own. He'd considered the cheesecake while ordering but forgotten to make up his mind, so he sent down again for a speculative piece, with a double Martel as a hedge. This time the waiter was named Dominguez and came from Guadalupe. He missed Guadalupe badly and sent forty dollars home each week. He had never been to Saint Sulpice but supposed it was very beautiful. He was not permitted to share the kind guest's wine, nor the coffee he'd brought on principle, but it was indeed exceptionally kind of the kind guest to offer and the gentleman should not hesitate if perhaps another piece of cheesecake or sirloin should strike his fancy before dawn. Dominguez explained the remote control and the various systems it commanded. On his way out he showed the gentleman how to affix the sign to his doorknob that would prevent the unfortunate disruption of one not yet accustomed to the hotel clocks. After Dominguez left, Nick watched some amazing things on television. One channel ran nothing but shaky videos of policemen wrestling drunks to the ground. Sometimes the policemen first had to run the drunks off the road and drag them out of their cars but eventually they got to wrestle them to the ground. Another channel did nothing but auction off bad costume jewelry at absurd prices. Finally he found a movie he'd seen before but not in English. He watched it for a while and then spent some more time at the window. Toward dawn he picked up the phone and said, "Nicholas Petraki, Nicholas Petraki, Nicholas Petraki" quite clearly; perhaps because he'd failed to touch any number of buttons or possibly because his bottle was empty, it refused to acknowledge him at all. After that he got partly undressed and went back to bed. He awoke a little after noon with not much of a headache, took a shower, shaved, and dressed even more carefully than he had the night before. With no difficulty at all he opened the door, retrieved the sign from the doorknob and walked off to find the elevator. For four days he rode up and down the elevator every few hours. He had gone twenty-five years without elevators. Two or three times he walked onto an empty one and forgot to push a button. Then it would take off on its own and open itself at some floor that looked just like Nick's but wasn't. People would walk in and look surprised to find Nick there with none of the buttons lit. They'd hesitate, then reach over and push one while Nick tried to become invisible; strangely, that appeared to work. At other times he'd walk into one in the lobby and ride all the way to the top before realizing that he hadn't punched his floor; then he'd have to become invisible for the people getting off and on but he managed that too.

Mostly he listened. He listened in the coffee shop, in the sports bar, in the lobby bar. He listened to young people from Georgia who called themselves data modelers and he felt that he should understand them but couldn't; then suddenly he could and felt an unlikely surge of despair for the degradation of his old trade. He listened to web designers from New York and California. He gathered that web designers are a type of artist, more important though less appreciated than the older kinds. One of the California web designers was also an actress but she'd taken a three-week data-mapping gig because things were slow in both her real trades. He briefly considered her but decided that her fantasy life didn't need external stimulus and, anyway, she'd probably think him too old. He listened to tired men his age who often wore suits but drank beer straight from the bottle. They talked only about sports. Mostly they talked about baseball because it was summer but many sports had been revealed to them entirely. The younger men also talked about sports but as a kind of warfare, to see who could confirm to himself that his opinions were the soundest and his knowledge the most perfect. The older men talked to make a kind of weak but vital contact with their fellows. He wished he could join them – he was sure he'd be welcome – but he could barely remember what he knew in 1975. *Ernie Banks – has anyone heard how Ernie's doing?* He passed, but he listened and even enjoyed himself and found himself wishing he'd seen players he'd never heard of, for instance, a man named Montana.

Once in the sports bar he heard the slow, essential voice of Texas say, more in wonder than in sadness and more in sadness than in anything else, "That was the worst call I've ever seen." He looked around and found his man – a tidy, corpulent, tweedy crew cut with turquoise cuff links and a rusty orange tie – but in that moment he lost any chance to see the outraged play itself. True, plays in various sports were winding down all over the room, but nothing about any of them suggested any kind of milestone. So he gave it up, and a nagging sense of loss stuck around for several minutes – but, *ce qui compte*, it *passed*. It was the nature of the sports bar that all manner of things *passed* in there, and quickly, even the guilt of missing the worst call ever. This made his sports bar listening the least strenuous listening of all, nothing like what he often heard in the lobby bar: for instance, a partner in some kind of pillaging consultancy instructing his identically dressed and coifed young band on the plan for tomorrow's raid.

Out in the lobby bar he found that the young women appalled him especially. Most were somewhat less obviously carnivorous then the men, and from some of them one might catch a glimpse of humor that wasn't irredeemably cruel, but true lobby bar men were easy to dismiss as jerks. He had never learned to think of glib, attractive women as jerks to be thrown away on sight and it put him in a distressful spot as an eavesdropper. I have so much to learn, he thought, and yet what could it amount to?

He listened to sleek men in jeans order Campari and tell sleek women in jogging suits how old the road could get. He listened to the women order Chardonnay and Merlot and agree about the road, but only after remembering to name their labels. He listened to conversations interrupted by chirping cell phones, watched one party sit blankly while the other talked for two or three minutes before saying, "Look, got to go, got somebody here," and never heard a single reproach for it. He saw people *make a call* between sips and never heard a slap or heels stalking quickly away. He asked himself how long it would take to get used to that and thought, maybe a lifetime, but not this one. He listened to people who sold *bandwidth* and *connectivity* and *seats* and mostly something just called *hours* and he waited to hear somebody who wanted to buy anything at all but he never did. He listened in the coffee shop and the sports bar and in the lobby and if he closed his eyes he soon lost all sense of who was speaking or how any part of their world might ever have meant anything to him.

In the coffee shop he ate pancakes and maple syrup and all kinds of fruit, every kind of fruit they had, every day, over and over again. When he'd had enough of it he'd stroll outside and tear up the pool for an hour of fierce laps, and though he was always full when he dove in and though he could barely stand when he hauled himself out, he never got a single cramp from it because there was always a lifeguard there, watching. Thus he'd be ready for the sports bar, where one could get pretty good beer from Germany and Holland but nothing from Alsace or Jamaica. But he was still most drawn to the lobby bar and always returned to it soon enough. In the mornings before his pancakes he sat out there, drank too much espresso and listened while people waited for people; the people they were waiting for joined them and then they all waited for others and complained about how hard they worked. They discussed airline schedules and airports and blamed the horror of the moment on travel departments or machinists' unions or accountants. They didn't always agree on the culprit but all were sure that somebody was to blame. After a while the laggard would appear and then they'd have to go find sushi. In the afternoons after the sports bar grew crowded and even the best beer lost its savor, a young man named Eddie showed up in the lobby bar to play the piano very well. Once Nick and what he'd learned over time to call music had been mutual enigmas. Then a dozen exiled Frenchwomen with a common musical pedigree combined to solve them both. What they hit on: keep playing the good stuff for him, always remind him what it's called and don't ever try to explain another thing. All agreed that the project has been a grand success: now, when the time comes for someone to get out of bed and change the record, one no longer hesitates to let Nicky do it all by himself. Now he figured that to their taste Eddie was a little too fond of Chopin, but so are many people. Occasionally he'd toss off a bit of perfect Satie but it never lasted long enough for Nick. Then he noticed Eddie's tip glass and took to dropping in a twenty when he especially liked what he heard. The second time he did that Eddie asked, "Rachmaninoff? Liszt?" Nick said, "No Rachmaninoff and maybe a tiny bit of Liszt." He suggested Beethoven but Eddie said he was a man who knew his limits, unless Nick was into *Für Elise*. Nick said he wasn't and they agreed to see how he liked Eddie's take on Gershwin. Nick liked it very much and, not knowing what a cliché it was, asked how Eddie came to be playing in a hotel lobby. Eddie looked a little blank and said, "Nashville, man." Nick decided that he'd best let that one go. In three days Eddie made a couple of hundred off Nick and always waited for him to leave before settling into his Beatles medley.

In the lobby bar people typed on laptops and read Burton and fished for angles and conspired. Everyone was invisible in the lobby bar, except to Nick, and nothing that was said was overheard by anyone but him.

He heard, "We're aggressively into B to B but nobody should

think of us as angels."

He heard, "I send you out to get a site license and you come back with twenty named users and you think I want to sit with you and watch you eat?"

He heard, "Everybody thinks they've got it but we're already at the next level" and watched three others nod smugly, as if to say they knew exactly what was meant. *Excuse me children but I'm an old man and out of touch – please, what was the last level but three?* But they didn't answer and he realized that he'd kept the question to himself. Something happened anyway. Immediately after this exercise in telepathy somebody finally met his eye (about five in the afternoon of his third full day) and then, with no thought of any kind, merely from a hard-earned reflex that hadn't been exercised in days, Nick had an eyebrow raised and a palm extended to the chair next to his and she was sliding into it in her traveling outfit, jeans, a liberal application of something from Chanel, a bronze silk blouse under tweed and, he was sure, a Hermés scarf.

"A fellow sufferer?" she said, a glance toward the leveling children.

"I avoid suffering at all costs, which is why you were sent. Something expensive and barely alcoholic to drink?"

"Why thank you. A double Hennessey would be nice."

A drink secured, he tried various guesses: thirty-eight with a couple of extra wrinkles? Forty-four and an hour a day in the gym? Fifty-two and some serious money invested?

"In the trade?" she said, another glance at the four little monsters.

"So many years ago I can't count them. I haven't the faintest idea what any of it means anymore."

"That's all right, they don't either. But still, you're here on business," she said, insisting, and after considering what it would mean to be sitting there for pleasure, he conceded with a shrug.

"Tell me what kind. If you don't at least mention it I couldn't take the shock."

"Waiting to spend someone's money. It's all that's left to me in my dotage."

"Spending it? And not getting more?"

"Isn't that what our twenties are for?" A nod toward young corporate America, who were now taking the supply chain out of the box and beyond the desktop.

"Alas, I neglected my twenties, and here I am."

"As?"

"As their den mother."

"I suppose there are worse fates."

"I'm sure of it. There are also better ones. Tell me about them."

"You're here alone?"

"If you don't count them."

"I don't count them."

"Then I'm here alone, if you don't count yourself."

"I see. Dinner?"

"That would be lovely."

"Perhaps an early one. That's Eddie. He gets off at nine. I have a certain amount of influence with him and he can play *Rhapsody in Blue* the way it was written. It *can* be danced to."

"I'll just go change. Half an hour?"

He went back to his room to shave again. He rinsed off his razor, he glanced at his mirror. He put the razor down again. He stared himself down and summed up what he'd learned so far in Nashville.

In considerable wonderment he thought that this country, this country has fallen from a predator's kingdom to a preserve for surly, posturing sheep.

Once, he thought, there was a touch of honorable frankness to our incivilities. Once, he thought, we made damn sure of it.

Back then when you got in our way you didn't like it one damn bit but at least nobody pretended they were sorry. Back then we saw you and we *sized you up,* and maybe you had it coming and maybe you were just in the way, but no matter why it had to be you, we never once took you for granted.

Today it doesn't matter who you are. Today, whoever you thought you were, you're really just the fool we ordered out for. We mumble and look anywhere but at you, we sneer "excuse me" and bluff our way through with a handful of slogans ripped straight from some kind of business school spelling bee.

Selling it everywhere we can but buying our fill whether we sell out or not. Hocking everything we own just to make the payments. With time running out we hit the road, following rumors, sniffing out new ways to fall for our own sad crap. Tonight he was hot on that trail himself, he was sure he could sell any damn thing in the world a hundred times over right down there in the lobby, if only he placed his own order then, without delay.

He picked up his razor again. Reflecting on the world like this was nice but he had things to do tonight. He got down to shaving. He looked in his mirror and he didn't hate a single thing he saw there.

He checked his watch, ran a brush through his hair and started back toward the elevator.

He'd have his fourth steak in three days and Isabella ordered something called shrimp scampi. "Well," Nick said, "which is it?" but the waiter looked blank and Isabella seemed to think he was making a joke she didn't get; still perplexed, he let it drop. They had a bottle of Cabernet that Isabella said was her favorite and Nick thought would have made a pretty good Chianti. She said she was a Senior Account Representative and among her wares was the chattering quartet in the lobby.

"And the less said about that," Nick offered.

"Precisely. Where have you been all my life and so on?"

So Nick told her a little about this and that – not too much *this* because he hadn't entirely lost his mind, but maybe overcompensating a little on the *that*.

"It sounds like heaven," she said.

"How could it be? It's a place where people live."

"But to be free of... all this. To know who you are and what you have to do today and have everyone accept that. That sounds so wonderful to me."

Nick sliced off a very thin piece of almost raw beef and dragged it through a more than passable *sauce marchand de vin*. He smiled, but he was thinking: one more believer in the curative virtues of ancient poverty. He held on to that thought just a tad too long and it exploded on him.

You people, you people won't rest till you've taken it all, will you?

It was spontaneous, and a savagely angry thing to have erupting in your head, but he hadn't had sex in two weeks and he fought to keep it down. "No, Isabella," he said, "no. Nothing's ever really quite like that." And he leaned forward and told her a story.

Chapter 6

Philippe Bondieu
May 25, 1969

This is the story that Nicholas Pope told Isabella over a steak, *crème brulée,* Cognac and Gershwin in Nashville.

In the France of 1962 the liabilities of empire had begun to overwhelm the balance sheet of state. Saint Sulpice must, alas, be made independent and for the seven years that followed, the transition to informal possession of France was handled with a minimum of grace. In France one was distracted. Bombs in cafés distracted one, mobs of crazy Parisians chanting *Algerie Française* distracted one, tanks clanking down the Champs Elysée calmed a few and distracted even more. Now was not the time to celebrate independencies and the French (in no way unique among nations) can fumble what they don't feel like celebrating. But a seven-year plan had been announced and, sure enough, seven years duly passed. By then France was distracted by rioting students and threats of a general strike but on Saint Sulpice they consulted the calendar and lowered the flag. A man named Mathis became President. *You are a democracy now: go and vote for a man named Mathis.* Mathis was a colorless toady, a barbershop Pompidieu. *Va t'en. You're your own country now, voluntarily de-Frenched, and colorless toadies are the way you've chosen.*

All this was before Nick's time but he knows it better than he knows his Valley Forge. Isabella is going to learn a little of it if it kills her.

There was, most of all, a sense that nothing was finished, that something very interesting and important had just begun. But if this sense was pressing and universal, the *what* of the something to come was trapped inside a thousand or more inexpressible private visions, and some of these were ecstatically hopeful and some were anything but. Consider morning. Early mass is long since over and Mme. Kunkel, the one M'sieur Bonnet so unfairly calls Fräulein Etwas-mit-Sprudelwasser, Mme. Kunkel (who tries so hard to be French) is on her balcony facing northeast, somewhat into the low but thoroughly risen sun to be sure, but for that very reason safely away from the untidy working vessels and shouting darkies to her west. This morning Mme. Kunkel has had to make her own coffee and therefore is in a mood so foul and rare that her years of practice at merely earsplitting foul moods scarcely enable her to approach it, and then only on tiptoe as it were – when all of a blow (*wie man sagt*) she looks up from last month's *Elle* to see, stock still and straight across the street, a somber black man dressed not *comme il faut* in a scant selection of once whitish rags, no, dressed instead in brazen, social climbing *bleu de travail*, yellow clogs and a wide straw hat, and gazing at her without pretense of doing anything else: gazing ever so speculatively, so that, of the thousand original thoughts this instantly provokes in her, the one she seizes and flings at M. Kunkel (emerging at last from the kitchen with a recent *Barron's* and a small *fine*) is this: "See? Take a good look. When they come in the night to hang us, that one will lead."

But poor Philippe Bondieu, standing there all blue and hatted, looks somber only because his sudden joy is too deep to express. The joys his face knows how to deal with are a full plate for every child or a mild, breezy evening with Colette after everyone else is in bed; anything greater than that overwhelms it, simply turns it off, and one of these rare excessive joys is repeatedly breaking over him as he stands there gawking up at that magazine, has been breaking over him since he first looked up and saw it, which he did because at just the proper instant the more-than-irritated Mme. Kunkel had murmured a thunderous *also!* and flipped two or three pages over in a spare little gesture that made no more noise than M'sieur Paul's whip when he's showing off for the tourists. M. Paul is one of seven licensed carriage drivers on the island but he is by far the best with his whip – even his horses think so, and that's saying a lot, but everyone who knows those horses agrees that when they hear that whip crack inches above their idle Caribbean rumps they flick their tails and toss their heads and go *wrrll, wrrll, wrrll* with their mouths and *clomp, clomp, clomp* with their hooves and then every little tourist child in sight yells, *Mommy, Mummy, Mamam!* Then the horse-prodigies get treats and only after they've finished them do they have to clomp around the square once or twice until the little heathens get bored and more ice cream must be found at once. But even though Philippe Bondieu knows this as well as anyone, he is not a horse and when he heard the sound of Mme. Kunkel's magazine pretending to be M. Paul's whip he did not toss his head or clomp his feet but looked up to see what it was – and what he saw was something he'd seen perhaps a thousand times (what kind of idiot would count such things?) but this time it instantly summoned the inexpressibly wondrous and joyful thought that should have come to him unaided weeks ago but which, evidently, had needed this admittedly crude prompt to get itself up and doing. Now it sang to him, over and over; over and over his thought sang to him, perhaps trying through repetition to atone for its tardiness, and each time it washed over him Philippe Bondieu's happiness increased by another impossible increment. Even M. Kunkel's strenuous good morning barely got through and M. Kunkel has a set of lungs on him. When he salutes you with an affable *"schwartzische Teufel!"* (probably *Top of the morning!* or *Won't you have a croissant with us?*) he can rattle windows up and down the street, but, today, so complete is Philippe's surrender to his joy that he can barely raise a finger in answering benediction and then slowly amble down the hill, leaving the Kunkels to their bizarre but doubtlessly fashionable style of bellowed endearment. At the foot of the hill – not the real foot of the hill, a good kilometer away and well into the shanty town of Belle Vièrge, but at the official end of the Rue Ste Madeleine and thus, in many ways, at the end of the world – he comes upon Anne Marie Marceau sweeping the horse apples away from the door to her gallery.

"M'demoiselle!" he cries. "Why didn't I think of it before? Now my children will learn to read!" Anne Marie has painted Philippe a dozen times and has yet to get him right. This makes him a serious person in her eyes (as good a system as any, one supposes). "Yes," she says, "and rich men on yachts will come and buy all my paintings!" "Ha! Old Rosambert says rich men from yachts will rape his daughters and poison the fish. But why shouldn't my children learn to read now?" "O, the younger ones perhaps. Claudine though, you'll not get her in any school room I think." Just about here one might have heard a cough or a squeak of some kind, and if one had heard it and then had been curious enough to glance the five meters across the street, one could have seen the back of a Belgian lad of twenty or so, pushing his useless and very expensive bicycle up the hill and thinking, *perhaps, soon, Anne Marie will sleep with me in the spirit of democracy…* But, possibly because one somehow knew that that was exactly what one would see, one carefully refrained from looking and redoubled one's interest in the proper color of M. Philippe Bondieu's lips: not the lips on his face, of course, but the lips on the canvas that was waiting inside, next to a pitcher of iced coffee and half a chocolate bar filled with strawberry jam. And in doing so one heard M. Bondieu's very judicious reply to that last bit of banter and, because one is at bottom an artist, one thought it summed up the sham of neocolonialism as neatly as is possible, at least as neatly as is possible outside the walls of the Sorbonne itself. "O, Claudine is as lost as Colette and me, M'demoiselle. She'll have a big belly by Christmas and we'll marry her off to her postman. But her kids, they can grow up reading with their little aunts and uncles." Such words will make one cry all night if one is not strong. In a very small house not fifty meters away, that same young woman and her postman even now are busy making a prophet out of Philippe. He has just thrown back the sheet, sat up and exclaimed, "I shall have a telephone!" And she has rolled over, howled and would collapse were she not already as prone as a Caribbean girl can be. "And what," she taunts, "will you do to make *that* happen?" "I shall become a constable and never take a bribe." *"O là!"* Claudine wails. "And I had such hopes!" And leaps on him, and starts to bite, so we'd best hurry back to catch the undeceived father say, "I know you like to joke, M'demoiselle, but tell me the truth. If we're a democracy now and most of us decide that the children should read, what's to prevent it?" "O, shit, Philippe, take me for a walk and I'll show you everything."

Of course it is Sunday. He will amble ever more slowly as the morning passes, for the truth is that he limps quite badly at times. He will say things like "The doctors will come see us when we're sick" and she will answer "The doctors have all bought tickets for France" and then they will laugh like idiots because what they're saying is what they hear all around them, day in and out, and somehow that makes it seem the highest of comedy. They will avoid the eyes of scowling crones who whisper, "Those two! Who'd have thought it, and yet, of course!" They will creep stiff-backed around the corner and then their knees will shake, they will squeal, look up and see even sterner gazes from even more forbidding eyes (surely now there will be voodoo in the streets). In the squeaky voice of Monsieur Maurice the curate he announces, "There must be clean water for everyone!" She jerks her thumb toward the bay, thrusts out her jaw and in M. Mathis's deadest monotone demands, "*Quoi, tout cela* isn't clear enough for you?" But then he pulls her aside and whispers, "But really. Why couldn't there be a school, just a little one to start with?" "Really," she protests, "people will believe it that we're lovers..." At the Café des Artistes Anne Marie leads Philippe to a table and dares the sum of authorities, past, present and future, to do something about it. Authority demurs while suspecting that the Café des Artistes is pushing the means of the town's only artiste, especially with fisherman – authority in this case being Antoine, least repressive of waiters, who is there with alacrity bearing menu and smirk. "Here, read me this," Philippe commands, and when she does, shouts, "Ha! So on Sunday my mackerel are worth ten New Francs..." Anne Marie will eventually decide on mauve and orange for his lips and will be selling about ten pairs a month by the time she and Nicholas break up, but now she is saying, "...because people have to agree that's what they want and they hardly ever do." Oh it is hopeless but Philippe keeps grinning at her, so sure she is joking. And perhaps because Philippe was limping quite badly just before or possibly because you like a nice coincidence, Claudine chooses this moment to exclaim, "My father will have a new cane and fish only when he wants to!" Her postman is watching more than listening and replies, "When they try to buy a woman we constables will shame them in the street." But they are way across the square and down the hill and anyway nothing like these dreams could ever happen.

Exasperated as ever by hope, Anne Marie crushes an expensive macaroon of the type called *bergamotes de Nancy* and hisses, "Look around you, Philippe. Tell yourself what you see. Show me this schoolhouse in anyone's face." (*"Annie Marie!"* It is a shout of mingled triumph and defeat and it comes from at least two streets away. *"Anne Marie, Anne Marie! They're pulling down Richelieu's statue and putting up a Coca-Cola bottle, in neon!"* But perhaps not yet because from above his fountain Richelieu still scowls beatifically at them, as do one or two shockable café dwellers: democracy is fine but, after all, if there is going to be shouting…) Philippe obeys and searches for his school. *"Tu crois,"* he asks at length, *"que les* Yankees will come and drag their scum back home?" "More likely that they'll leave the scum and just take their money." Perhaps a little loudly, that, for the next table joins in: "The Yankees will send the rest of their scum and then forget us." And who should be surprised that it's the Belgian lad, and who should be surprised if he leans a little heavily on *scum?* Not Anne Marie, who puts her hand over Philippe's and leaves it there. Not Antoine the waiter, who winks at Anne Marie and says, "Oh, yes, until Fidel shows an interest," and, suddenly spotting a couple who've been waiting half an hour to order their usual *omelette aux fine herbes,* marches briskly off across the terrace. He has contrived to leave them someone else's milk, which Anne Marie hurriedly pours into both their cups.

In the time that takes, silly Nicole Malzac has run noisily ahead of her frightful family – *Maman! Papa! Ici, ici!* – to claim for her whole tribe the remainder of the besotted boy's table and announce, still (or always) out of breath, "Oh, he has, he *has,* already there are six Cubans at Mme. du Fresnes's!" Then to glare at Anne Marie through her absurd pink sunglasses and sneer at Anne Marie through her absurd pink lips, quite prepared for all steps necessary to forestall the theft of her beloved little Belgian. Then to disappear from Nick's story forever, which is not to disparage her in the least but rather to demonstrate with the most apt precision her entire effect on everyone she would ever meet. And if Isabella should be the least inclined to doubt this, she can consider how nobody in the entire café, in the entire town or even, for that matter, Mme. du Fresnes herself, ever showed the slightest interest in Nicole's extraordinary news. Except, momentarily, Papa (as Papas will), and he only to eye Philippe sideways and remark (possibly in jest but the case is not certain), "Never mind. If Mme. du Fresnes's is lost, I will build another hotel, become ten times a millionaire and we shall all move to Johannesburg." Mme. Malzac prefers to notice Philippe more frankly and even studies him a moment but contents herself in the end with an inward *"infamous!"* that barely carries across four or five tables. Half bowing to madame, Philippe announces, "Yesterday a submarine cut Rolland's net." While Anne Marie cringes, M. Malzac spots M. Delormé a scant dozen meters behind her and commences an intimate duet. "They dismantle the power plant next week, engineers have arrived from Tobago." *"C'est rien, ça.* They have frozen half the bank accounts already." "That is not so; instead they have confiscated *Le Matin's* press and are printing money around the clock." Mme. Malzac keeps her eyes on Philippe and her purse on her lap but leans toward the Belgian, for callow though he is and to his considerable distress, his father is somebody. *"Regard ça.* From now on fish will rot before they'll sell them to us." On cue and to be expected perhaps, Philippe whispers to Anne Marie; insupportably, she whispers back. From the bottom of a well of pain the boy tells Mme. Malzac, "Then I will buy the Prefecture and open a restaurant. For people of taste." (At this a wheezy, mouse-like noise emits from someplace quite close by but no one can seem to locate its source and in a moment conversation resumes.) What Philippe has said is, "She might try paying cash. If fish were sold for cash there might be shoes." But he would not wish to be offensive about it, so he whispers. What Anne Marie has said is, "If you're not rude to her soon I'll tell Colette you made a pass at me." The Belgian boy thinks that possibly suicide would strengthen his case. Mme. Malzac tells him, "I think the maid will quit. Perhaps she already has, it's become impossible to tell." Philippe says, "I am in your power, then, but beware. She would say it is your fault." M. Malzac takes pity on the Belgian, tells him, "I had to pay ten thousand old to get the telephone fixed. Informally, you understand," but Mme. Malzac hisses, "Be quiet, they listen to everything." Anne Marie says, "Why won't you do what I want?" Choosing life and aiming for irony, the Belgian says, "Possibly it's not so bad with your maid. Perhaps all the young women will come to their senses." Aiming not at all Mme. Malzac spits back, "More likely she'll steal the flat and we will starve on the beach." Philippe considers. M. Delormé shouts, "While there's still time I will buy old Rothstein's papers and move to Tel Aviv," which all the visible Malzacs think is *very* funny. In addition to her bag Mme. Malzac clutches a rosary. Philippe smiles, then Anne Marie smiles. M. Malzac says, "Tell that one to your father. He'll appreciate it." Philippe begins to open his mouth. Anne Marie says to Mme. Malzac, "Lovely day, isn't it?" Philippe says, "*Tu sais*, next Sunday, if I want it, I shall have a pew in the front. I think Colette might like that." M. Malzac blanches. Mme. Malzac gasps. "Always," she breathes, "they rape the nuns first." "What *I* have heard proposed," Anne Marie offers, purely as a matter of interest, "is that white people will be made to tithe and for a change the nuns will be fed." But at that point, possibly because the sun is almost directly overhead, spirits begin to flag and the festivity of the moment begins to dissipate. On the slow walk home she explains, "You see? Whatever they might come to agree on, it won't be that they should pay for a school before they steal another sou." But he is imperturbable. "Pray God you are fooled, M'demoiselle. It has happened at least once, I believe, or why would you be here with us? But do you not at least find them invigorating? Just listening makes me want an outboard motor, like a white man's."

None of this was the essence of it. All this together was not the essence of it. The essence of it was too unfamiliar to have a name. The essence of it was that for one year of its four-century history, collectively and universally and apparently without cause, Saint Sulpice had finally experienced impatience.

For collective sins there are collective punishments, and there is nothing strange if their agents should be diabolical, nothing strange at all if God should seem to let the devil have his way in them. A man named Gérard arrived from Martinique, as colorless in his rumpled colonial linen as any Mathis but with *ancien regime* stamped all over an especially acerbic crew cut and wearing those steel-framed glasses affected in those years by the worst kind of police.

M. Gérard set up office in a vacant bakery next to the Prefecture, as if to say, *See? Is it not clear that I have no official function?* Of course officials of one kind or another were always visiting him, probably for only the most unofficial courtesies, but all agree that he stayed religiously off government property. It is also true that at one time or another every member of that comical gang of functionaries known to all as The Khaki Brothers spent his hour in M. Gérard's office, went in sweating and came out nearly prostrate, but too much can be made of such things. Indeed, undeniably, important visitors of all kinds sought him out, and many were the people who, having been to see him on vaguely described visits of no moment at all, reported that M. Délibes or *Commissaire* Proudhon himself had sat, and silently, mind you, throughout the interview: well, there you have it. In the face of such coincidences, conclusions will be jumped to; indeed, when all the known facts are so strikingly innocent and trivial, the jumping of conclusions provides all the interest to be had. Thus, for instance, people said the most outrageous things about the repeated visits of the Belgian lad, pretending to reveal the most shocking particulars while disagreeing, even, about whether he had barged in unannounced or been dragged screaming by three fat constables. And so much was made of the visit of the lad's father, and the three hours he stayed, and how he and the boy left together and how the next day the boy flew off to Martinique and was never seen again – well, that kind of thing is the very stuff of gossip but who, really, can claim to know the truth? And in the end the disappearances were remarkably few. A cobbler, a curate, a mechanic: all, unfortunately, useful men. And a postman, more easily replaced. And of all people, an eccentric fisherman, and concerning him, for a while people would stand quite apart from any crowd and whisper, *why? Why* that *one? You don't suppose…*

When Anne Marie couldn't sleep in later years she would take to asking, "Have you never murdered anyone, Nicholas? Has someone never trusted you, and you killed him with café au lait and little cookies?" At first he would say the things she seemed to expect. Together they explored the mysteries of a world so malign that even Anne Marie could be an instrument of evil. Then once he heard himself say, "Well, not really. Of course I did betray everyone I knew but I did it for money and probably no one died, so I guess that doesn't count." When he heard himself say that, he was pretty sure they were nearing the end, and so they were, though Anne Marie rated civility very high and they merely shook hands and parted friends – which, if he didn't understand it, was still fine with him. But, look, we have wandered almost into modern times. Back in the year of independence we abruptly take less philosophical approaches. Overall there is a swift foreshortening of perspective and a lessening of interest in the problems of existentialism. Most of all, certain kinds of talk go out of fashion with breathtaking speed. *That which hath been,* saith the Preacher, *is that which shall be,* and suddenly one wonders how that had ever been forgotten. Anne Marie, for instance, has a visit to Gérard's little office and both Délibes and Proudhon sit in, each, she thinks, probably there to spoil the other's nonexistent chances with her. In her view it is all cryptic, surreal, repressive, fascistic and inept, and in these terms Nick will hear quite a bit about it. (In his view it was meant to scare the shit out of her and did; Nick, as you see, is not much of a thinker in her eyes and for a so-called child of the sixties he has no revolutionary consciousness at all.) In any case Gérard hands her a copy of *The Myth of Sisyphus* and asks, "Yours?" Anne Marie already knows that it isn't (it's far too new) but looks inside anyway before saying, "No. See? I sign them there, in my own name." Gérard next gives her a *Nausea* which she doesn't even open. "Mine has a coffee stain on the cover," she explains. It is Proudhon who manages the leap. "But, then, you've read this book," he pronounces. "I'm not one of those who say it's his best," she allows, "but I admit I've more or less memorized it." "Coffee stain and all," Gérard murmurs, perhaps to prove himself unshockable. But shockable Délibes blurts out "But Sartre is a traitor!" and Anne Marie thinks there's a scandal brewing deep down in his fantasy life, in which she, probably naked, is preparing to submit to his lust in return for his name on some secret Marxist blood-oath. Proudhon gawps at him in annoyance and Gérard says, "Well, yes, but the formalities seem to be lagging in his case, don't they?" and then Proudhon smirks and Délibes, knowing he's defining himself to her as both a prig and a killjoy but unable to see another way out of his own trap, mutters, "Nonetheless, one's duty remains…" "Yes, it does," Gérard agrees with unusual good humor, "but, as you see, we are dealing here with one who does not share your views on duty and treason. And as we all formerly lived in France where certain political realities may have become habitual, and as we now live in a country so new that political reality is not to be found in any book and where we cannot expect it to be reflected in the lifelong habits of intellectuals of any stripe at all, well: under those circumstances, don't you think we owe it to her simply to explain how it is?" "Yes but—" Délibes begins but Proudhon cuts him off. "What he's asking her," Proudhon explains, "is whether she wants to stay here. I admit you have to listen closely but believe me, that's what he means." "Yes," Gérard adds, not the least put out by Proudhon's critique, "and everyone we talk to *wants* you to stay, don't they?" "Oh, yes," Proudhon puts in, "and so do we, emphatically. But the economics of it concern us for your sake. Do you really think you can get by, selling the occasional piece to the occasional citizen of consequence?" And suddenly all three are giving her their fullest, blandest attention while she teases the intended meaning from the text. "You mean," she says, feeling her face redden in spite of herself, "can I maintain the sort of reputation among—" "You see?" Délibes exclaims in triumph, as if she has suddenly shouted, *ce beau Étienne Délibes is right about everything!* "One *knew* she'd understand at once!" And Gérard and Proudhon are also on their feet and shaking her hand and patting her here and there almost paternally and sweeping her through the door with assurances of their own and (less plausibly) their wives' most distinguished sentiments and vague promises of visits to her gallery with money in hand once this exhausting season of reform has (someday!) run its course, and then she is standing between the forecourt of the Prefecture and the much less grand forecourt of the *Mairie* and beginning to realize that over the next several decades she must try to come to grips with selling out to the ludicrous vanguard of the murdering bourgeoisie without having offered a single word or gesture in defiance or even, for that matter, in acquiescence.

In more or less this manner, though perhaps with less personal engagement from the party of reason, many dozens of civics lessons are delivered and understood. With the basest of one's inferiors a certain jauntiness is appropriate. "Can it be true, Angelique, that you'd consider leaving Mme. Malzac's employ? Oh, we didn't think so either – how these stories spread! But look, you'd better tell her at once, shouldn't you, before she sends for your replacement and you're on the barge for Fort de France!" "Ah, Rolland, encountered any submarines lately?" "So, Rosambert, your daughters are all locked up for the night, I suppose?" But it isn't all perfunctory. Not a fisherman, for example, escapes being asked where he thinks that crazy Bondieu might be keeping himself; but, also, not one fails to shrug most elaborately and confess his utter incompetence even to guess, and that seems to be the correct answer, for all return home, well after midnight, to one sort of undignified and excessively emotional homecoming or another. With the lesser whites and the elevated blacks a franker tone is taken, one that serves to reestablish clear thinking in the face of so many confusing slogans and loose, enthusiastic nonsense about new orders and such. *"Écoute-moi, Antoine.* You are amusing and one is willing to pay a small price to be amused. But do not think that you will stay on this island one hour past the time your *patron* becomes bored with your antics, *tu me comprends?"* And, surprisingly to some but never to its objects, this spare, god-to-bacterium mode of address is only a little tempered for even the haughtiest of expatriates. "Listen, Kunkel. A man in your position requires a certain amount of respect if his life is to be tolerable. And that means that his entire family must act in ways that others of his station deem respectable. I'm sure that I'll not have to speak to you like this again…" Because, of course, one has almost failed one's headmaster before and can be put in mind of life's earliest watersheds. Of the voices of reason, only Gérard seems to appreciate that it is all an enormous bluff. With those few he deems capable of resistance he is shrill and unbending – perhaps he can be beaten but not without casualties. With the vast majority who believe what they see whether it's true or not, he allows himself a touch of humor, a poor one to be sure but welcome in any case under the circumstances.

Nowhere is this truer than in his encounters with *les frères khakis,* those unlovable little dun-suited parasites who are always under their betters' feet, so damnably ostentatious and mediocre, so damnably necessary. After their personal interviews they are brought back in batches to discuss the arrangement of society, the economy, the very state itself. They see it as no less than their due; Gérard and his few confidants see it as the most distasteful slumming of all.

In theory what passes is privileged but, socially, *les frères khakis* reinforce their conversation with certain well-established formulas. It is not terribly hard to construct plausible alternatives to their accounts if one knows how (as, in fact, everyone does) to interpret such phrases as "Monsieur *le Commissaire* requested my advice" and "Monsieur Délibes agrees with me that…" Thus translated, it is put to them: the system of informal taxation inaugurated (or at least accelerated to an unprecedented scale) immediately upon independence (i.e., upon the withdrawal of the last competent police) must now cease without delay. The rich, on whom, after all, everything depends, will not tolerate it. And it benefits only those in positions to arrange each individual levy and therefore does nothing to serve society at large, meaning, especially, M. Gérard's peers and advisors. This message is rendered abstractly. As it has already passed to each of the assembled brethren, privily and concretely and accompanied by dangerously apposite examples of what is now to be collectively regretted, the gathering accepts its scolding as the choir takes to their sermon. Accounts vary but it is quite possible that along in here Gérard achieves something close to genuine eloquence; unlikely as that is, there is no doubt that he reaches for it. If, in future, our fine and necessary public servants (vast relief at this sarcasm) are to live well on Saint Sulpice, then they must be adequately compensated by salary, and so, gentlemen, let us turn our attention to how that desirable condition must be sought. Compensation by salary implies an influx equal to the communal reward (a disturbing adjective that keeps one a little edgy). Since it is the function of governments to spend wealth created by others, the money must ultimately come from some form of taxation. True, one can print it but only at the cost of radical inflation – and, if one will look at the roster of souls on Saint Sulpice, and, especially, at who is on top and who is on the bottom, one will see that inflation is about the very worst fate one can imagine. So one is looking for a kind of tax, is one not? But wherever one looks there are difficulties. One may not tax the rich because they will simply move away. One may not tax one's self and one's brethren because one is about increasing one's share of the wealth, not diminishing it (usually, at this point, one recalls a certain amount of nervous laughter and applause). One may not tax the blacks because, logically, one must then permit them to acquire the funds from which to pay. Here we may assume that Gérard is rhetorically adept enough to pause, and it is not reaching far to imagine that some bold Khaki Brother obligingly steels himself and babbles out the critical question: *but who, then, is left?*

Gérard instructs them. If one must tax but may not tax whom one has, one must have someone else, *ne c'est pas?* What one desires is a new kind of wealth, one that will come but will not go even when the taxes become significant.

But, the same or another *frère khaki* surely persists, what is this elusive species and how will it be lured to Saint Sulpice?

M. Gérard had an answer for that too, and on 23 October 1969, President Mathis signed Amendment One to the Constitution of the Sovereign State of Saint Sulpice, rendering it henceforth and forever illegal to extradite anyone, citizen or foreigner, to any country whatsoever.

Not even the country to which Saint Sulpice was so long attached by bonds of kingship and fealty? *That Far Off, Gracious Land Which in*

So Many Ways Is Still Our Mother?

No, not even to that one.

Then M. Gérard strolled into the Café des Artistes and let himself get royally drunk. As afternoon strayed into evening and no one else was permitted to pay for a round, he let it drop that he would be staying on in town, to open a travel agency.

Chapter 7

Aunt Mary
June 25, 2001

After the third dance she went off to the head and Nick went up to the bar for refills. A potentially interesting blond of the same elusive non-age as Isabella was sitting next to the spot you'd naturally pick to place your order – he couldn't tell exactly how interesting because he didn't have the angle – and while he waited he looked down and she looked up and smiled and said, "Hi."

"Hi," he said in return, and she said, "I just wanted to tell you, before you decide to close that deal? Any friend of Johnny's is a real good friend of mine."

Nick took a second to decide whether he was supposed to say something and concluded that it didn't matter much.

The blond nodded toward the dance floor. "I can get you prettier if that's what you want. We're a full service enterprise."

"You think I need help?"

"You'd be amazed what's changed since you left. Bumps in the road to love that your old man wouldn't even know what to call."

"You're prettier yourself."

"See, lines like that?" She nodded. "They're over."

"Jesus. Does it have to be a line?"

"Hotel. Bar. Drinks. Hell yes it has to be a line."

"And do lines always fail?"

"On me. Sorry. We specialize."

"Pity."

"No ego damage I can see, anyway. So here we are. You just snuck back into the country after twenty-five years of hiding and you're picking up the first loose woman you see. Got any questions you might like answered first?"

"Do they still make Roman Meal bread?"

"Sigh. Any more?"

"When did we give up on whitewall tires? In my day only cheapskates wouldn't pop for–"

"All right. Have your romp with Isabella–"

"My, my."

"You think you're playing with the kids in the alley? Isabella Giachetti, forty-five, rep for the same body shop for six years, which is forever. One bust for pot in college so there were prints, which match her glass from before dinner. Which means she's real because nobody who'd want you would ever plant anyone for six years. That's why you're talking to me and not your Uncle Roger. He's somebody you really don't ever want to hear from."

"So who are you?"

"I'm your Aunt Mary, of course. And speaking as your aunt, you could be the victim of false advertising. She's been married twice and they both left her."

"Auntie dearest, did I say anything about marriage?"

"Cad. Roué. Go have your romp with Isabella but in a couple of days we go to work."

"We?"

"Mr. Pope, so far you're an inspiration to us all but somebody needs to make sure that doesn't change. Get used to me."

The morning after the morning after next Nick was pouring the coffee when a twittering bird broke into the room and hid. Nick was looking around for it when Isabella said, "It's yours," and handed him his pager.

"I hate these things," he said.

"Who doesn't?" she yawned and turned back to her mimosa.

Nick picked up the phone and looked at the pager. There seemed to be too many numbers but he dialed them all and the blond answered before it rang.

"Say, hi Aunt Mary, I'm in Nashville."

"Oh, hello, Aunt Mary. Noon *already* in the Poconos? I'm in Tennessee for the bird watching and here it's barely light."

"Wonderful news, asshole. Look serious and a little shocked, like when you saw her the first time without her makeup. Great Aunt Bertha is desperately ill. In fact, it doesn't look like she's going to make it."

"Aunt Bertha?"

"*Great* Aunt Bertha. Your auntie is much too young to die."

"How sick is she?"

"Sick enough that the doc says you'd better get up here, not so sick she can't change her will if you don't."

"I'd better fly up there today."

"Smart boy. You make it a quickie, you just have time for a farewell matinee."

"I'd better leave right now."

"See, I tried to tell you but would you listen?"

Wherever she'd been when he called, by the time he was packed she was waiting at the elevator, reading the paper and snarling to herself. "Car keys and papers, love, then go down and check out." He dug them out for her and held the elevator door but she was walking away. Downstairs she slipped in behind him as he walked out the revolving door, grabbed his bag before the doorman could get it and tossed it into the back of a black car, not half as big as Ruiz's but still bigger than anything on Saint Sulpice. She climbed in and waved him in after her and as soon as he shut the door the car was off and into traffic.

"This isn't mine, is it?" he asked.

"You don't really have one, you know."

"So, Aunt Mary, where to today?"

They were already at a red light and the driver turned around and said, "She ain't really one of your aunts. You can call her Cousin Olga."

Nick stared at him.

"Damn," Cousin Olga said, "you shut him up."

"Think of me," Johnny said, "as your other good old cousin Sugar Lips. You kids ready for a nice long ride in the country?"

Chapter 8

Roddy John Hall
1974 – 2001
Nikolai Nikoláevich Petrov-Pope, Johnny W.
Summer, 2001

Nick first heard Cousin Olga's voice on a cassette that Johnny brought to Anne Marie's gallery one afternoon not a month before they drove off to Kentucky. Of course he didn't know whose voice it was and in fact wouldn't figure it out for some time to come, but it did impress him.

"It turns out," Johnny said, "you got the story nearly right. Listen to Mrs. Simpson," waving off the question raised by Nick's eyebrows.

Nick listened. It was a very pleasant and just perceptibly mocking voice. After a couple of minutes Nick reached over and turned off the player and said, "I was getting to that part."

Johnny said, "Sure but we couldn't wait" and turned it back on.

Halfway through Nick stopped it again and asked, "How does she know?"

Johnny said, "She asked. When she asks, she gets told. It's a real big part of what she does."

Here's what she told them:

Roddy didn't exactly notice this but his life continued like a weedy patch beside the road or a bank of fog that didn't burn off quite on time. You could tell him anything you wanted to but if he didn't want to hear it, what could you say next?

A couple of years went by, Schrenk blowing in and out like a whirlwind every couple of months. Schrenk officially worked out of Lexington, Kentucky, but he never seemed to be there. When he wasn't in Chicago you could almost track his progress around the country as he called for details of every conceivable kind of transaction. It was almost more restful to have him leaning over your desk.

In spite of his luck Roddy held his department together. If anything it ran better and better, reaching its apogee on September 24, 1976, the day that provoking innocent named Nicholas Petraki left town for good and Roddy made the biggest wire transfer in the company's history.

A shipload of active ingredient, brewed up for Himmelskirch by one of the most famous companies in Europe, had left Hamburg in mid-August. By the time the customs broker in Baltimore had the paperwork together, the pile was over an inch thick. The price was stated in DMs – it was summer and the DM was high – and Roddy settled on a rate with the bank on Thursday afternoon. By then Roddy was checking the calculation of duties and the Material Manager and the Moron had signed off but when they all were done it was after three and too late to wire the payment. The next morning Roddy entered a wire transfer request for $4,562,388 even, no cents – he always felt he could round off the cents on wires. A few minutes later Mrs. Macmillan brought him the printed voucher and he called it in to the bank. That night he and Nick Petraki went out to dinner, as they often did on Fridays. In Greek Town they ate a pile of braised lamb and okra and eggplant and killed a bottle of Retsina. Nick was off to Key West for ten days and Roddy lectured him on marlin fishing, which he'd never done but had read a lot about. Nick had a couple of Greek coffees because he was driving to the airport and while he drank them they kicked around a fanciful plan for a program to detect and isolate the Moron's personal trips from his expense reports. Then Roddy went home and started calling around for someone to watch the Bears game with him on Sunday.

On Monday morning Roddy walked in to find a puzzled twix inquiring into the whereabouts of Europe's four and a half million. Roddy swore and called the bank but the bank was all reassurances – transfer sent, transfer confirmed. Relieved, Roddy cheerfully typed this out on the telex, pressed send and prepared to forget about it. Five minutes later the telex was clattering as it had never clattered before and Roddy was pulling papers out of cabinets and comparing them to each other. Everything seemed to tally, and it was only as the hapless bank clerk read him back everything he'd told her on Friday that he realized that the account she'd sent the money to was utterly different from the one blinking at him from his terminal. Ready to explode, he laid the phone down and, just to be sure, retrieved the printed voucher from his outbox where it was waiting to be filed, and almost started his tirade before he found the account number on it. Then he stopped. Then he hung up. The telex started in again. Roddy began to imagine a snide little paragraph on the front page of tomorrow's *Journal*. He called the bank back and the clerk went off to find a supervisor. It took five minutes to get one and another five to convince her that Roddy really had ordered four and a half million dollars wired to the wrong account. Right bank. Wrong account. Waiting for her call back, he tore off the new twix but didn't read it. He called Schrenk in Lexington, knowing full well that he'd miss him. He left a message and worked on praying that the bank would call to tell him how the Swiss had found the money before Schrenk phoned in from God knew where. But when the bank called, the supervisor had a vice president on the line with her, so there could be no disputing what she said when she told Roddy that a half hour after landing, the money had taken off again per standing instructions whose confidentiality was protected by the most sacred of Swiss banking laws.

For two days various authorities prowled through Accounting. It was difficult to know who was government, who was insurance, who was subcontracting to whom. On Tuesday morning Schrenk appeared and for the first time ever he did not shake Roddy's hand. "Hall," he said, "where is Petraki?"

Roddy thought, all these experts and they need him back here to get inside the computer. "Key West. He flew to Miami Friday so he must have made it by now."

"He went to Miami but he does not seem to be in Key West. He had reservations at a hotel but they cancelled them when they heard nothing by Sunday night."

Of course Nick had met a girl, probably on the plane down or maybe waiting for the next one, but he didn't need Schrenk knowing too much about his favorite hobby and Roddy tried to cover for him.

"He'll show up," Roddy said.

"Is this intuition, Hall?"

Roddy did not like that and just looked back.

"Because if it's intuition, I can understand that. But if you know where he is, if you have a basis for this confident assertion, then it is already very late for you to be telling us your informations."

Two men arrived. First Schrenk announced that two men would arrive tomorrow, then tomorrow came and they were there and all the others were gone. Schrenk showed them around each department, all except Accounting. They went away with Schrenk for lunch. They spent an hour with the Moron and then Schrenk brought them to

Roddy's office, introducing them as Hölle and Teufel. By then Roddy knew many scraps of German and didn't really believe that Hell and Devil came calling, though maybe this time they had. Hölle was a from-the-mold Hollywood Nazi, six-two and built like a halfback in his tight gray Berlin suit, whitish blond hair in a brush, transparent skin and impossibly blue eyes, over which he wore round, rimless glasses with gold wire temples. It is possible that he knew how to smile but Roddy wasn't convinced of it. Hölle couldn't have been more than thirty, which made him too young to have been in the Hitler Youth, and that was the only kind thought Roddy could ever summon for him. Teufel was supposed to be the other kind, the one you longed to be alone with so he could protect you while you got it off your chest. He had perhaps five years on Hölle, was short, slight, balding, with lank, mousy brown hair that would not stay combed. He compensated with a bandito mustache that would have done any *cucaracha* proud. He wore a loose tweed suit over a colorless but once green cardigan and carried at least five fountain pens. He did smile. He had quite a repertoire of smiles: tentative, expectant, reassured, pensive, puzzled and rueful. Rueful, Roddy learned, you did not want. Puzzled was nearly as bad and pensive could turn into it. Pensive and puzzled were accompanied by questions that were impossible to answer, though, always, one realized that there should be answers, easy answers, if only one could think of them. Teufel spoke near-perfect Oxbridge English. Hölle spoke English like a brain-damaged drill sergeant and did most of the talking. It was absurdly effective. "I do not understand this word as you use it." Well, he didn't, and Teufel for some reason wouldn't explain it to him – perhaps he felt it impolite to speak German in front of his hosts. Everything that troubled Hölle was something that *he did not understand* and somehow his ignorance was always your fault. There was nothing to do but explain it over and over again until dawn broke over Prussia and

Hölle would say at last, "So. That much, now, is clear."

In retrospect, it seems their method was designed to defeat any prepared line of defense. Contradictory instructions followed one on the other with no acknowledgement that some must be disobeyed:

We have all the time in the world, expound, leave nothing out; we have no time at all, get to the point at once.

Please include all trifles, it is not for any of us to realize at this soon point their possible importance; but then – so, Mrs. Macmillan and not Miss Rosenthal brought the documents: explain, please, why you deem this suspicious.

And, if given the chance, all of us, guilty or innocent, prepare defenses for moments like these. We do it whether we know it or not, we seem to be born knowing that even the best of us must defend ourselves someday, if only before God. Roddy's strategy was a meticulous recital of the facts, down to the smallest detail, and a refusal to discuss what he didn't know for sure. It was shattered in minutes and he found himself making elaborate guesses about who might have made the coffee and who might have turned out the lights. When asked, he replied that Petraki had keys that opened every office but Roddy's. This admission (for it was taken as one) seemed especially significant. But how else, Roddy pursued, really puzzled and really sweating, was Petraki to work, then? If he couldn't get *in*. If he couldn't unlock his own door. But this earned him only Teufel's most rueful smile and Hölle's darkest scowl, and they moved on.

Herr Schrenk has provided us with an account, based in great part on yours to him, we think (possibly, the tone implies, an offense worth twenty years). Tell it to us your way. Tell it from the beginning, include every detail, also your conjectures and opinions, but do not fail to be succinct and pertinent. They excused Schrenk – the man had duties after all (possibly unlike Roddy anymore, though in fairness they didn't say this), and then they sat back, ostensibly to listen.

Where to start? Roddy will begin with the process that was subverted. It has a history, not an especially tidy one. Fifteen months earlier the company had changed accounting firms. No audit is ever easy, especially any good one, but Roddy had no complaints about the firm they started with. They lost the account by being too thorough. Himmelskirch dictated that, because their own statements were due in March according to German company law, all subsidiaries would submit audited statements by the first of February. This is not realistic. It is worse than not realistic. The old firm balked. Which tests should they omit, then? Which standards should they relax? Along comes this other... this other band of... *firm*, and steals the account. *We* can do it. *We* know the answers to all those questions without asking them and we guarantee an opinion by the end of January.

It was... to start with, it was ridiculous – maybe we should leave it at that. The company had property in thirty-two states! Mostly pickup trucks and filing cabinets to be sure but they are fixed assets nonetheless, to be depreciated according to several different methods and in two currencies at once. All ought to be at least *seen* once in a while and the previous auditors *did* that, whereas–

"Well, yes," Teufel murmurs, "the regrettable decision to comply with German company law was made without your endorsement," while Hölle grunts and glares and scribbles furiously and Roddy despairs of ever being understood.

He trudges on: in any case, the new firm had to seem to do something to make up for what they wouldn't do in fact, and what they proposed was an intensive pre-audit review of all procedures and controls. The inspiration was a fantasy about self-auditing companies that anyone but an accountant might find plausible. One part of this would be a so-called computer audit that scared him and Petraki half to death. The auditors would sneak arbitrary test transactions into the system and follow them through; if they emerged correctly at the other end, they would identify them to Roddy, who would somehow make them go away – after he had reported them to the whole company and to Berlin as real. No, Roddy told them, they wouldn't do that. If they said they would review controls, then they could review the damn controls. If they said they would follow transactions, then they could follow real transactions. Roddy could not choose his accounting firm but he still had approval over the audit bill; he won. An expanded, intensive and, Roddy suspected, vindictive witch hunt for potential breaches of control would happen instead. Roddy summoned Petraki and Morris, the accounting manager. We have two weeks, he told them. Think like thieves. Think of every way we could steal and we'll come up with a way to block it. They found very little: Roddy had paid attention in class and the controls he instituted were good. Morris suggested that when they added a new vendor, someone in Accounting should make a call to prove that the company actually existed. Roddy himself had the receivable and payable clerks moved to different ends of the floor and secured the programs they ran, such that it would be obvious if one was suddenly doing the job of the other.

It was Petraki who found the mother lode.

Wire transfers, from the least to the greatest, were recorded informally. A voucher was approved. Morris or Roddy called the bank. The bank called the other one back to confirm the order, and if it couldn't get him, it called the Moron; if he was out, they called the Director of Research. A journal entry was made from the original voucher. If that journal entry was not made, if Morris or Roddy or someone pretending to be either waited until the right someone was out and called the bank and moved a few million to himself, and then answered the phone he knew would ring right away, and then did nothing at all except go on about his business – well, then the theft would probably go undiscovered until the bank statement arrived.

"A few million?" Hölle breathes "A few *million?*"

Well, yes, at least in summer. Infratox was permitted to keep six or seven million from July through October to pay the initial costs of the next production campaign. Anyway, Roddy says they came up with what they thought was an effective safeguard. Petraki would write a couple of programs. Roddy or Morris would enter a request for a transfer into a terminal. It would print exactly as entered and become the official voucher, from which the telephoning would be done. More importantly, it would immediately appear as a disbursement in the accounts payable, where many people would see it and where it would find its way onto the cash control sheet at the end of the day. Most importantly of all, on the voucher would be a control number assigned by the computer. The bank was instructed to ask for this number, both in the incoming call and the confirmation. The confirmation would take place while the original caller was still on the line; whoever confirmed it would call up the transaction and repeat the control number and the amount, and only when the bank heard both men speak at once could it proceed.

That's what they put in place, that's what the auditors grudgingly agreed was excessively thorough, and that's what happened the day the money was stolen. Roddy entered the order. It printed – nobody doubts that. Miss Rosenthal gave it to Mrs. Macmillan and *she* gave it to Roddy. He called it in. Morris got the call from the bank and confirmed it. The rest they know.

Here Teufel becomes loquacious again. Ah but this *rest* contains matters of extreme moment. It is not possible to identify every computer printer but impact printers such as the IBM model thus and so acquire idiosyncrasies much like a typewriter's. The remittance instructions were undoubtedly printed by theirs, on a sheet of single-ply green bar such as they use by the dozen of cartons per week. Now on this kind of printer the ribbon of course wears and must be replaced. It was replaced early in the afternoon of Thursday the 23rd and again late in the afternoon of Friday the 24th. This is established by examining the reports so meticulously stored in their color-coded binders throughout the department (Mr. Hall's files really are a model). One easily sees that the cash requirements report printed before noon on Thursday is faint, one sees that the aged payable report printed in the afternoon is coal black and even smudged. Then the ribbon begins to wear again.

But still, Hölle erupts, Mr. Hall may perhaps instruct them further, even in this well-understood matter. Two particulars remain unclear. First. Why did no one notice the discrepancy in the account number? Second. Having arranged for the fraudulent document to be printed, how did Petraki quickly and safely return the computer to its original condition?

The first question is easy. The account number doesn't display anywhere except to users of the highly secured program that sets up permanent information about the vendor. It *prints* on the voucher, because it must be read to the bank, but nobody has anything to compare that to, you see.

Perhaps they see. Perhaps, their looks say, they already see too much. Hölle is dumbfounded but by now Roddy realizes that it's pretense. Teufel is puzzled and Roddy knows that's trouble.

"Mr. Hall," he says, "I find that quite incomprehensible in one respect. You design such an elaborate procedure, and then you would not validate this critical record that determines the destination of the funds? Why? Why, especially, could Petraki be so confident that you wouldn't?"

Roddy tries. The account number, you see, is not *needed* in the normal course of business, not for any of the approvals, nor for the authorization or the confirmation. And what one does not need, one shouldn't show. It confuses people. The Moron after all... Even the Director of Research, they couldn't be expected... Amid both glaring and smiling disbelief, Roddy peters out and fights for breath, then regroups and tries again. These programs were *tested*, they had been *used* for months: everyone *knew* they printed what they were supposed to, no one *imagined* that suddenly they'd stop doing that. To backtrack all the way to the vendor record would be... and he gropes, perhaps for *excessive* but to his own horror blurts out *paranoia*. And has shocked himself into silence but for some reason Teufel makes none of the obvious rebukes and Hölle seems to be waiting to open another front.

Roddy must force himself to start again. He can also answer the other question and knows as he does it that he's damning Petraki irredeemably in the minds of these clumsy thinkers. Assuming it was Petraki, he says heavily – and Teufel nods, says yes, please accept that hypothesis – well, assuming it was Petraki, he'd have known how. Suppose Roddy, for example, or Morris, or anyone else had changed the account number in the normal way, and even if they'd then changed it right back again: here, come around, look at his screen – it will only take a minute, see, he calls up a vendor, this is Dow Chemical, see, the record shows the date and time it was last changed. Now watch, he adds an X to the end of the address and then he rubs it out and look, see, today's date and time. But the victim's record says it hasn't been changed for eighteen months, so this isn't... but they've straightened up and are no longer peering at his screen.

"Yes," Hölle says, "we have seen this demonstration."

Tuefel says, "We've even tried it ourselves and we believe you entirely."

How? Roddy seethes. *Who the hell has...?* With difficulty he finds his place. With Petraki it was different. Petraki had access to difficult special methods that allow highly trained technical people to bypass all the programming and make changes directly to the data itself. He has had to use them occasionally to fix broken files; in fact, it was the occurrence of such problems, Petraki's ability to fix them and the need to direct him when he did that led to locating him right here in Accounting. So some such thing must have happened that Friday and of all the people in the building, only Petraki was supposed to know how to do it; at least, no one else had any legitimate reason to learn. Suppose he did it early on Friday morning. He would go about his business all day and change the account back at three o'clock. Even if the wire hadn't been sent by then, it would be too late to send it until Monday. After that he merely had to wait for the daily reports that ran at four-thirty. A brief glance would tell him whether he had succeeded: if he saw an item for four and a half million on the daily cash summary, it was his. And he had an opportunity to look. For months, for as long as Petraki had been there in fact, he had fallen into a certain habit. If he were waiting for something of his own to print, he would walk to the printer and catch all the paper that came out of it. It was actually a way of flirting. He would stand there and separate the reports, tear them apart and fold the front sheet down and give people what they were waiting for. Whether that's what really happened or not, Petraki did give the cash summary to Miss Rosenthal. It was remembered because, as he had done before on Fridays, he asked her to run away with him to a tropical paradise. It was remembered and resented by a very proper young lady that he neglected to invite. It was remembered, that is, with care beyond imagining.

"Flirting," Hölle demands. "Flirting is socially correct sexual overtures? This is Petraki's practice for one year and more, in bureau?"

And Roddy tries to explain: the hours he works his people, the standards he demands: somewhere, somehow, he must allow a few harmless releases… And while he's talking this nonsense he thinks, Paranoia was okay with them. They don't care what the answer is as long as they get one.

"And you, Mr. Hall," Hölle continues, hearing nothing he's told, "do you flirt also? Perhaps with other unmarried people of similar culture, with Miss Rosenthal perhaps?"

Oh yes, very much the Nazi then but also, Roddy is suddenly sure, mostly fishing for the unconvincing denial.

"Have you seen Miss Rosenthal?" he inquires. "Because if you have you'd be suspecting any man who didn't at least try."

And gets for that one of Teufel's rare smiles of reassurance. And gets from Hölle a look so offended that certain of his history lessons instantly multiply in clarity. And at last admits that they are on opposite sides and will remain so forever, and finds this not so difficult to accept though there is now no doubt in his mind that his career is finished. As if refusing the blindfold he says, "Let's continue, okay?" and draws from Teufel an admiring grin for his sangfroid.

The inquisition doesn't end in any logical way. Suddenly it is simply over and Hölle and Teufel are promising to return in the morning. And they do but somehow Roddy is now exempt from their interest, somehow just a little beneath it or perhaps not quite trustworthy enough to include anymore. Would he please arrange *this*? Would he please be so kind as to do *that*, and at once this time if he can manage it? One by one his people are summoned to meet Hölle and Teufel. People come to work shaking from the flu so as not to seem to evade Hölle and Teufel. Miss Garcia walks out of Roddy's office and slaps Miss Montgomery. Miss Montgomery had preceded Miss Garcia with Hölle and Teufel and Miss Garcia has drawn a hasty conclusion from her own summons. Hölle and Teufel look on silently while Roddy tries to deal with the mess.

After two days of this Hölle and Teufel take Roddy to the Moron's office. "Now please, Mr. Hall," Hölle says very loudly to the whole department. "We go now to Dr. Petersen's room, at once, yes?" The Moron and Schrenk are waiting, the Moron behind his teak barge of a desk and Schrenk in the privileged armchair at its side, but both are instantly dismissed. "Go now," Hölle says. "We do this alone, yes?"

Schrenk marches to the door and holds it for the Moron, who hangs back, unwilling to leave. Hölle and Teufel say no more, offer no smiles or glares of reassurance. "Come, Doctor," Schrenk says and the Moron finally leaves. Roddy expects one of them to take the Moron's chair but they stay where they are, on either side of him and far too close in the big, empty office.

"They can think what they like," Hölle says. "In their way they are as guilty as you."

"Only in their way, though," Teufel reminds him but Hölle has prepared a speech in whole English sentences and has no time for equivocating.

"There are two points to be established," Hölle says. "One. As you certainly have wished, you are unlikely to be prosecuted. You may have anticipated the reasons for this and you may even have evaluated them properly to a point. If so you are more lucky than clever. Many of us, and I speak here for my colleague also, would accept further public humiliation if you could be imprisoned. That is one point, of two as I have said."

Roddy is in a very strange state. On the one hand he is quite sure he's heard all this correctly; on the other hand it can't possibly have been said.

"The second point," Teufel offers mildly, "is by far the more important. Please don't let your relief at remaining at liberty interfere with your judgment on this matter. I'm afraid that wouldn't be wise at all."

"I intend," Hölle says, "to make all misunderstandings quite impossible. I hope you will give me every opportunity to impress you with the reality of your predicament."

"And he really does hope so, too," Teufel says. "He's talked of little else for days."

Hölle is off. "So pay attention now Mr. Hall because this is what I've been waiting to tell you. Now I explain your punishments. Principal of these is that you will never, ever spend one penny of what you have stolen. If you do you will be imprisoned for violating the taxation. We will see to it. We will always see to it. This is so today. It will be so a year from today. It will be so after twenty years. It will be so in your eighty-fifth year when you think we have forgotten you, which we shall never do."

"If you should ever get lucky at the races," Teufel says, "be sure to have plenty of witnesses about. You'll need them."

"If your aunt or uncle sends you a check for Christmas," Hölle says, "I beg you to forget us and cash it at once."

"Keep receipts for everything," Teufel says. "It's astonishing how petty the authorities become once they learn of someone who thinks he's eluded them."

"This also I would say to Petraki," Hölle says, "but of course there is no longer a Petraki, is there?"

"No longer–" Because, impossible as it should be, that is still a surprise.

"You see," Teufel says, "my colleague thinks you did it all yourself and then killed him."

"Had him killed, surely," Hölle protests.

"Very well, had him killed. It is consistent with many things. A man with your resources didn't need Petraki. That's rather a strong point, you see: without a Petraki to blame, you'd be the man everyone would think of first. All that nonsense about special programs that only he could use! Every night a copy of every file is made on tape. It is called a backup and some are on a rack in the computer room and some go home with trustworthy people to defend against the risk of fire. Once a week one of them goes home with you, Mr. Hall. Every Friday in fact you take the Thursday night tape home. So on Friday you changed the account in the usual way, and yes, had anyone looked, it would have plainly shown the date and time you did it. But that evening you took your tape to the computer room and copied the pertinent file back onto the machine, and you thought all trace of what you'd done would vanish. Careless, that."

"Very careless," Hölle agrees. "Because of Bensenhurst Motor Freight Lines."

"Installed," Teufel says, "as a new vendor Friday morning before entry of their one hundred dollar invoice for a single delivery, but missing from the vendor file yesterday when Miss Rosenthal tried to pay them. It caused the machine to become quite ill, I think, and delayed the whole check run."

Hölle says, "Many people have mentioned that, but not you of course. Everyone else noticed right away. What are we to do? Checks must print, our machine is sick and we have no Petraki!"

"Of course," Teufel says, "others had these tapes also, Dr. Petersen, Miss Rosenthal: your barrister would no doubt make a point of that. Yours, though, was by far the most recent, and we find vendors' records that were changed between that Friday and the creation of any previous tape. But what really settles it for Hölle and those who side with him is all this silliness about giving him a key. All this need to cast suspicion, to show that Petraki could go where no one but you had any right to, no matter what the time of day or night. They find that especially unconvincing."

Teufel pretends he is arguing but Hölle has a glow on him like a kid lying about his first hot date.

"Oh," Hölle says, "I think that is unfair. There are many other indications, many things that fail to convince. This fantastic idea that Petraki must peek into the staff's reports to see if his money has gone to Switzerland! After you go to such pains to show that he sees into the machine whenever he wishes! As if he would not use his powers merely to look, to discover when he becomes a millionaire!"

"Hadn't occurred to me," Roddy says quietly. "He did stand at the printer that morning and for a while I thought you wanted the truth."

"Of course it hadn't occurred to you," Teufel says. "I told them that but they like the logical way so much better."

"But not you," Roddy says and, not remembering what anger at anyone but the Moron felt like, wonders why he bothers.

"Not me," Teufel agrees. "I am more sympathetic toward the desire for an accomplice. I think you told that silly story because he didn't *tell* you exactly how he'd do it, and therefore I think Petraki is still somewhere among us. My advice is, call him at once and tell him to take it all and never return. Do it quickly before temptation strikes again. Above all, please, for all our sakes, suppress any desire to repent. Play the match out, Mr. Hall. Play it to the end. It's far too late to think we can reach any kind of settlement now."

The Moron was inordinately fond of tigers. There were crude china tigers on his desk and credenza and expensive porcelain tigers visitors sometimes found tasteful on the empty shelves a gullible decorator had thought Herr Doktor would need for his many wise books. There were prints of tigers scattered across the walls and behind his desk a very large, very expensive and very, very badly painted tiger, all luminous green eyes and International Orange stripes, leapt from a phosphorescent jungle.

It is either look at this thing, which was the Moron's essence, or look at Hölle or Teufel. Teufel's mock sympathy is like a puddle of sweetened filth. Roddy turns to Hölle.

"He's right. If I'd done it I'd have done it with Nick. But I'd have run away too. Nothing on earth could have made me wait around for this."

Roddy stands to go.

"Mr. Hall," Hölle says. Roddy stops. If it had been Teufel he'd have kept going.

"What?"

"That was only the most obvious punishment. There will be others. Don't resign. Don't ever think you can leave us. Above all don't ever take your holiday in places that don't talk to your own government. We would know about it and we would find it far too convenient for the good of our souls."

Roddy walked out of the Moron's office believing so thoroughly that his life was finished that in most respects it was. Hölle and Teufel were intimidating anyone who could possibly have had a part in it. That was all they were doing because that was all they could do, apart from waiting for Nick Petraki to wash up somewhere within reach. They had gone after the Moron one way and Schrenk another and had chosen this way to seal Roddy off from both the others. But Roddy didn't know that was what was happening. Roddy supposed they really thought he did it and he wondered how they could. Thinking it over, he realized that the Moron must have told them so. Thinking it over further, he arrived at the only reason he could have had for doing that. This was the moment he might have quit. He could have done it without carrying much of any cloud with him, he could simply have gone for the understandable reason that his job was reorganized away. He would not be a treasurer again any time soon but he would land a far better spot than he had dreamt of ten years earlier, and he would still be young enough to advance. It did not even occur to him to go. One thought he did have made many other thoughts impossible. It was a thought that recurred so frequently and so insistently that not once in twenty-five years did he consider evaluating it for sense. *If you go*, it shrieked, *the Moron wins; as long as you stay, he hasn't got away with it.*

The company was reorganized into HAGUS, Inc., which Roddy pronounced haggis but without his old enthusiasm. Bricker Thresher simply disappeared from their world and Roddy never learned what, if anything, they were paid for their share. The Chicago offices were closed and the headquarters split between two sites in Kentucky. Accounting and Research moved to Louisville, Marketing, Sales and Operations to Lexington. Most of the inventory was already in a public warehouse in Lexington anyway, so Schrenk could visit it often. Research didn't really need a headquarters – all the real work happened on three dozen farms, scattered across the continent. Roddy, as Controller, no longer needed real accountants and presided over a dozen clerks in three adjacent strip mall storefronts. There was no more treasurer but there was a CFO and his name was Schrenk and he stayed in Lexington and would stay there forever: Hölle and Teufel had seen to that. The geography had its own significance. Louisville, Lexington: not really so efficient a way to divide a headquarters, even if every decision that mattered arrived after midnight from Germany on one machine or another. It was all so Schrenk wouldn't have to look at Roddy, and the motive for that was simple mercy; they granted Schrenk just that much. Had they known how much not looking at the Moron was also mercy for Roddy, they might have rearranged it. As it was, the Moron got the office next to Schrenk's but went into semiretirement right away, planning his life as one long vacation punctuated by bogus meetings in city after city. He never showed up in Louisville and Roddy made the trip to Lexington only twice a year to consult with Schrenk on the Master Plan. At the office Schrenk treated him with icy professional courtesy but Mrs. Schrenk insisted on having him to dinner, once per visit. She actually seemed to like him and in her presence Schrenk played the affable host, considerate, confiding even, as he reminisced over long-dead social trivia from the days when they had futures. It did not seem at these times that Schrenk was putting on any kind of act at all, which made it all the more unsettling when, the next day at work, he would turn back into a self-absorbed functionary addressing the least distinguishable of his subordinates. One day around 1982 Roddy drove to Lexington, arrived early and went to the office instead of his hotel. The Moron was just getting into his car. They stared at each other. They hadn't met in six years. Finally the Moron said, "I didn't expect you till tomorrow." Roddy said, "I was early." The Moron said, "Well, I have to go to Charleston." Roddy never showed up early after that and they never met again.

So much time passed without seeming to. It didn't seem like the time we used to get, where unusual things could happen and almost everything could turn out to be important. It was a watercolor kind of time where week bled into week without contrast. Everything that happened had happened before, or was a clumsily disguised variation of something from the time when Roddy's luck was good. In a way this was merciful because Roddy's luck did not change back again. Because of the way time had changed the bad things didn't jump on you anymore. Now you could see that they were links in one long chain dangling back to the days of the Moron's malfeasance, and it was possible even to see a little humor in each new manifestation. Dishwasher freezes up: oh, hi there. Late for an appointment and, yep, here comes the freight train.

By the twenty-ninth year of his bad luck Roddy John Hall was bald, weighed two hundred and sixty pounds, and had been convinced for more than two decades that the Moron stole four and a half million dollars from the company and, not incidentally, murdered and then framed Nick Petraki in the process. What he hadn't known for much of that time was the part played by Alois Schrenk, or even if there had been one. But then the Moron retired for real, fell out of his canoe and drowned, and Schrenk's guilt began to seem more than merely plausible.

Roddy was thinking about these things as he had done for twenty-five years, he was thinking about them and above all talking about them to two or three gossipy underlings, when the FBI finally took pity and rang him up. First there were preliminaries and it was, he realized, a very pleasant voice demonstrating great power in a stylish way. Roddy never forgot that he had once been treasurer of a corporation. Since then he had taken hundreds of calls from the IRS and thousands from authorities in dozens of states and even before his time with Hölle and Teufel he had forgotten how to be intimidated on the telephone. Those who tried got straightened out – after all, they were basically clerks and he was a professional working accountant. With those types you hold your temper and bring them back to the facts. But this woman was one of the good ones, just said who she was and took it as a given that he'd grant her his respect. In spite of that she seemed to hem and haw a bit but then she said, "We'd like to see you today, sir, to discuss Mr. Nicholas Petraki and the consequences of his return to this area."

Well. After that Roddy did bounce around a little but who wouldn't?

The tape stopped. Nick looked at Johnny for some time before asking, "Roddy told her parts of it himself, didn't he?"

Johnny said, "Sure. Part of it. But most of it was from other people he told first."

"But not that last part. Roddy didn't tell her that."

"Right again. The last part was kind of special. See, I believed you and things are happening because I did. So it's real now, Mr. P. We're going to have to start working a little harder at it."

Chapter 9

Hector Ruiz
May 14, 2001

Sal Ruiz's father, who still thought gentlemen sometimes removed their hats, accepted a tall cold drink and, leaving the women inside, followed his host out onto the veranda.

"How does this sound?" he asked Fuentes. "In Cuba, things are rather strange these days. I have to tell you that we'd hoped we'd seen the last of deals like this one many, many years ago."

"Then the Russians left," Fuentes prompted.

"Then the Russians left," Ruiz agreed.

"Then I say, with us it's the Yankees except they never seem to go. Or something like that, some collegial expression of hemispheric solidarity."

"That's always appreciated," Ruiz said. "Anyway, it's the way I see us starting out. Think you'd be tempted?"

"Oh, I'm easily tempted. They understand that well enough, I'll never have a problem convincing them I was *tempted.* It's the next couple of parts that need work."

"Ah yes. Remind me, please. Which parts are those?"

"First comes the part where you convince me you're the kind of Cuban who has actually seen Cuba sometime in the last thirty years.

Then you convince me you really need to place this order. Finally you convince me that you'll pay. Those parts."

Ruiz reached into his jacket and offered cigars, and mulled *those parts* over as they went through the cutting and the lighting and the anticipatory puffing phases. When Fuentes had taken his first serious taste, Ruiz said dreamily, "It's as Fidel was telling me only last week…"

"Stop!" Fuentes almost choked with laughter.

"They'll really quiz you about these things?"

"They always have before."

"Can you remember what you told them last time?"

"I think so. I think the last few times, in fact, the successful answer to every question has been, *they're still offering twenty percent over list, my brothers.*"

This time they both almost choked. When the hilarity died down and the curious Señora Fuentes had retreated to the kitchen, Ruiz moved in for the close.

"You'll need eleven million. You can promise an enormous return."

"I'll need eleven million for ten million dollars in goods? And I'll pay back enormously more?"

"Ten for the Germans, one for you. I'm afraid we'll not be contributing anything, so you won't be able to pay anyone back, even a little bit. You'll have to choose your partners very carefully."

Fuentes studied a very pretty lizard perched on a potted cactus. It thought it was invisible because it hadn't moved for several seconds, but Fuentes was remembering how his wife had shopped for that pot for a month and he stared anyway.

"I doubt very much," he said at length, "whether such partners exist anywhere in Mexico."

"I would tend to agree. Have you considered Berlin, though?"

Chapter 10

Roddy John Hall
June 7, 2001

The duo from the FBI remind him somewhat of Hölle and Teufel, and Roddy throws a sucker punch before they even sit down. It's one hell of a wallop, even though they will eventually decide it's their salvation. *How is Nick, is he all right, can Roddy talk to him, at least send him a message?* It doesn't seem like much to Roddy but it certainly does to them, and they cover by forcing him to examine their ID while the man Curtis does some opening riffs on the classic theme of *we ask the questions here, sir.* He throws the usually effective *sir* four or five times while Roddy tries to feed them Coke and coffee (see, he knows they can't have anything to drink, but maybe a beer before they go?) Still clenching, the woman accepts a coffee, black, while Curtis wastes a glare at her that Roddy fails to notice.

Of course any two interrogators would remind him of Hölle and Teufel but there really are similarities. Curtis takes the Nazi role, though he looks very much like an iron-pumping Malcolm X. The very pretty woman named Gonzales (she's the one who called) is also black but mainly Spanish, though she doesn't any have accent he can hear. She does Teufel to perfection, with one important change that Roddy thinks is an improvement. Instead of smiling, ever, she uses varying shades of concern, playing off Curtis's incredulous hostility and hammering down the point that this could be the end of your life come calling, yes it really could be. Roddy thinks he might have bought it if he had anything more to lose. Instead he can see it for what it is: they're doing a job that somebody still cares about, and for a while he works on ways to thank them for that. Soon, though, all that is driven out by these suddenly familiar feelings he can no longer name: mostly relief and curiosity, and even a little of what might fairly be called hope. He doesn't know it but merely by feeling these things he is ruining their act. There are acts for scared innocent people and for tough guilty people but this is an act for the frightened white-collar crook (emphasis on the white) and how do you make it work when the victim wants to hug you? They are backing up and improvising like crazy but that's all right with Roddy; he doesn't even notice as long as they keep talking, and talking is mostly what they're here for.

"Mr. Hall," Gonzales says, "you don't seem surprised that he's back."

"Surprised? I was sure the bastard killed him. I've been sure for twenty-five years."

"The bastard, Mr. Hall?" Gonzales is deeply worried for him now, sticking to the script just that much.

"The Moron. Petersen, the man who did it all."

Curtis is finally off the ropes and seriously into sneering. "Well, now you see he didn't. So how does that affect things, sir?"

"It means he's alive, that's how. Where's he been? Witness Protection?"

"Sir—"

"Hey, I know, you can't. But you have to understand. I hired him, I was responsible, I put him in that spot. Then we were friends. He was pretty much the only friend I had at work. We'd go out, have a beer after work and bitch. I bitched, he listened. I was, see, I had kind of a bad spell there. So I thought, anyway. I found out about bad after that," and demonstrates a laugh that isn't the least bit healthy.

As Mrs. Simpson pictures it, by now Gonzales has had time to look around. She sees the most mundane executive class house imaginable, spotless, boring as oatmeal, except that it contains about half the things it should. A green suede couch on which Roddy sits, bursting with impatience. One picture over that, a retriever with a pheasant. Two red leather wingback armchairs, one for every visiting government employee. A painfully expensive and tasteless coffee table, plate glass over driftwood, wouldn't be too awful except for the hunting scenes etched into the top. On it, one big picture book about famous shotguns (there's a thought for you), perfectly centered. At the edge a *TV Guide* and a remote. Behind her, the TV, maybe thirty inches, in a once very nice and now gutted armoire. No stereo, but a VCR. To the right of that, one bookcase, entirely filled but no books anywhere else, as if someone had said, *let's see, need a bookcase here, plus I got to fill it up...* Further to the right, the dining room: no table, no chairs, no rug, no curtains, no pictures, the bad factory parquet gleaming in the sunset in front of a mahogany china cabinet with a Wedgwood plate showing through polished glass. To Hall's right, the staircase, with a flowered runner (the only carpet in sight) and one small print in the mandatory place at the landing. Over that a ridiculous chandelier. To the left of that and down, on a humid ninety-four degree evening in Kentucky, a fat, bald man in brogues, dark blue pinstripe trousers, damp white Oxford shirt with gold cufflinks, club tie still high up in perfect four-in-hand knot, and eyes jumping straight out of his head.

"Mr. Hall," she says, not needing to fake her worry very much now. "People get into Witness Protection for being witnesses. There have been no trials here, no indictments even. What do you imagine he's told us?"

Roddy gapes in admiration. He doesn't even have to grope for her meaning, it just comes to him. "He told you all about Schrenk, didn't he?"

"Are you playing games with us, sir?" Curtis demands, but Gonzales says, "Suppose he has, Mr. Hall. What do you think he would have said?"

Roddy tries his very best. It is thrilling how quickly they pick up on it, it is fascinating how they take him back over things they must know as well as he does. Watching them work is like having a really good movie right in his living room, and it's all Roddy can do to keep from giggling. Once he just bursts out in happiness, "Nick's alive, I just can't get over it," and Gonzales almost smiles and Curtis has to work hard on his scowl. In the end they won't take the beer because, after all, rules are rules. At the door Roddy says, "I know you can't make promises but I'm just saying this. I really would like to see him." And even Curtis finds a way to bend a little and says, "Believe me, sir, we're doing our best to make that possible." That's a really clever line if you consider the demands of his part, and Roddy isn't in the least displeased that Curtis has pulled it off while staying in character. He watches them back out and drive away, and realizes that in the seven years he's lived there he's never watched anyone do that before. That also is a kind of omen and he is now fully prepared for his life to turn weird again.

Chapter 11

Cousin Olga
June 27, 2001

Tennessee flowed past, looking like a place people might live in though from the interstate it was hard to be sure.

Johnny said, "One thing I've always wondered about. Say something in French, Mr. P."

"*Pourquoi?*"

"More."

"I dearly love," Nick said, but in French, "the role of performing monkey. I've always aspired to it and now that I have it I am truly content."

"Well?" Johnny asked.

"Well," Cousin Olga said, "it's unique all right. There's a kind of Parisian swank to it that isn't badly done. There's the expectable tone-deaf Midwest underneath. But the rest of it sounds like it should be African, except it's not exactly any real country."

"So guess," Johnny insisted.

"A long time in North Africa—"

"Ha!"

"—or the Caribbean. Basically living with Europeans but going native on the side."

"See," Johnny demanded, "what did I tell you?"

"Nothing at all," Nick protested.

"She's the one's been teaching me, aside from you. You said I was getting better, yourself."

"Oh sure–" he started but Cousin Olga wasn't having any.

"Like hell you'll hang that on me. If your parents had ever taught you to say one word correctly, maybe there'd be a chance but–"

"See," Johnny said, "Olga's a snob about how everybody talks. She hears somebody say something once, any language at all, and she can fucking say it perfectly. And once they noticed that they started teaching her to sound like all kinds of people. I guess there wasn't much else to do back home. What's the name of that place, anyway?"

"Atlantic City?" Nick guessed.

"Close," Olga said, "Sverdlovsk."

"Oh," Nick said, and decided to shut up for a while.

"Say, Cousin Olga," Cousin Sugar Lips said, as if a fanciful whim had just struck him, "why don't you tell your Cousin Nicky how we met?"

Cousin Olga raised an eyebrow. "Once when I was a real Russian, I used to work for a man who worried a lot. Every once in a while he'd get drunk and say, 'You could follow instructions once too often.'"

"That's not something we say very much," Cousin Sugar Lips admitted.

"There are other things we don't do very much. Before I go ahead and tell Cousin Nicky exactly how we met, is that really what you want?"

"Sure," Cousin Sugar Lips said, like, *what could be the problem?* "We're all family here, aren't we?"

"Oh, shit," Cousin Nicky said.

"Wow," Cousin Olga said, "you *can* say it."

Chapter 12

When Johnny bought Olga Kopeikin from three Russians in Brighton Beach, they called her into the room and said, "You don't need to hang around here no more. You get to go with this Italian Mr. Johnny Wonders now." They probably wanted to add a parting shot in Russian but weren't sure how Johnny'd take it, so they passed. They might also have imagined that, in his ears, Italian Mr. Johnny Wonders would sound respectful. Anyway, the room was a pigsty. Olga remained standing and said, "Can we go then?"

"You want to get your things?" Johnny asked.

"Hell no."

Johnny nodded to the men and held the door for her. The last they heard from the Russians were a snicker and the start of a guffaw. In the car she looked straight ahead and asked, "Did you just rent or buy me?"

"Buy."

"Do I want to know what I'm worth?"

"I hear I can't afford what you're worth. You definitely don't want to know what I got you for."

She turned to look at him. "You hear." Olga Kopeikin was thirty-six years old and for the very first time it seemed that someone had heard.

"In D.C. On the street, more or less."

"Excuse me but under these circumstances I imagine I'd be worth very little."

"Not if you really think about it. At least not when I do."

"And what do you think when you really think like that?"

"I think," Johnny said, "that tomorrow you're going to call the FBI and square it."

"Square it? Do you know what *it* is?"

"First you give up the three bears back there. Then you tell them, they leave you alone, you'll call in every so often with stories that'll keep the Russian outfit on the ropes for years."

"There's a lot they badly want to hear from me. On the other hand I know very little about any Russian mafia, except that from the bragging I've had to endure it's something like the Roman Empire."

"That's all right, 'cause we know way too much, believe it."

Right about there, Olga Kopeikin decided that possibly, just possibly, Johnny Wonders might not be still another irredeemable fool.

In the morning they rode off to Queens in a van and parked in an alley. A man named Rudy climbed a pole and tapped in. When he got down he was shaking, it was that cold. "Go get some coffee," Johnny told him, "I'll buzz you."

"You want serious Rooski accent, dah-link? Known to fool even moose and squirrel."

"Why? I heard you do Boston and Beverly Hills, no problem. If I know it, so do they. Here."

He'd already dialed. "Federal Bureau of Investigation," it said.

She smirked and gave them her Lady Di. "Good Morning. This is Olga Kopeikin. K.O.P.E.I.K.I.N. Olga."

She paused a second for the computer to catch up. "That's right," she said, now Tallulah Bankhead, "that one. I'm a retired citizen of the world now but back when I used to be Russian, I lived here as a resident agent of the GRU. For, oh, just the longest time. I lived here for so long that I rose from Praporshchik to Captain, always somewhere between sea and shining sea. Do you know, I'll bet a month's pension that in as little as ten seconds you can connect me to someone who'll understand everything I just said."

Chapter 13

Cousin Sugar Lips
June 27, 2001

That didn't take long, did it? Johnny once said to Nick, "The more stories people tell you just to tell them, the uglier your future looks." On the other hand Mr. D'Annunzio told him, "If I tell you about somebody, it's 'cause you're going to do business with him someday." Tennessee rolled right on by outside and didn't seem to have an opinion. Nick licked his lips. "If it's not intruding," he asked Olga, "just how close to my would-be friends at the FBI are you?"

"At first they were skeptical. When I explained that perhaps I'd been working for them for a dozen years they were confused. When I explained that perhaps our friendship was so secret that no trace of it could be found, they began to see the possibilities. It was Johnny's idea, who would have thought it?"

"True," Johnny said, "but the beauty was in how she played it. Gave them that and then said, 'So. I'll call this afternoon at four, yes?' and just hung up."

"If there's one thing I know," Olga said, "it's bureaucracy. You have to let ideas percolate. Good ones need a little time to rise to the people who really deserve to think them."

"And since then you've been a regular correspondent. I see."

"No you don't and stop fishing. You have nothing to worry about. I haven't told them a thing about you in days and days."

"Oh, well," Nick said, "in that case…"

"The guy she gave them," Johnny said, "is Nicholas Petraki. Nothing about any Caribbean Russian."

"Russian?" Olga said doubtfully.

Nick said, "Oh, as long as it's only Petraki."

Johnny said, "And Pope too of course."

"What Russian?"

"That's the Pope I seem to be?"

"Relax. They have to know to leave him alone till after they sting the Germans. Anybody could see that."

"My Germans? The FBI wants my Germans?"

"A man ignored me once before," someone mused, possibly Bette Davis.

"Yeah, you'll like this, I forgot. Back home Cousin Nicky is Mr. Nikolai Petrov. Say something in Russian, Mr. P."

"Yes, please do." *Very* possibly Bette Davis.

"Sorry. Don't speak a word of it."

"That should be such a relief," Olga said, "but somehow it isn't. There could be so many complications." No, it was Myrna Loy.

"For that you'd need Russians," Johnny said, "and where would he meet one of those?"

"Where indeed?" Myrna agreed, and stuck out her hand. "Olga Nikolaiova Kopeikin, at your service."

"A pleasure," Nick said. "I don't think it will be a problem. They only need a couple of names to indict you. Sometimes they actually make do with one. More than a few just confuse them."

"True," Judy Garland said, "but how they love to be confused."

"Lucky them," Nick said. "Then it didn't bother them at all to hear how someone sold a friend a new identity for about a quarter million and then gave it to them." It was fascinating, once you saw it, how she flitted from one film star to the next and never got past the 1940's.

"What quarter million?" Johnny asked doubtfully.

"I don't think so either," Judy said, "but there'd be nothing confusing about it in their world. You see, criminals do the darnedest things."

"You know," Johnny said, "it did add up, didn't it?" but Judy didn't seem to hear.

"And," she said, "sometimes they actually catch criminals, did you know that? Say, for instance, a miscreant claimed to be a Russian just to get their attention and then turned out to be a phony Frenchman from Chicago: I wouldn't be surprised at all if they caught someone like him."

"Nobody thought I was Russian."

"How could anyone? I was referring to what you claimed to be." Katherine Hepburn. Once you caught on it was easy.

"I never claimed it, either. It was just a name some ex-Frenchmen thought up for me."

"Oh. Ex-Frenchmen now."

"See," Johnny explained, "France found it could almost live without them, so it made them independent. Which I think they pretty much were anyway."

"So many Frenchmen are but they don't usually make it official."

"Well, these guys were in the right place at the right time, what can you say. Anyway, Cousin Nicky helps himself to what he thinks is a lot of money and then gets down to figuring what to do with it. And these guys explain, well, what you do now is give it to us and you get to live like the King of Portugal. And just so everybody can be sure of where they stand, they keep his passport and give him papers for a Nikolai Petrov."

"It's a real *Carte de Séjour*," Nick protested. "It has a seal on it and everything."

"And no one found your name peculiar?"

"Well, there was a waiter named Antoine who used to call me *tovarich* but I think somebody had a word with him. A word goes a long way there, believe me."

"But the name didn't even bother you?"

"Why should it? I was born Petraki and I don't speak a word of Greek."

Kate said, "Cousin Sugar Lips, however did you meet this innocent?"

Johnny said, "Don't call him innocent. He hears it and then he has to prove you wrong."

"How on earth would he do that?"

"Well, by thinking up something like this, for one thing."

"*He* thought this up?" Rosalind Russell demanded, truly alarmed. "I thought you did."

"Sure but only after he came up with his version, which I think we won't discuss."

"We won't?" Nick asked.

"Maybe in a year or so, when we have a reunion or something. Till then it's best forgotten, believe me."

"I believe you," Scarlett O'Hara said, "with every beat of my heart."

"Then what are we doing?" Nick demanded.

"Driving to Louisville, of course."

"I meant, we're still stealing ten million dollars, aren't we?"

"Sure. Pretty much. It's just, we thought it might be better if the FBI did most of the work."

"Oh," Nick said. "And why would they do that?"

"To give it to us, of course," Johnny said patiently, while what's-her-name, Sam Spade's nemesis in *The Maltese Falcon,* looked pityingly on.

"Cousin Sugar Lips," she said, "you know I don't ask much."

"Oh, no. About half of Fort Knox every month but other than that you're free as air."

"Well, I'm worth it, aren't I?"

"Sure, but… Okay. Sometimes I forget my place, I mean when I'm driving and all. Okay. You don't ask much."

"But now I want to know something, so you'd better tell me. Because you know how I can get. Or maybe you don't. I can get–"

"Stop. I heard about the cold war. What?"

"I want you to please tell me how I acquired my new cousin Nicky. Nothing in my previous lives has prepared me, I'm afraid."

"Okay, but somehow I don't think it'll satisfy you. I inherited him."

"I see. And you know, you're right."

"Mr. P, you better tell it. It might make more sense."

"It won't make sense coming from you, Sugar Lips? I've always hoped you'd never tell me that."

"Oh, sure it would," Johnny said. "It'd just lose a lot of atmosphere and all."

"Well," Nick said, "it's a rather long story."

"Good," Lauren Bacall said, "it's rather a long ride."

Chapter 14

Mr. D'Annunzio
April 24, 1982 – April 25, 2001

One fine Saturday in April of 1982 – every day is a fine day on Saint Sulpice unless a hurricane is blowing and hurricanes don't blow in the spring – Nikolai Petrov was absorbing *un gros rouge* at the Café des Artistes and wondering why Charles the cop was hanging out in front of the cathedral when a lively, balding fat man of more than a certain age bounced up to his table, twinkled, and purred, "Hey there, fella, guess what I got that you don't?"

Nick considered. "The loudest shirt south of Miami?"

The fat man laughed and twinkled some more and said, "Hey, maybe I do, I paid enough for it. But nah, I got something else and since you're never going to guess, I'm going to have to tell you."

Sighing inwardly with what he later told himself (and Anne Marie, and then several other people, and eventually Olga Kopeikin) was the onset of premonition, Nick gestured to the seat across from him.

Settling in, the fat man said, "What I got is two things really. One that you might have too from what I heard is a great sense of timing. But what proves I got it is I'm here and yesterday you were declared legally dead. The other thing I know you ain't got is a copy of your obituary. You want to read it before we discuss your investments?"

And sat and beamed, and even found it convenient to yawn just a little, seemingly not at all from boredom but purely from a touch of expectant weariness and all the glorious fresh air.

M. Gérard had told Nick, "Our rules are strict and our terms are harsh but we brook no interference with those who agree to them, from any quarter whatsoever. From time to time it has been tried. You have only to report it at once but that you are required to do." Later *Commissaire* Proudhon added, "Our friend Gérard thinks he talks man to man but he can't order spaghetti without a code book. Someone comes looking for you, they get told once. The second time they go under the *quai*. But there's another side to that. *You* don't tell us, you try to handle it yourself, then as far as we're concerned you're one of them. Because we will *not* let them get established here. And this is your one warning, right now. Understood?"

But the fat man smiled and twinkled and looked at Nick and Nick's table and Nick's glass like they were all we could ever need, and in just a couple of seconds Nick drew some conclusions from that. A little while later, when he had to decide many things very quickly, he recalled how Gérard and Proudhon had seemed to be on stage for him but that never, not for half an instant, had it been possible to doubt a thing the fat man had to say.

Nick said, "I'd love to read my obituary but as for the other, there are people with a proprietary interest in my investments."

The fat man said, "Scary people too I'll bet. I'd get scary myself, I was getting two and a half percent on your money plus I get to play with the principal and then somebody else came sniffing around. Between us they ain't what they think they are but I can see why you might not want to test that on your own. I'll make you a promise. Any deal we make, they get to approve it. They say no, I go away and don't come back. But they won't say no, I promise you."

Antoine the waiter marched up, grinning as always. Nick said,

"*Un autre pour moi et...*" The fat man pointed first at Nick's glass and then at himself.

"Hope that's as good as it looks," he said. "Some of this French wine they go on about, an Italian would swear they water it. Here."

And handed Nick a page from the day's *Chicago Tribune*.

Nick read. After a while he said, "I see I'm still alleged. They have to know I did it by now."

"It's their lawyers make them talk that way," the fat man said. "See, your old man pushed it through. You remember you had twenty-five large insurance from work? Company fought it but his lawyer filed and the court went along. Our first thought, see, I'll be frank, was that would be leverage for us. It comes out you're here, he loses that and maybe they start looking at him for fraud. Then we hear he's telling everyone you did it and to hell with you, and our leverage don't look so good."

Charles *le flic*, born in Belle Vièrge, studied Saint Sulpice's statue like any visiting nun of the Order.

"He said to hell with me a long time before that. To hell with him. I wonder if I could talk to a reporter."

"I think you'd probably piss your friends off a little."

"I think they'd kill me but it might be worth it. All this raises so many questions."

"Then why not skip them and I'll just start answering, okay? No, I ain't talked to anybody else here yet. Lots of questions been asked and answered but all by somebody else. I'm just a tourist. All the same they'll know who I am by tonight if they don't already, and they'll be watching me by then if they ain't watching us now. So you got till close of business this afternoon to rat me out and that's something you got to do, no question, no hardship coming from me. You decide you don't want to do business, all I ask is you let me walk back to the pier first. But that's not what you're going to decide."

Charles the cop had bicycled away from what, in spite of the plaques and the brochures, is technically just a church – once it really was a cathedral but, frankly, that calls to mind a certain stature that it no longer quite attains – and found something of consuming interest in the window of Mme. Bousson's dress shop. Three or four passersby stopped to gawk but he managed to ignore them and seemed to be staring up the mannequins' skirts.

"Another question is how we know and all. Sorry but all I can tell you is it's our business to find these things out."

"It's many people's business," Nick said, "but they don't seem to do it half as well."

"See? That's what I was trying to say. We're the people you want to do business with. My name, I should have done this before, is Mr. Carmine D'Annunzio. No bells, huh? That's all right. But that's my name and here's a card, so they know how to spell it if they haven't checked already which I expect they did. Even if they go through channels they should get a good reference back in half an hour, any agency they try. I'm not saying this to brag, you understand. You got a right to know. You got to ask yourself, is this old man who he says? 'Cause if I believe him and he ain't, then I'm screwed. And if I don't believe him and he is, then he screws me worse. That's a no win situation and that's why you got to rat me out. What I'm asking you now is, if the people you been doing business with tell you I'm the real thing when you do, will that be good enough?"

The waiter was back but, unaccountably, this time he was a nondescript city employee, a Khaki Brother named LeGrand that Nick recognized only because he was rumored to lose spectacularly at dominoes every few months. He seemed to have difficulty walking while balancing his tray, towel and bundle of checks.

"If you're not the real thing," Nick said, "I can't imagine what they'll do when it shows up."

"Messieurs?"

"Deux."

LeGrand fled with his towel over his shoulder. The fat man nodded after him. "Flatfoot?"

"I always thought he was a clerk."

"Maybe he is. Place like this they probably do double duty. This is good. At home there's other people you could ask but they're not people you want to be talking to. Anyway, who we are is also the closest you get to how we come to talk to you. I mean, it sort of explains that."

Ah ha. M. Délibes' Mercedes pulled into the square and of course would need a place to park. At that very moment Charles *le flic* turned casually away from Mme. Bousson's window, wheeled his bike away from the curb where it had been blocking the head of the carriage rank, and M. Délibes casually swung in before the first carriage could move up to its proper spot. Well, under the circumstances, what could have been more natural than for M. Délibes and Charles to exchange a languid and democratic Caribbean greeting before going about the business of their fantastically disparate stations?

Mr. D'Annunzio saw Nick looking and glanced around. Nick said, "I think I'm supposed to notice. I think I'm supposed to be strong because help is on the way."

"Help's already here. Let me prove that to you 'cause what you want to know is, what's the deal? And I got to explain that we're not really negotiating here, and it isn't because we don't do that, I don't care what maybe you heard. This is pretty much a take it or leave it proposition because there's only one way it'll work, which is how I'm going to lay it out. But I'll say this part up front. What you get out of it is a hell of a lot better than what you got now and it's a hell of a lot safer in the long run. Let me explain that part first 'cause from where you sit it's probably more interesting than our side of it and I want you paying attention when I get to that."

Charles was no longer in sight. M. Délibes and four men dressed for the office were out of his car and walking away from the café, counterclockwise around the square. Out of the Rue du 23 Octobre came the black shark's nose of a Citroën DS.

"I don't mean to rush you," Nick said, "but *Commissaire* Proudhon just pulled into the square."

Mr. D'Annunzio might not have heard.

"You got four and a half million at four percent, right?"

Commissaire Proudhon double-parked in front of Délibes and his men. One man stayed with the car while the rest cut straight across toward the café.

"Four million. It cost something to move it. You didn't know that, so at least the bank's not talking."

"Why the hell would they? They take two and a half percent, you get one point five, that's sixty grand a year, right? And a hundred for them, forever."

"Right. And I'm doing well to spend twenty. If I tried a lot harder than I want to, I might manage thirty."

"There's always your charity work but we'll let that pass since you're so modest. The point is, what you don't spend goes back in the pot and then they get two point five on it. But it don't work the other way. No matter what you take out, you owe them their hundred a year forever."

Commissaire Proudhon was a third of the way across the square. Délibes and one man split off to the left. His other two men split off to the right. *Commissaire* Proudhon walked on, staring straight at Nick.

"Right. Those were the terms and I agreed to them."

"Okay. You agreed to them but now you buy a certain piece of property for us for two million dollars. Basically you just give it to us. After that they don't want your hundred anymore. After that you got a special arrangement where you don't owe them anything. That leaves you two mil at four percent which is eighty a year to you, plus you can do anything you want with the principal and nobody gives a shit unless you tap out. You in?"

Nick was silent. *Commissaire* Proudhon was sixty meters away, buttoning his jacket as he walked.

"These people here, they're a bunch of thieving Nazis, got no use for anybody."

Nick said, "Nazis is about right. Nazis is good." But that was all he said.

"We did our homework, we asked around, we heard about you, mainly your mouth. You stand up to them pretty good."

Nick's famous mouth stayed shut.

"You stick with them, you're on the shelf for the rest of your life. Come in with us and you're back in the game."

Twenty meters.

"Come on, Nicky. They're crooked cops. They're unclean. They hate themselves. You're a real crook. We're your people, Nicky."

Nick stood up. *Commissaire* Proudhon walked onto the terrace and said, "Good day, Monsieur Petrov."

Nick said, "Good day, Monsieur *le Commissaire*. May I present Monsieur D'Annunzio?"

He said it in French of course but what was there to misunderstand? Mr. D'Annunzio stood and offered a royal paw. Proudhon took it.

Nick said, "I've invited him to discuss a very interesting business proposition with us. I'd intended to introduce him to you later, after we've completed our own preliminary discussions."

"I would be delighted. Don't let me disturb you. Would three o'clock be convenient?"

"Three would be ideal."

"Until then, gentlemen."

Another round of shakes and this time a curt, military bow. Then *Commissaire* Proudhon strode back to his Citroën, one of six private cars on the island and, after M. Délibes', the second newest. Mr. D'Annunzio turned around to watch. "I seen pictures of those cars," he said. "How much time he give us?"

Two of M. Délibes' men sat down at the opposite end of the terrace. Another now leaned against the Mercedes. Nick couldn't see Délibes or the last man. "Enough," he said, and it was. By three o'clock, when Proudhon led Gerard and Délibes onto the terrace and announced that he'd reserved a table indoors, Nick was pretty sure that inside of half an hour Gerard would be pretending it was all his own idea.

Over dinner Monsieur *le Commissaire* indulged himself a great deal and as the evening wore on he absented himself for longer and longer periods, always with one or another of his own guests. During one of these retreats he took Délibes and all three of the bankers off with him on some pretext and, by coincidence, the room briefly tired of spinning. Nick said to Mr. D'Annunzio, "So. I'm the partner you always dreamed of."

"Oh, you ain't so bad. You know, what you did with that money, a lot of people would say it was wrong. I mean a lot of good people would say that without looking into it at all. They'd think, where was his loyalty? How could he do that to the people trusted him? And I got to tell you I can't criticize those people 'cause I was thinking that way myself. When we started looking at this it was just for an angle, something, I'll be truthful here, we could hold over you – like we needed anything else, you think about it. I mean, we didn't see you as any kind of partner. But we looked into your situation 'cause it pays to be thorough and then we find out about this place. And we figure,

I figure really, I may as well take the credit 'cause I deserve it, I figure you did it 'cause nobody ever gave you anything you could be loyal to. You never had no proper loyalties and then you end up here where they ain't allowed, and you try to buck that but what can one guy do? Let me put it to you like our people always see it. Loyalty's something everybody needs. What we bring to this table today is something you can be loyal to forever, be part of, have a purpose again. It ain't a chance too many people get twice and after living with these shits on their terms, you just about got to be starving for it. Anyway, that's how we see it."

"Mr. D'Annunzio. Try to answer me something. We've been sitting here all day and most people would say that you've threatened me a dozen times. So why do I want to start singing and kiss you?"

"Because I walked in here and told you the truth, kid. And it's a well-known fact, and not just something I always say, that the truth, it sets you free."

Six years later Mr. D'Annunzio retired from the resort business and brought Johnny out to introduce him around. Later he and Nick had a private and somewhat sentimental drink at the café. In the course of it Nick said, "There's a question I've had for a long time that you might find offensive, though I hope you won't. On the night we drank the government under the table, you said when you started planning this you didn't think of me as a partner. What was I supposed to be instead?"

Mr. D'Annunzio looked around the square for a couple of seconds and said, "Nicky, this is something we both could take offense over, we were looking to be offended. But we ain't. This business has turned out pretty good for us, wouldn't you say?"

"I would say. I have. I will again. Thank you. Now offend me."

"Well, Nicky, we were going to threaten your life."

"What good would that have done? I'd have run straight to

Proudhon."

"Sure. Then we'd have killed you and gone on to the next guy. He probably would have listened better."

In a few years Mr. D'Annunzio died and the heap of wreathes overflowed the funeral home's lobby and halls. M. Délibes and *Commissaire* Proudhon each sent one, as did two men who thought themselves important at the bank; also Mme. du Fresnes' daughter sent one – neither Mme. du Fresnes nor anyone in her family had ever met Mr. D'Annunzio but they had made inquiries and knew who to thank for the hotel's unexpected fortunes. The bank of course sent its own, specifying the largest size available, which duly went to the very back of the chapel. Bored to tears by two days of visitation duty, Johnny was reduced to reading sympathy cards when he came upon a very small wreath beside the ormolu clock on one of those useless side tables at the far end of the hall, under one of those equally useless gilt mirrors that nobody ever looks in; really, it was little more than a bouquet and hardly appropriate for any funeral, let alone a funeral of state. Bemused, he picked it up and learned that it was sent by "the family Bondieu and Anne Marie Marçeau, with deep sentiments of extreme gratitude for his favors." He thought for a moment before he was sure he had them right. Then he carried it inside and showed it to Mr. D'Annunzio's impossibly sentimental widow and her coterie of dutiful sycophants. "You see," he said, "this is from some little people on that island he took so much interest in. You see how they loved him." Mrs. D'Annunzio cried and put the bouquet in her lap and refused to part with it. The card was given to her daughter, with instructions to compose a fulsome and eloquent reply. The daughter promised that she would but Anne Marie must have somehow garbled her own address because nobody on Saint Sulpice ever heard a word from her.

Still, Mr. D'Annunzio had something left to say to Nick. This occurred quite recently while he and Johnny were in Anne Marie's back office, taking a break from his lessons. Johnny got the idle, speculative look in his eye that means he's concentrating totally and only on business; then he pretended to reminisce. He said, "You know, Mr. P, in a lot of ways the old guys ran a simpler kind of operation than we do. You look back on how they did it and it seems almost funny, no disrespect to them. They'd come up with these off the wall ideas so simple you'd ignore them if you got them yourself but the thing is, they made them work. Sometimes it scares me they even tried the shit they did and sometimes it scares me we don't think like them, but whenever I think about it something always scares me. Mr. D was like all those old guys and nothing he did ever went wrong.

"I'll give you a for instance. When he brought me into this side of the business he ran over the players to me and pretty soon he got to you. And I said, 'This guy's a front, right, a pretty face at the bank, what do we have on him?' And Mr. D said, 'You got it wrong, Johnny. Nicky,' that's what he called you, no offense 'cause he didn't mean none, 'it's what Nicky needs from us that matters to Nicky. He can't live without it now he knows the truth.' And I say, 'What truth's that, Mr. D?' And he said, 'He thought he could stop being a player but he can't. If he ever stops playing again he's going to curl up in a little ball and die. So don't ever let him think he could lose that 'cause if you do, he'll go looking for it someplace else.' That's what he said, Mr. P, and like I said, I never heard of him being wrong. So my question to you is, did I let you get bored? Are you looking for it someplace else right now? Is that what we're doing here?"

Nick thought for several seconds. "Yes," he said.

"What I thought," Johnny sighed.

"But at least I'm letting you play too."

"Appreciate it, Mr. P. Glad we can still play together. But to be honest with you, to us the ten million matters almost as much."

Chapter 15

Mr. P
June 27, 2001

From the highway Kentucky looked a lot like Tennessee.

Olga said, "So Sugar Lips calls you Mr. P. Would you like me to call you that too?"

Nick said, "Not much."

She nodded. "But it's okay when he does it."

Johnny said, "You looked in a mirror lately? You want me to explain that to you?"

Olga said, "No. I wanted to know if he could. In particular I wanted him to know if he could."

Nick said, "Have you ever met anyone named Dolly?"

Olga shook her head. "Not from me. Not unless he tells me to."

Johnny said, "Sure. Why not?"

Olga stared. "You're saying he already knows it all. How does that *happen?*"

Johnny said, "You were right there with him, weren't you? You're here with him now, aren't you?"

Olga stared some more. "Maybe you should have made that clear before."

Johnny said, "So I'm making it clear now. What's the difference?"

Nick said, "Do I want to know what you're talking about?"

Olga said, "No, but I'm going to tell you anyway."

Johnny said, "Mr. P? What she wants to say is don't fuck up. You really don't have that option."

Nick said, "I never thought I did."

Johnny said, "I didn't think you thought so either, Mr. P. What about Dolly?"

Nick said, "Nothing, really. She said stupid falls right off my radar. Now Olga says pretty does too. That's all."

Johnny said, "Well, they notice things, Mr. P. You and women, it does stand out you know."

Olga said, "Then let's try this instead. The day you met the old man. You sat looking out on the square. Why?"

"It's where I always sit."

Johnny laughed. Olga ground her teeth and said, "Yes, Nicky, it's where you always sit. You sit that way to watch the square. That's obvious. But when you watch the square, what are you looking at?"

"People, mostly. All kinds of them. Other than that there's a fountain with a statue, another statue, a few dozen old buildings, some palm trees, flowers everywhere even in winter. Some carriages usually. It's a beautiful view that's always changing, or I could turn around and look at the front of the café all day."

"You didn't mention police. You didn't say you sit that way so anyone who joins you will have his back to the whole damn world."

"Why would I?"

"Oh, why indeed? But that old man thought you did. He even said so. He called you a real crook. Now this one calls you mister. It's incredible when you think about it."

"Olga?" Johnny said pleasantly.

"Sugar Lips, sir?"

"Is your point that he's an idiot or I am? 'Cause if it's about him, I could let it slide."

"You don't usually favor me with trivialities. Believe me, I can see the sliding you do for him."

"Sometimes you don't need to know my reasons to believe I have them. What's different today?"

"Perhaps I'm building up to a crisis of faith."

"This'd be a bad time for that. Back home on his island Mr. P does things we can't do. Mr. D saw that and showed me and now I see it too. Fourteen good leg breakers couldn't do what Mr. P does. You couldn't do it and I couldn't either and it's all because of how he is. So he doesn't understand it. He don't need to understand it. I do."

"Give me something, damn you. I'm shivering, I really am. Tomorrow we sneak into four different places the FBI are watching because we told them to so we can steal millions with little more than our superior finesse, and suddenly what used to happen on Cousin Nicky's island *matters* to us? To you, to me?"

"This isn't a new job. It's an old one. It's what we have to do to keep Mr. P and our thing on his island going. It doesn't work, we go on a while there. It works and in twenty years we own our own country."

"Riddles!"

"But it's true. It works and in a couple of years we don't need him anymore. He puts himself out to stud and everything sails on without him. We sit back and clip coupons on Park Avenue and only ever steal again when we get so bored we just can't stand it. That so, Mr. P?"

Nick thought it over. "It was really clever of you to ask for so much. It kept me from seeing that. But sure, if you're careful. If you learn a little more French and do a better job of staying in touch."

"You have a problem with it?"

"Only what Mr. D'Annunzio said about staying in the game."

"You'll have lots of better games now."

"I didn't think you'd notice."

"Not my day for respect, is it?"

Olga *hissed*. It got quiet. It got scary. She let it build a little and then she said, "Cousins, you started this. Finish it. Tell me about my Cousin Nicky's games. Tell me why on earth they matter now."

Nick pondered. "The problem," he said, "is that I usually throw in a couple of comments about, oh, the meaning of life, and there are people who find them, ah, distracting. I'm sure you know people like that."

"I'm not one of them. From the time I was a child I've sought the meaning of life in everyone I meet but all have failed me, even my own dear Sugar Lips. Reveal it to me at once or I'll become even more annoyed with you both."

Chapter 16

The Meaning of Life – Part I

Ma chère cousine,

If like some tiresome philosophe *we mean by* necessity *merely that which is not restrained from becoming, then all crime is necessary because all crime happens. But if we mean (as we so often do)* that without which disaster must follow, *then only a few crimes are truly necessary, and of these the recurring theft of civilization is the most needful of all…*

Explaining this idea (which is now the meaning of his own life) to Cousin Olga, Nick no longer remembers how he came upon it. Maybe Anne Marie let it slip years ago. If so, she would deny it. She would deny it because she doesn't believe it, or at least she doesn't think she does, although it *is* the kind of thing you could pick up just by listening to her. Maybe he even figured it out for himself. Whether he did or not, he knows that he's added a few features of his own by now, foremost of which is the stipulation that civilization's proprietors of the moment rarely last three generations before they're besotted with lazy arrogance, nor more than five until they're paralyzed by it. He can defend this part of the thesis; he remembers perfectly well how he came to appreciate it.

From two queer London "antiquarians," who after forty years together still share digs at the top of the Rue Ste Madeleine with the smallish remnant of their old wares that they didn't have manufactured to order, he learned the various declines and falls of Persia, Greece, Carthage, Rome and, five times a week if he'd let them, of dear old England herself.

From their sometime lover "Jaime," a "Spaniard" whose overwhelmingly Germanic appurtenances are no mystery to any Nikolai Petrov, he learned both the surprisingly short duration of the *real* Germany and an especially caustic version of the brief flowering and long, slow dotage of Iberia.

From his own forged ancestral memories, aided in part by *le Compte* Léon Tolstoï, he has mastered most of Russia's spasmodic forays into prominence.

Three far flung Italian ladies (and two of their nearer flung husbands) have revealed, if only by their mutual foreignness, that *there has never really been* such a place as "Italy."

From half the expatriate riffraff of Mitteleuropa he has gleaned a vivid if tangled notion of the Hapsburgs' centuries-long decline – though he is a little less clear on what they took so long declining from.

And of course he has plucked the history of France from the very air he breathes. Maybe not *all* the lesser parts that *some* little bootlickers can recite when Teacher calls on them, but he's certainly got the background music down pat.

From the bread he eats and the jam he spreads on it he has absorbed the rest of Europe's various *régimes, ancienne* and otherwise, *tous les Belges* and *tous les Hollandais* in their bickering, frigid north, and *les* sunny *Monagasques* and the happy *Luxe-oom-bourgeois*, nestled snugly in among the *Piedmontese...*

On top of which, he has heard reliable rumors of a vast, bewildered region called the Orient. If he ever learns any more about it, he is confident that these parts, too, will conform. (And if all that weren't enough, why, just this week he's been to Nashville…)

From all these stories from all these trustworthy *auteurs* that he's spent half a lifetime plying with wine and conversation, he's been pretty sure for quite a while that civilization's recurring theft is the only renewal the world ever really gets.

He's almost certain he'd have thought of this even if he'd never seen it happen, but we'll never really know, will we?

Claudine Bondieu
March 20, 1978

So to one fine Monday, not yet midway between the arrivals of Messrs. Petraki and D'Annunzio. Nikolai Petrov is reading on a bench on the *quai* when a strikingly beautiful woman tows a sheepish but somewhat menacing young boy up to him and demands, "Sir! Do you speak French!"

"An all small little," he replies. Glibly. Knowing that he's somewhat better than that at it, and she'll see this soon.

"Then teach my boy to read, please. Like he was in school. I see you here every day, I know you have the time."

"But Madame. I speak a little French but I read it very badly."

"Then teach him to read English!" screams the madwoman. "What difference could it possibly make?"

"What do you – you have an idea that I'm not sure I can follow."

"Oh, it is too simple for you! You see him! Teach him what you learned when you were like him, that lets you sit on benches all day while men of Belle Vièrge drown catching your dinner."

And she begins to cry and the boy bends down and picks up a rock and stands over Nikolai Petrov.

"It was my grandfather," the boy explains. "It was his idea there should be a school but he died for saying so and also my father.

Nothing else would make me talk to thee, thou may believe it."

Nikolai Petrov looks at the woman for several seconds.

"I believe," he says carefully, "that I know who you are."

Chapter 17

The Meaning of Life – Part II
June 27, 2001

Olga said, "I can see the possibilities already but I have to tell you, I don't fancy any of them as the meaning of life. Today we'll conjugate three verbs that will pass, respectively, for a pair of nylons, a chocolate bar and 20 cigarettes. And so we go screwing our way across Normandy."

Johnny seemed to know where this was headed. He moved to cut it off fast. He jumped straight in and he barely paused once for breath.

"That would be if your Cousin Nicky was the kind of small minded jerk who could never go on vacation with us. But Nicky's never been that way. When he was a kid and wanted ten minutes to himself he cut school for the whole day. Later when he wanted to sneak one drink he'd steal a whole bottle from his old man's basement. After that he just got worse and here we are.

"Go on Mr. P, tell her how you did it. Before she, *you know*, all over again."

Yes, Nicky *knew*. He wasn't about to forget. He *sank* back into the soft leather cushions but he *rose* to the occasion. He looked her straight in the eye and he did not blink once. He *told*.

Dieujuste Rosambert
March 24, 1978

One talked to Old Rosambert in the evening while he pretended to mend a perfectly good net. Old Rosambert said, *"Mets-toi en bateau…"*

For a second Nick thought he'd heard *get in the boat* and that the man was as crazy as they said. But even then he was learning to hear all of it, and finally did – *put thee in a boat and what could thou do?* – and then he thought it was the start of a pissing contest.

"It's true," he admitted. "I couldn't get out of the harbor."

"You see that and still want to pass your condition to the children? What kind of devil are you? You think they can take their books to the *Mairie* and all the nice Frenchmen will say, *Oh, look, how good you are! You don't have to work anymore and we don't have to eat!* You think boys can learn to live for the sea if they grow up like rich white fools? You think girls can dream of living like your ladies and still want any man from this place?"

Old Rosambert's insanity was mostly an uncontainable surplus of rectitude. He was complicated and no one ever denied it but it wasn't complication as some people have. He was not an unstable mix of outer strength and inner weakness. The principles you saw ran clear through to the other side. He pretended to mend a perfectly good net in the twilight to show that there was nothing wrong with his eyes, also to be the last man home from work. Others wandered slowly back to the beach to let their dinners settle. Families sat in little groups and communed with their neighbors. Kids still ran around but they were getting tired. Couples joked at spooning and prepared to spoon in earnest once the elders wandered off to bed. They would start to do that when Old Rosambert sneered discontentedly at the vanished sun, folded up his net and carried it back to his boat. There he would rummage a bit, demonstrating how one makes sure that the last possible bit of work has been done. Then, picking his way through the gaps, he would exchange a brief word with each family he passed as he made his way home. He would even tell mysterious jokes to the children, because true rectitude needn't be standoffish, as some falsely believe. Sometimes, ten or twenty years later, profound thoughts would come to these children, perhaps becalmed, baking in the sun without a sign of fish all day, or washing tin plates at the pump and worrying about a sick child of their own: and then they would think, *that's what Old Rosambert once said to me!*

It was now well past that time but Old Rosambert's net was still in his lap.

Nick said, "I didn't see Monsieur Pichet. Do suppose he's gone home already?"

Rosambert glared, but perhaps was prepared to be amused. "One knows where to find Pichet. Even you know it. You play cards of a fine evening yourself."

"Yes, now I remember. Sometimes for stakes as great as your catch."

Rosambert glared on but his thoughts no longer seemed amusing.

"Of course," Nick said, "to be just, we account him poor. It's strange, isn't it? He takes more than half what you get. He has a fine house and eats like twenty men. He loses two boatloads of fish at belote for pleasure and drinks up just as much, I assure you. But he's nothing to us. No one says, 'Say – let's have a party and invite Monsieur Pichet!' It's simply that at the café standards are much less rigid."

"More than half! You know nothing, do you?"

"True, but I know that much."

"You know less than nothing."

"You see, he is a braggart, I'm sure you must have noticed. He says such amusing things about all of you. Would you like to hear them?" Nick was sweating. He had no idea how well this might be going. Old Rosambert's knife grew longer by the second and they both knew that he really wouldn't need it. "He says you live not so much from day to day but meal to meal and bed to bed. He says that is why your fish are always fresh, from your hurry to get a handful of coins and spend them at once on the appetite of the moment."

Rosambert said, "What is it then that Pichet has done to you, that you're trying to arrange his murder so cheaply?"

But Nick mused on. "In many ways he agrees with you. He says that if he paid you fairly on Monday, then on Tuesday you would not fish…"

"Pichet or another Pichet: what you can't know is how it doesn't matter to a man…"

"And if all the Pichets were to become unnecessary?"

"You pick a strange place to try out your silly philosophies. No one here has time for them. Fishermen sell their catch. It's what fishermen do, and all the Pichets in the world are so much dirt to us."

"Yes, that's right. Fishermen must sell their catch and the rest of us must buy it, but neither of us needs Pichet between us, pretending to you to be a hungry mouth, and to us to be the man that wrestles fish from the sea. The man without whom no fish would ever find a plate."

Rosambert put down his knife and leaned closer to Nick. "There is now no doubt that you are trying to enrage me. Think, first, that there is no Pichet at hand if you succeed."

"I'll take the chance. I have a proposition. There is no *reason* for you not to hear it."

Rosambert considered. As suddenly as that it was as dark as it would get. There was the sound of breakers. There were whispers off to the right.

"All right. Since you take the chance."

"I'll sell your fish for you. I know where every one of them goes and I know how much is paid for it. I've been instructed. I know Vachon who buys for the cruise lines, I know all three brokers for the canneries and I know every shop and restaurant on Saint Sulpice. I learned it all before daring to approach you and if you doubt me I'll recite it. Instead of keeping anything, I'll give the money back to you. All the money, not what Pichet can bear to part with. Maybe some of my friends will help from time to time but we'll never take a franc. A fish perhaps, but only if it's offered. When one or two of the older girls have learned arithmetic and a little reading and writing, they'll take it over and I'll go find another pastime. But from the day you say yes, no one will cheat Belle Vièrge again."

Rosambert hadn't moved. The breeze was delicious. Nick was excited. Was it possible he was getting away with it? Perhaps the breakers were getting louder but he could still hear giggles off to his left, and he prayed that he didn't seem to hear them.

Rosambert said, "How long?"

"We'll call it a cooperative. I'll go when I'm not needed, one year, perhaps as much as two. It depends on how well I teach as much as anything."

Rosambert said, "Don't imagine anyone could forget such a promise. Don't think gratitude will make idiots of us."

From nearby came what might have been the cry of a gull.

'L'École Dieujuste Rosambert. You'll admit it has a certain ring to it."

"You are trying to bribe me."

"Of course."

In the starlight Rosambert no longer looked old, just immensely strong. His person grew to fit his voice, which said, "So the children learn to read and write and count. All the fishes fly one way and the money flies the other and you stand in the square with your umbrella and nothing falls on you. You'd have me think you're some kind of missionary. But I don't think so and, believe me, you do not want me to."

If our corrupters are to succeed in suppressing our sense of sin, they must be worse than we are yet not intolerably wicked. Nick had been fairly called. He told Rosambert his price.

Rosambert's shirt had disappeared into the dark. He was now a giant draped in seaweed. "Good. You ask too much but no one has to pay it. I suppose you know you're a fool, and doomed to disappointment?"

"Of course."

"And our school will continue if she remains sensible?"

"Of course."

"Good. At least that part of it is none of my affair. In the midst of all the clever fidgeting you do instead of work, do you think you can remember that?"

Chapter 18

Entre Acte
June 7, 2001
"…but I digress from my digression."
- Henry Fielding

After leaving Hall, Gonzales said to Curtis, "You notice? Everything he does and has is perfect but it's only half what the rest of us have and do."

Curtis said, "Does the stuff he thinks they left him. No woman, no friends? Okay, won't need a dining room then. Still got to pass his own time? Okay, he'll need a nice couch and TV."

"Somehow spotless bothers me."

"Hell yes spotless. Place got to be clean, your mother told you that."

"Say he's the same at work."

"Why doubt it?"

"Then we trust what he says."

"About debits and credits. The rest is Looney Tunes except the details all come from something he's seen somewhere."

"Something real we have to get out of him some way."

"Something real he can't wait to lead us to, soon as he remembers what it is."

"That outfit."

"What he's supposed to wear. What you're supposed to do doesn't change until it just goes away."

"Not a textbook case, is it?"

"It will be, we got anything to say."

Chapter 19

Important Lessons
June 27, 2001

Johnny said, "See, what sticks out here is, however crazy Cousin Nicky's plans may seem to us, he always finds the people who can make them happen. This is an important lesson for you."

Olga said, "You're talking about yourself, of course, so one can only agree."

Johnny said, "You too."

Olga said, "Nicky didn't find me, Sugar Lips. *You* remember how we came to meet."

Johnny said, "Well, in a way he did set it up. It's just not any way you can explain. But sometimes the people he needs just come to him and afterwards even he's not sure just what he did to make that happen."

Étienne Délibes
April 1, 1978

It was getting a bit dark for reading and Nick closed his book. He would, perhaps, have another, and looked around for Antoine. Instead, M. Délibes rose from his own table, glass in hand, and wandered over, wagging his finger. Well, Nick thought, it might as well be now.

Seating himself across from Nick, Délibes said, "I've come to scold you."

"In effect," Nick said, "we all think of you as our conscience."

"One doesn't see you anywhere at bridge."

Neat, Nick thought, and tried hard to look like a desolated man. "I play very badly. I play many games badly but around here at bridge, one has a partner of substance to enrage. It's not tranquil."

"You prefer belote with the shopkeepers."

"Most of whom rejoice when I blunder."

"Dominoes next, I suppose."

"I don't even know the rules."

"Perhaps someone should start a school."

"There's a thought."

"Look, Monsieur Petrov. Have you thought it through? It's like pulling loose stones from an old wall. They all seem so useless but who knows which one will bring it down?"

"Well said. Possibly that's why walls are sometimes repaired."

"And you play all games badly. Perhaps I should speak plainly."

"I beg you."

"What do you hope to accomplish?"

"Teach a few idle kids to read picture books." Délibes nodded but Nick wasn't through. "Possibly do a little good."

Délibes nodded and opened his mouth but Nick kept going. "Amuse myself and some of my friends. Feel like we're a little useful."

Délibes nodded earnestly and waited. "Mostly, though, keep *them* from doing it," and Nick nodded toward the church. "I'm one of those that think once a week is enough."

Délibes stopped nodding because his jaw got in the way. "Them?

They are forbidden!"

"In France," Nick agreed.

"But nothing has changed! There is the state and there is the Church."

"So it appears but it's just a trick of relativity. It's the proportions that matter." That's what he meant to say but his French was still in its infancy and he'd called it a *joke* of relativity, but that said it too for Délibes.

"What do you know?" Délibes demanded.

"Nothing but talk. Hours and hours of it. What's amusing is that I started talking to them for my own education. To improve my French."

"Such French!"

"Perhaps it will improve all around."

"They wouldn't dare."

"Monsieur Délibes. You are the Frenchman and I am the stranger. But can it be that there's anything they wouldn't dare?"

Délibes was not only a Frenchman but a Frenchman with a father who had said, *There are worse things in business than having your affairs discussed in the street. They might make it to the church*. He changed course. "Why *École Rosambert?*"

"Better than what *they* have in mind, don't you think?"

Délibes was unable to ask.

"*École Bondieu*. You really hadn't heard? I had to argue with Rosambert for hours. He wanted nothing to do with it. You said walls, he said loose pegs in a boat, did you know how much he agrees with you? He thinks it will ruin them for the simple life."

"He's right!"

"Not if we do it as he would if he knew how. Is he really such a bad ideal from our point of view?"

Délibes considered. After all… "What do you need?" he

demanded.

"Pichet must have known," Nick mused idly.

"Pichet! Tell us and lose another precious fisherman!"

"Still, for those who like to eat, he's an invaluable man. He often says so himself."

"Invaluable! He's a grocer we've made rich because it was convenient. We could get another man in a week."

"I suppose he could always fall back on tinned guavas."

"They supported him once and he'd best remember it."

"You know," Nick said, "what I miss most of all here? Coming home from a modestly busy day at work. Say, as a fish broker, perhaps. It could make all this" – here he gestured, taking in the café, the square, the universe of Saint Sulpice – "so very much more satisfying. Make me feel more a part of everything, you know? Somewhat like bridge, I suppose."

Délibes was back in his element. "I can't imagine anyone objecting. And you'll... *control* this thing about the school?"

"Won't be hard," Nick agreed. "Know where we can pick up a few arithmetic books? Count the pins and fishhooks, right? Maybe learn to count change so the maids can't say they're cheated when they're sent to do the shopping."

Délibes had had maids of his own. He said he'd get right on it.

Chapter 20

Margarite Schrenk
Lexington, June 27, 2001

After kicking it around, Gonzales and Curtis made a date with her for coffee. When you intrude without a warrant, a nervous woman in her own home can always tell you to leave. Morning coffee in one of her public spaces has its own dynamics. The best and worst are that she can get up and walk whenever she wants. This makes panic almost impossible to handle but sometimes it gives her the confidence to keep panic at bay. Also one stays aware of manners out in public, and part of manners is answering questions if they're politely put.

Margarite Schrenk walked into the Starbucks to find them waiting, Curtis smiling expectantly and in the red tie he'd described, Gonzales in the emerald blouse and glowering like the bitch she doubtlessly was. She hadn't realized from the call that they were black – and at any moment an acquaintance of her husband could walk in, but Margarite Schrenk was always prepared. All she had to do was put her briefcase on the table and there she was, real estate lady on the job instead of real estate lady being where she wants to be. She reached in and plucked out two business cards, which forced the bitch to take one. Curtis gave her a card of his own, then Gonzales did, but sullenly. "We have ID too," Gonzales said, "if you want that."

"Yes," Margarite Schrenk said, "perhaps you should," and studied each just long enough to be sure. "Don't you hate it," she asked Gonzales, "when they keep using an old picture after you get your hair the way you really want it?"

"You speak English very well, Mrs. Schrenk," Curtis offered, possibly noticing an appealing detail or two but only in the most professional way.

"I should, I think. I've lived here many years and before that I went to school. I know I have a terrible accent but I've given up fixing it, you see. When I try to talk like my friends everyone starts laughing and can't stop for hours."

"Interfere with your business, being foreign?" Curtis asked, as if interested, while Gonzales almost groaned in disbelief.

"Not in real estate, for some reason. Once you get beyond the trailer-trash category, you find people here who seem to associate Europe with taste and class. One's most ordinary opinions become strangely valuable at times. And, technically, as I'm sure you know full well, I have not been a foreigner for seventeen years."

"So get on with it, right?"

"Well, one is curious after all."

Gonzales leaned forward. "Coffee or something before we start? Because once we do we'd kind of like to keep it going. *You* understand, business lady yourself and all."

"Oh," Margarite Schrenk said, "perhaps our businesses are somewhat different. In mine I find that comfort is almost everything." And walked to the counter and ordered.

"No pastry," Curtis said.

"No bet," Gonzales agreed.

"One of those dry biscotti things, though. Show she isn't

spooked."

"She doesn't need to. She isn't."

"A quarter."

"Oh, hell, sure," Gonzales surrendered. Margarite Schrenk was forty-eight. Had she not known that, Gonzales would have put her at forty-two and bet most men would say thirty-eight or forty. She did it with nothing but her figure and her walk, which was not the least bit suggestive but simply announced an awareness of being exceptionally attractive. "What you see?" Gonzales said. "That takes more work than you can imagine. She's had it down since way before anything we were going to talk about."

"We've got some new questions, now she's not the lady who sold you your condo?"

"Damn right. That package ended up selling houses in Kentucky, and it was *not* designed for that."

Margarite Schrenk came back with a small black coffee (points) and two biscotti.

"Fifty cents," Curtis said.

"Fifty?" Gonzales demanded.

"Two biscotti. Twenty-five each. Fifty."

Gonzales dug in her purse and slapped two quarters in front of Curtis, then leaned back, folded her arms and glowered.

Margarite Schrenk gave them a real estate lady's smile. "In my trade also," she said, "people often seem to forget why they come to us. Would it help if I try to sell you a house?"

"Told you," Gonzales spat. "This interview belongs at the office, anything does."

"We have time," Curtis reminded her. "Mrs. Schrenk, we have some questions for you."

"Start with the money," Gonzales told him.

"We could—"

"The money."

"All right. Mrs. Schrenk, you have your own checking account and it has quite a balance in it. We're interested in how you manage it."

Gonzales leaned forward now, ready to enjoy whatever came next. Curtis looked on mildly as though he'd just asked what time dinner would be served. This was the moment for Margarite to panic, get mad, get tough, start lying, break down, become outraged, walk out, call her lawyer, blather or turn on the bewildered innocence. Instead she considered a moment, then murmured, "Well, you do have the correct credentials after all. Is this a tax matter?"

Gonzales said, "Could be."

Curtis said, "Not really. I'm afraid that for some people it's quite a bit more serious."

"Well. I have two checking accounts actually. One I use every day. It has about a hundred dollars in it so I don't think you mean that one. The other is for the income of my business. I put it all in, pay the taxes from it each quarter and after Christmas we decide what to do with what's left. In between we live on my husband's salary. It's not really complicated."

"And you always get money back," Gonzales said, as though that were at least a misdemeanor.

"It's not difficult. I don't deduct my expenses until next year at tax time, you see. That way we're always covered even if my husband gets a bonus or something."

"We'll get back to *or something*," Gonzales promised but just then Curtis made his move.

"So except for taxes coming out and distribution at year end, all the activity is the deposits from your real estate business, Mrs. Schrenk? Is that what you're saying?"

"Exactly."

"And how do you get paid, Mrs. Schrenk? Sale by sale or at month end, for instance?"

"Oh, one commission at a time, unless I'm lucky enough to earn two in one day."

"And that's what, Mrs. Schrenk, three percent of the sale?"

"Two, Mr. Curtis. I pay for the privilege."

"Two percent," Curtis mused.

"You sell many houses for three point five mil?" Gonzales asked, with a look that said, *all right, people, I'm taking over now.*

"Never. Not even close to that amount."

"How about twice this month?" Gonzales said, but Curtis waved her gently down.

"Mrs. Schrenk," he said, "how much do you think is in that account?"

"Around ninety thousand I should think."

"Two hundred thirty-two thousand and change," Gonzales said. "And the check for your last taxes has cleared."

Margarite Schrenk looked calmly from one to the other, apparently waiting for Curtis's punch line.

"Mrs. Schrenk, on the first and the twelfth of this month identical seventy-thousand dollar deposits went into your account. Can you explain them?"

"Not at all," she said, looking not exactly stricken but far from happy.

"Could your husband have made them?" Curtis asked.

"Of course but why would he? And certainly not without telling me. I have heard of mistakes – but twice, and so long with no correction?"

"They weren't that kind of mistake," Curtis said. "They were wires and the bank got the account number right."

"From Grand Cayman," Gonzales said. "You know where that

is?"

"The place that doesn't talk to you. Yes."

"Yes?" Gonzales.

"Yes, so you'd have to come to me. I see. Only I don't, not at all."

Curtis was now in a speculative mood. "Suppose you found the money on your next statement and the bank said it was definitely yours. What would you do?"

"Keep it, I suppose. Perhaps consult a lawyer."

"A lawyer would tell you to pay tax on it," Curtis said.

"Well, yes, we'd have to."

"So that's what you'd probably do? Declare it and keep the rest?"

She just looked at him.

"Just like it came from your business," he said.

She kept on looking.

"Ma'am," Gonzales asked, "do you know what money laundering is?"

Curtis winced. "Mrs. Schrenk," he asked, almost with a trace of desperation, "do you know how much your husband makes?"

"Of course." She thought a second and nodded. "You suppose he's come into something he can't explain. So he turns it into something I can't explain. Yes."

"Yes?" Curtis, this time.

"It would seem to make sense. I of course know that it does not but how could you? I think, by all means, that you should pursue this conjecture. In fact I think I insist on it."

"You insist, ma'am?"

"Yes, Agent Gonzales. It is your right to refuse of course but it is certainly my right to insist as much as I please. Right now it pleases me very much."

Curtis looked at Gonzales. Gonzales looked at Margarite

Schrenk. First she looked at her hair. The cut was lower maintenance than it looked but it looked dynamite. The hair itself was one of those combinations of color, mostly red and bronze, that don't really happen naturally but let women of a certain age keep control without seeming to be trying to put anything over. From the hair she moved on to the face. The face, she thought, had always been a little hard but probably not many men would care. The arms were tan and firm. Not a machine, Gonzales decided, and certainly not gardening. Probably golf, then, hours and hours of it from the results she got. At golf, you weren't looking to buy a house of course, she could probably surprise you. Gonzales often said that some people wouldn't give it up because they were waiting for you to take it. She made up her mind. "I'm not usually this crude," she said.

"How could you be?" Margarite Schrenk said and Curtis broke out laughing.

"It's what we do," Gonzales said, quite gently in fact.

"I'm sure that I'd usually find it fascinating," Margarite Schrenk said. "I hope very much that I don't start crying now."

Curtis leaned closer. "Do you understand what you'd be asked to do?"

"Of course not. Is it really him?"

"Almost certainly," Curtis said, but the new Gonzales added, "That doesn't mean he won't be able to explain it."

"Oh, no," Margarite Schrenk said, "it certainly doesn't mean that at all. May I have some more coffee please?" And Curtis was up and on it, fast.

"A good explainer, huh?" Gonzales said.

"Pure at heart, you see, utterly so. The very worst kind, I think, but then I was spoiled as a child. Men in my own family actually made mistakes from time to time."

Gonzales agreed. "You're right, you were spoiled rotten," and when Curtis got back he wondered what the laughter was about. They talked business but took a few breaks. During one of them Margarite Schrenk said, "When I came here, I was twenty-one and Alois was twenty-seven. Already he had been chosen for the Board. Americans have trouble with that idea, to choose a man for a job he'll have in twenty years but in Germany it was done, perhaps it still is. So we had to live here for three years you see, because the North American market would always be very important. In Berlin we lived on the fifth floor. We walked up, there was no elevator. This was considered a good apartment, you understand, there was simply no housing in Berlin. There was everything else you could want, though, except heat in the winter and peace and quiet almost any time. Alois is a Berliner and didn't notice. I was an ignorant country girl from near Munich who couldn't even talk right, which I believe will be my epitaph. We came here and moved temporarily into a big apartment complex which has now gone condo. It had a swimming pool and a clubhouse, I couldn't believe it. I spent every afternoon at the pool. People said hi and I said hi back but no more than that because no polite person came along to make introductions. Later I learned there was a great debate about me. Either I was the most stuck up bitch in creation or just a poor dumb clueless foreigner. On a bet two girls walked up and asked if I could drive them to the store. I said I'd love to but didn't have a car. Something like *oh yes but I haf not car,* I suppose. One girl yelled, 'Jesus!' and the other said, 'Honey, your husband? Maybe he's new here too but if he's going to leave you alone then he's *got* to buy you a car.' These girls took me bowling which I had heard of but never done. I was pathetic and we got a little drunk. It was wonderful. The next day I showed them tennis and they were pathetic and after that we were friends."

"You get your car?" Gonzales asked.

"Eventually. Eventually I got everything. I had three years, then back to Berlin. People said, don't worry, you have nothing to worry about, you can have your same apartment back when you get home. Two things I understood almost from the start. One was that Alois would do anything the company asked, any time, to anybody, including me, which indicates my self-centered view of our marriage. The other was that I was not going back to that apartment. Perhaps, yes, back to Germany, because I couldn't control that, could I? Not married to Alois with the visa we had and anyway Germany was my country that I loved. But not to that apartment. Of course I asked him. Could we not stay here? Could we not try Bavaria? He was incredulous. Not return to Berlin? When already he was selected for the Board? After two years I cried every morning before I was able to go out. Nothing could save me. They'd send me back and then I must leave Alois and even that might keep him off the Board because a wife is important. Then that man came along and saved us."

"What man?" Curtis asked.

"A man named Petraki. He ruined Alois's life. After that there was nothing to do but stay. But two things have still not changed."

"What are those?" Curtis asked while Gonzales nodded to herself.

"Alois will still do anything those people tell him to and I am not going back to Berlin."

Chapter 21

Parlor Maids
June 27, 2001

Olga said, "You know, Cousin, in everyone's upbringing a certain number of vulgar stereotypes and prejudices inevitably take root that no amount of experience can entirely dislodge. Mine hardly ever bother me anymore but if you really made a trade school for that man's future parlor maids, then I think this would be a good time to tell me a very different story."

Johnny said, "Don't worry about it. Don't you see by now that Mr. P never gives anyone exactly what they want?"

Olga said, "Oh, Sugar Lips. Just when I thought you knew what reassurance really means to me."

Lucienne Bonnard
May 15, 1978

The schoolhouse was made of four poles with a heap of old nets thrown across the top. They cut about half the sun and when it was more or less overhead the school was a shady place to rest. For several days a lot of resting was done while Nick struggled to explain the alphabet. Then two things happened. A raiding party of six screaming mothers swept in, slapping and pinching where it hurt. So much for restfulness and inattention but Nick was just as stuck as ever and now he had a garrison of mothers observing his futility. At the first hint of noise, or of thinking noisy thoughts, one of them moved up, ready to smack. To prevent another riot he established that questions were okay, questions were good, questions are what we're here for, but first one must raise one's hand. Thereafter at least three hands were up at all times but he could hardly back down. Trying to not look at the glowering women, he was groping to answer a small boy's earnest and woeful, "But, sir, what is P *for?*" when a voice cut across the dock and saved him: "P is so your Papa can catch fish. If it weren't for P he would be your *ah ah* and he could only catch *'oisons.*"

The class squealed in delight and every hand came flying up, which was all that prevented a final maternal massacre.

"And R?"

"And Q?"

Nick fled to seek his savior and met a tall, furiously severe lady in a bell-shaped, cast bronze coiffure and brilliant yellow dress and shoes. Uh oh, he thought but there was no helping it now.

"Have you the faintest idea what you're doing?"

Perhaps forty-five but, mainly, a *grown up*. "No."

"Thank God you know at least that much. What on earth do you hope to accomplish here?"

This was not a woman Nick felt he could say *get laid* to, so he prevaricated. "I was hoping it would come to me."

"Well," she said, "it has. Lucienne Bonnard. You're Petrov or something. We've not met."

"Or something."

"Pardon?"

"Petrov, exactly. Of course I've seen you in the café. Tell me you're really a teacher."

"Headmistress too, by the look of things. What time do you start?"

A teacher, so lying had been the thing to do. "Promptly at ten."

Mme. Bonnard, a tower of respectability whose husband once enjoyed considerable prominence on the Paris *Bourse*, said something unprintable and turned to the squadron of mothers that now surrounded them. "Is there a reasonable objection to eight?"

Most of them just smiled but Claudine Bondieu said, "What's wrong with six? Once the men leave they start playing and after that they're spoiled for the day."

"Seven it is," Lucienne Bonnard said. "Certain men leave later than others."

"Er," Nick began but Claudine had him by the hand.

"It is impossible," she said, "for us to thank you as you deserve."

Not really, Nick thought, while five other women repeated the lie in exhaustive variation until Claudine signaled her readiness to continue.

"And to think you even doubted yourself. Now you've even found us a true expert, something everyone said was impossible. We will remember you forever."

Nick started shaking hands, saving Claudine Bondieu's for last. "No more than I'll remember thee, I'm sure," he said, and thought that just possibly he saw a spark of something there behind the laughter.

They waved and shouted as he backed on down the dock. Lucienne Bonnard glared on.

Chapter 22

Entre Acte
June 27, 2001
"…but I descend to particulars."
Robert Burton, *Anatomy of Melancholy*

"Mrs. Schrenk," Curtis asked, "what can you tell us about your husband's business with Cuba?"

Margarite Schrenk put down her last piece of biscotti. "This isn't getting any funnier."

Gonzales said, "We weren't really hoping you'd know but you have to tell us so."

"Cuba. I don't really think it's possible."

Curtis asked, "How about Mexico?"

"Oh yes. Mexico is very important."

"For Mexico's sake or for who they might be selling to?" Gonzales asked.

"Oh dear. This isn't going to get much better, is it?"

"Sometimes," Gonzales said, "when it's like this, you need to starting thinking long range. Short term is probably going to be a little rough."

"Tell me. Is that something you know or did someone just say it to you?"

"Oh, it's true all right. Isn't it?" To Curtis, who nodded.

"Fascinating," Margarite Schrenk said.

"How?" Gonzales asked.

"It's something my husband believes, and it turns out to be true."

Curtis said, "It's the dates that are the problem. The way they line up with those deposits."

"Dates?"

Gonzales said, "The dates of Fuentes' last order for Cuba."

Curtis said, "It was confirmed on May 31st."

Gonzales said, "It shipped on the eleventh."

Curtis said, "The deposits happened on–"

Margarite Schrenk said, "Yes. I don't plan on forgetting for a little while longer."

Chapter 23

The True Bourgeois Within
June 27, 2001

Olga said, "Just rode off into the sunset then, did you?"

Johnny said, "How could he? He hasn't got the girl yet, has he? Plus look at all the stuff he hasn't got his fingers into, now that he's back into sticking his fingers where they don't belong."

Nicky said, "I had a girlfriend after that, Sugar Lips knows her, who said that by not thinking about what I was doing then I forfeited my only chance of shedding the true bourgeois within me. Or evicting it. Or something good like that. Back home did you ever–"

Olga said, "No, Cousin. We didn't talk that way even in school, rather we did not commit individualistic deviations of that kind, for the simple reason that we admitted to harboring no inner bourgeoisies and all they would have meant. But I'm glad that you later had a girlfriend. I'd come to fear that Isabella was your first."

Johnny said, "Isabella?"

Nicky started in again, fast.

The Chairman, the Vice-Chairwoman and the Honorary Advisor
June 22, 1978

First Mme. Bonnard had declared that, as in any civilized place, there would be no school on Thursdays. Claudine Bondieu had negotiated fiercely. These children were already very *late,* was that not true? What was to be gained from denying it? Why pretend that this was Paris and they had wholesome games to go to? Mme. Bonnard considered and announced a compromise, in a tone that not even Claudine dared dispute. On Thursdays the children would come to school but instead of their studies they would learn instructive and stimulating pastimes. In the mornings they would sing and draw. In the afternoons they would tell stories and perhaps act them out. As their learning advanced, they would begin to get their stories from books.

On this Thursday morning Nick had the whole co-op management committee sitting in the lee of a palm at the foot of the dock. In the middle distance the children sang, *On the bridge at Avignon...*

The management committee consisted of Dieujuste Rosambert and Colette Bondieu. Not being a fisherman, Nick was merely an honorary member and as Rosambert saw it Colette's was mainly an auxiliary position.

The children sang, *There one dances, there one dances...*

Colette Bondieu smiled at the sound.

Old Rosambert said, "I've got to hand it to you. In four hundred years nobody from here has ever sung that stupid song before."

On the bridge at Avignon...

Colette said, "You know, on Thursdays..."

"Oh, yes. Thursdays are for stupidity, not work. Therefore I sit here like an invalid."

There one dances all around!

"Hey," Nick said, "I never sang it either. Let's talk about money, all right?"

Rosambert said, "You have some numbers to confuse us with, I think."

"A report, then, if you please. First of all, it's been a month exactly. Every man has been paid for his catch, yes?"

"As before, though now with considerable fumbling."

"I hope to get better with practice. With what was left I bought ten hammers."

Colette Bondieu started and Old Rosambert gaped in outrage.

"To go with the nails. Five kegs."

Colette looked puzzled. Rosambert said, "Oh, *five* kegs. That's all right then."

"Because of the lumber, you see. It seemed to be about five kegs' worth."

Colette began to smile.

Rosambert said, "The lumber…," but now in a serious way.

"Sure," Nick said, "for the sidewalks. Lumber is dear in this place, I had no idea, but I think I got enough for about two hundred meters, one meter wide. I was thinking from there to there, then along there, then around there till we run out. After we get more we can branch out and cover each lane."

Colette whispered, "Each lane."

"First one side, then the other. If we wait a few weeks, two or three, we can buy it all together and only pay for shipping once."

Colette said, "Two or three weeks."

Nick said, "I had to get some saws, of course. And a crowbar and a level, a how-do-you-say, you dig post holes with it, and a couple of spades. I'm no carpenter myself but I assume that men who can keep boats in good repair can manage hammers and saws."

Rosambert stood and removed his hat. "It begins to seem," he said, "that one has falsely accused you of lying about Pichet."

"Pichet," Colette said thoughtfully.

"May he visit again very soon," Rosambert said. "One begs your forgiveness."

"One has nothing to forgive. Who has done more than you?"

"There remains right and wrong."

"Then let's keep on being right, shall we?"

Colette said, "And next? Your thoughts on that?"

Rosambert sat back down.

Nick thought, so it is possible to look fiercely remorseful. He said, "A storm sewer for that ditch. Build a shed. Get a scale. Real ones are expensive but we can make one ourselves. It will do for our needs."

Rosambert asked, "How long?"

"Three more weeks. At most another month."

Colette asked, "And then?"

"It begins to get beyond me. We can start paying out more but I suspect we can do more useful things ourselves. Fix all the leaky roofs for instance – we could do that before winter. Work on the dock. But as for real plumbing and electricity, for instance – those things need serious planning and consideration."

Rosambert put up his hand. He sat for several minutes while the others listened to a children's song that neither of them recognized.

"How's Claudine?" Nick asked.

Colette said, "Intolerably pretty and vivacious I think but then again I'm her mother."

Nick was still recovering when Rosambert came out of it.

"It appears," he said at last, "that, after all, I will not be able to rest for quite some time yet."

Chapter 24

At last Margarite Schrenk swallowed her biscotti. "Fuentes," she said.

"Diego Fuentes," Gonzales repeated.

"Oh, I know who he is. Tell me, is it possible he could get in trouble for this?"

Curtis considered many things. "It's possible. He's also one who might be guilty and walk away."

"Because he's Mexican," Margarite Schrenk said.

"There are violations we can extradite for and those we can't. I'll be honest. Some we could, we hardly ever do."

"Making clumsy passes at married women?"

"For some reason I can't fathom," Curtis said, "Congress hasn't got around to that one yet."

"How clumsy?" Gonzales asked.

"I'm here, I'm available, I'm irresistible, you're but a woman and life is short. Where's the bedroom?"

"That kind," Gonzales said.

"That's a kind?"

"Oh dear me yes."

"What did your husband say?"

"You very clever young man. Yes, I told him. He said, 'So? He's a Mexican.'"

"And he came back anyway," Curtis said.

Gonzales looked at him. "You're a little too sure you understand that."

"Let her answer, please."

"Yes, he came back anyway. Read nothing into that. He was a major customer in good standing, of course he came back. He could have stolen the silver and burnt the house and he'd have come back. I take it back. Read everything into it."

Gonzales said, "You won't like this but you have to try. We need his words. We need your husband's words to him."

Margarite Schrenk sighed. "You flatter me. And if I could remember it all, it would only be what they said in front of me. Nothing about business."

Curtis said, "Never about business?"

Gonzales said, "Never once? Maybe you were walking out of the kitchen with the salad. Maybe your husband took a call from Fuentes at home."

Margarite Schrenk thought about it. "Never," she said. "I mean, there were many calls, many dinners everywhere. But not a word about work."

Curtis and Gonzales seemed to fall into a somehow shared and very satisfying reverie.

Margarite Schrenk began to feel a draft.

Chapter 25

Polish Sausage
June 27, 2001

Stopping for gas, they looked over the snacks in the little mini-mart. It was late afternoon, they'd left it too long, they were vulnerable to the packaged crap and they knew it. Nick saw Polish sausage on the sign over the hot dogs and Johnny had to bring him down gently. "It's industrial tube steak, Mr. P. Stick to the chips, at least they won't break your heart."

Nick said, "You wouldn't know about Polish."

Johnny said, "That's a natural mistake, you being from Chicago. But what all you people forget is that there's two places to get any kind of good food: where it comes from, and New York. Plus, on top of that, I'm educated in the ways of the world. I even heard about the celery salt."

Olga said, "Think, Cousin. Have you not at least one grand memory of some peerless Caribbean sausage to console you at moments like this?"

Nick thought. "No," he said, "but there's a whole plate full I didn't eat that bothered me for years."

Pierre Bondieu, Emile Bonnard
December 29, 1979

The Café des Artistes had invested heavily to counter the usual
pre-New Year's lull. On Friday night there was *choucroute garnie* in the
Alsatian manner. Lucienne Bonnard left her party's table, stalked
across the terrace to Nick's, kissed him on the cheek, sat and
demanded, "Do you even know what prudence means?"

"Possibly not. Usually you enumerate the indictment."

"You gave Pierre Bondieu that book for Christmas."

"It wasn't new. I read it first myself."

"Oh, he knows you approve it. He is close to shattered."

"There are some long words but–"

"He can read it all right. Can't you imagine what Hugo can do to
someone like him, especially *Les Miserables*?"

"I thought I could. That's why I gave it to him. What does *like
him* mean?"

"You know too much to confuse me with these pigs. It means an
exceptionally precocious and sensitive but barely literate provincial
child living in intolerably oppressive circumstances and hearing for
the first time that the world has long had a concept of justice it
remorselessly withholds from him."

"I'm a different breed of pig myself. The best I can do is blunder
forward but sometimes I manage it."

"And how thrilling that must be, and how one envies you for it!
In effect it's only because one knows this that one can speak to you
so frankly, can bring you one's little cares. One hopes only to not
mire you down, one prays that the grand sweep of your conception
will sustain you and bear you onward."

"At present the grand sweep of my conception awaits a glass of
wine. If you'd finally accept one yourself it might feel free to reach for

better things."

"But no, I invited myself."

"Faithless vixen! I invited you so long ago, you think you can pretend to forget."

"In front of my husband? Perhaps he's a jealous beast."

"He's nothing of the kind. We're almost friends in fact. It's only your low opinion of me that separates us."

"My opinion of you is too rich in particulars to be called simply low. I'll order for myself if you permit. You appear not to believe it but there *is* a difference between one bottle and the next."

"Then you must order for me too. How can one learn if one is not taught?"

"That part you seem to understand. But how can one be taught by one who hasn't learned?"

"Surely you know the answer to that. One mumbles along for a while and a true teacher arrives to do it right."

"*Par example!* You'd flatter us both into imbecility, wouldn't you?"

"I didn't mumble? You're not a true teacher?"

"You know perfectly well what I mean. Try a little seriousness. You may not need it very often but you're intolerable without any at all. You have started something with Pierre Bondieu. Go fix it."

"Can you—"

"I could and I won't, unless you decide to get out of his life for good. In that case you can stay away from mine as well. You're the one to do it, accept that I know."

"You can't even—"

"No I can't. He'll tell you or he won't. If he won't I suggest that you find a way to make him before you come crying back to me."

"Tomorrow I'll—"

"Ah, yes. You can always do it tomorrow. He was close to tears this afternoon and so agitated that he couldn't sit but what's another night?"

"Do you suppose they'll save a plate for me?"

"Are you telling me it would matter?"

"Only to me, Madame."

Antoine was there at last. Lucienne Bonnard said, "Alas, Antoine, my dear colleague has remembered a forgotten obligation and has changed his mind about ordering. But don't be so distraught! We'll eat and drink everything he meant to, and a great deal more beside."

Nick stood and bowed. "Madame, if ever I am tempted to regret the fearful responsibility that I burdened you with, I will recall this very moment and be reassured."

It was early but almost dark and those too accustomed to the climate might have thought it cold; but Nick did not and there were still plenty like him who remembered what real winters are like. As he left a couple was already moving to his table and it would be a good few hours until he could get it back. He kicked his scooter to life and sped across the square and down the Rue Ste Madeleine, staying on the crest of the cobblestones because whatever lay in the gutters was now invisible. Where the cobbles turned to gravel he slowed to ten kilometers. When that turned to dried ruts he slowed to a crawl. He turned onto the dock, rolled past the co-op's office and shed and saw that they were locked and dark, and coasted down the mud lane to Claudine Bondieu's tiny house. Out front he gunned the motor, turned around and climbed back to the co-op. He parked next to the office, unlocked the door, went in and lit the lamp. Fetching the ledger, he pulled what was left of the last two days' tickets off the spike and looked at them. Nicole had sorted through them and got all the way through the O's before leaving – but then Nicole always was known mainly from the traces of her last disappearance. He spread the tickets out in the little pool of light and began to make his entries.

Panet, François Xavier, Thursday 28 December, sixty-seven kilos,

10 F advanced. Friday, 29 December, eighty-one kilos, 50 F advanced.

Paul, Luc Pierre … forty-four kilos…

Pinot, Jean Baptiste … fifty-one kilos…

Rolland, Pierre Paul ... 200 F advanced…

Rosambert, Dieujuste, Thursday, 28 December, ninety-one kilos, 0 F advanced. Friday, 29 December, ninety-nine kilos, 0 F advanced.

Claudine said, "It is possible–"

Nick stood.

"–to approach a house on foot and knock. One is not invariably offended when that happens."

In the doorway, and with the lamp beneath him now, she was nothing but an exquisite silhouette.

"I've been sent. His teacher says Pierre is disturbed and it's my fault and I'm to fix it now."

"Disturbed how?"

"The book I gave him."

"*Disturbed?* He won't put it down. I can get him to eat but it has to sit next to his plate. I can't get him to sleep till after midnight and then it has to go under his pillow."

"She says it's too powerful. After all, he's an oppressed and sensitive child."

"The cow! How can such a fool perform these miracles with the children?"

"Confidence, perhaps?"

"There is certainly enough of that. Have you eaten?"

"I have pickled cabbage waiting at the café."

"Pierre will bring you something. It can be why I send him, not so?"

St. Boniface, Jean Marie …

St. Boniface, Jean Pierre …

"Why do they make him wear the iron shoes! Why does he keep

them on, even when no one's looking! Iron shoes are—are—are—"

"Iron-soled shoes in France at that time were not—"

"He didn't see the money! He had the iron shoes on and he just stepped on it by accident and he couldn't feel it! It's not fair, he couldn't, how could they—they—they—"

It was necessary to take the plate away almost by force. The book could not be taken away but with difficulty it could be made to close. One resorted to the crudest of threats. If one did not sit on a stool and listen, the other would not eat. If the other did not eat, certain mothers would draw certain conclusions, and the results could not be good for anyone.

"Now listen. Iron-soled shoes. Jean Valjean is poor, he is an ex-convict, and he can't afford boots like rich men wear. But he'd rather wear iron-soled shoes than go barefoot. It gets cold in France and there are sharp rocks in the road. It would be better if he didn't have to wear them but there are even poorer people who wish they had shoes like his."

"Because of them he couldn't see the money. He—"

"That was bad luck. Bad luck happens. It was bad luck for the kid to lose his coin, it was bad luck for Jean Valjean to be standing on it. If he hadn't been a convict he might not have been accused for it but on the other hand he might have been anyway. A hundred years before he would have been hanged, Pierre. That's not good. But that's what happened to people."

"What were galleys for then! Why did they make him row around in them, what is the use of that, why do they—"

"Pierre! I don't know. Maybe they used them for tugboats but I'm not sure. I can look it up, all right? Now…"

Pierre had brought grilled mackerel with curried plantains. Nick ate it all and almost licked the plate. Pierre offered to go fetch more and looked relieved when Nick said he'd prefer to sit and talk. In all it took a couple of hours to work the whole thing out. Nick gave him a ride the forty yards to the hut and Claudine stepped out when they stopped. Heads poked out of other huts as well.

"You advertise too well," Claudine said. "Time for bed, then," and led Pierre inside.

Nick took it slowly riding back and tried to think of anything he'd failed to tell Pierre (if it was important he might have to go back) but if there was something it refused to show itself. The Bonnards were still on the terrace. Nick was on his way to the bar because every table outside was taken but M. Bonnard called him over.

"Take Lucas's place," Bonnard said. "He turned into a pumpkin not ten minutes ago."

The rest of their party had gone and all but one of the empty seats had been carried off to other tables.

"Then I shall stay off pumpkin pie a while, even though it's traditional with us at this time of year."

Lucienne Bonnard said, "*You* invited him."

"*I* find that quite amusing. So Petrov, eater of pumpkins – your crisis is under control?"

The ashtray in front of Bonnard overflowed with butts. The table was strewn with cardboard coasters that Antoine would have to count and there were two or three empty wine bottles, but their own glasses were also empty. Plainly, they had waited for him. Bonnard must be bored silly. Lucienne must think him every bit the fool he played for her.

"Eminently so. There was a slight misunderstanding but now he sees things clearly."

Lucienne Bonnard said, "Explain. Rather carefully, I'd suggest."

"Oh, it's simple enough. He thought he could talk to everybody like he talks to me. We're straight about that now."

Lucienne Bonnard said nothing for several seconds. Finally, "Did you agree to something, or just talk through your hat until he shut up?"

"I had to make some promises. They weren't anything I wouldn't have done anyway."

"Can you remember to go through with it? In a month perhaps, when the next young lady is jealous of your time?"

"Why not? Probably the next young lady will care no more for literature than the last. I keep telling myself I hope they will but they never seem to and I've given up wondering why."

"You don't fool me for an instant."

"Of course I don't. Why would I want to?"

"Oh, for practice, perhaps, or to keep some pledge you made when you were ten years old yourself and feeling whiney."

"What makes—"

"But since that is how you are, one may as well take advantage of it. I decided today that there are three other boys who would like to talk to a man about their reading. I'd have arranged it myself but I wasn't entirely sure of your mysterious schedule. Be at school Tuesday when it closes and we'll settle with their mothers. Emile, buy the man a bottle of watered-down Sauternes. One must be careful not to elevate his tastes too quickly but it would not do to leave him here entirely sober."

Bonnard craned his neck and beckoned. Nick bowed and Bonnard bowed back, but when he looked up again he scowled and swore.

"Bastard looked right at me and walked the other way."

Lucienne Bonnard said, "Then you'll just have to go to the bar, won't you?"

Bonnard gave her a calm but very married look. "If a man must be made to drink, surely he may choose his own."

Bonnard wore a yellow sweater under gray tweed. He suddenly

looked like a man who has been cold for a long time and something in his manner sent a spasm of caution through Nick. He wondered if perhaps the man might not be drunk and he had failed to notice, but then he saw that it was not Bonnard he should have been watching. Lucienne Bonnard put her face a foot from her husband's and leered and started in, as only an angry drunk can do when it's been building up for hours.

"Go. Now. Go inside to the bar and buy my friend a bottle. Who cares if you don't like the service here? Who cares if you don't like this place at all? Perhaps you'd prefer the Place de l'Opera! Well, I'd prefer to teach at the lycée! It is because of you that we will never see them again, it is because of you that we are here tonight and it is because of you that we will be here tomorrow and tomorrow and forever." She was close to shouting now. She was close to losing every pretense, close to deciding that everything but lust for retribution was pretense. Retribution is often like this and drunken retribution always is. She got to its edge and hung there. Then, instead of screaming, she whispered. "So. *So,* if we must sit here for the rest of our lives, one of us must go to the bar and get the only man in sight a drink."

Then she was on her feet and through the door and into the café. Nick turned and stared after her; it seemed like a good direction to be looking. The bar was bright behind the varnished double doors with their many little panes, such as one sees throughout France and all its true possessions. Everything was clear inside but it was crowded and he lost sight of her at once. Neither he nor Bonnard spoke. Around them people talked very carefully in normal tones about carefully normal things. Then Nick told himself *what the hell* and turned to face the man. He wasn't sure what he expected but what he saw was a frantic desire to talk.

"Petrov," Bonnard said. "Lucienne is disturbed tonight. You

must make allowances."

"Of course. I should go."

Bonnard shook his head very sadly. "She'd never forgive me if you did. I'll go myself, but first I wanted a word."

"Oh, now, that is hardly–"

"Petrov. Lucienne is taken with you. Perhaps you realize this."

Nick gripped the edge of the table tightly; that, too, seemed like the thing to do.

Bonnard, also, had to force himself. "I must ask a favor, man to man."

At that he turned away and something rippled across his shoulders and when he turned back his face was a horribly composed mask of sincerity.

"You're a young man, used to the company of young women. One remembers that. One remembers how one looked at things. If you could see it–"

He stopped again. Nick could barely breathe.

"If perhaps," Bonnard went on, his voice much stronger now, "you could see your way clear to be her friend, we would both be very grateful."

He nodded once, rose, and nodded again, and Nick realized that he was trying to bow. He put on his hat and picked up his umbrella, though why he had brought it tonight Nick could not imagine. There had not been a cloud all day and in the absence of a moon the stars were as brilliant as they ever got. Nick studied them for several seconds to be sure but he'd been right. The imbecile! To carry an umbrella on a night like this, it was simply incomprehensible, it was... The door to the bar opened, the opening notes of a merry, drunken, New Year's weekend washed quickly across the terrace and the door closed again. If you thought about it, it was simply unnecessary to own an umbrella in winter! When he finally looked back down,

Bonnard was a shadow halfway across the square and her footsteps were tap, tap, tapping toward him from behind.

Chapter 26

Entre Acte
June 27, 2001

Curtis cleared his throat. "Let me put this as professionally as I can, so try not to be embarrassed. Your husband had no problem with Fuentes propositioning you because he was a Mexican he had to do business with. Does he have other ideas about ethnicity that could get in the way of doing business with us? I mean, if we're not prepared for them?"

Gonzales said, "We have a lot of training, you understand."

Margarite Schrenk nodded. "So does he."

Curtis sighed. "That kind?"

Margarite Schrenk said, "That kind of training, yes. His mother was a sentimentalist and the thirties had been fun for her. Having a child in Berlin in 1945 was not. Nothing was by then. So she talked to him about better times, what mother wouldn't?"

"You're a fan of hers, aren't you?" Gonzales asked.

"She was a dangerous, spiteful fool who saw right through me. She told Alois that if he brought his hillbilly to Berlin she'd either ruin him or leave him in five years. If not for Petraki it would have been five years exactly. So yes, my feelings toward her are a little powerful."

"He defied her," Curtis pointed out.

"About everything," Margarite Schrenk agreed. "He never has been any kind of Nazi. He will disbelieve in something just because she said it's so. My God, do you know what Berlin was like? And his father died somewhere in the east months after any sensible general knew the war was lost. She thought she was telling him about great men and he was learning who to blame for his world. But still, she was so sure about so many things…"

They waited.

"Yes, your question. About ten years ago Alois announced at dinner that he no longer believed African people to be inferior to us. There was an implication that I was to take note and perhaps revise my own opinions but I cannot say that he actually said it. A few years before, the Asians were also pardoned. Some people must continue to wait."

Curtis brought her back. "But African people are not inferior anymore."

"Not abstractly or scientifically but your position, like everyone's, is defined by culture, you see. Here your cultural position is inferior, so, naturally, that is how you behave."

"It's such a relief," Curtis said, "to know that I didn't embarrass you."

Margarite Schrenk raised both eyebrows. "You asked for this. I never did."

"Okay," Curtis said.

"It's not okay, Agent Curtis. I never said that either."

"Okay," Curtis said.

"I too am well instructed. It is not your fault that you were not raised in Berlin. I was not either and that is not my fault." She made a sweeping glance around the room. "Nobody here was and nobody here is at fault. My husband is a very fair man. He will manage not to blame any of us, I'm sure."

Chapter 27

La Bohème
June 27, 2001

Olga said, "And how long did *that* go on?"

Nicky said, "That kind of thing is mainly why I couldn't say no to Mr. D'Annunzio."

Olga said, "How on earth did Mr. D'Annunzio stifle the exquisite hothouse temptations of *la vie Bohème*?"

Johnny said, "Got him back to stealing, Cousin. Nothing like simple, barefaced stealing to overcome the temptations of true love and honest toil. Especially if you get to get over on a few idiots who think they've already got over on you. That's your cousin's very favorite way to do it."

Mr. D'Annunzio's Caretaker
November 25, 1982

Gérard's office was empty on Saturday mornings and, six months into the D'Annunzio era, he still had to make the coffee himself. There were other places to meet but on the whole he preferred his own domain: turf, naturally, though he'd have used a hundred words to explain it.

It was not going well for Délibes. As to the matter of short-term financing for construction payrolls and materials, the bank of course would forgo its usual fees. A simple interest charge at prime would satisfy the regulations, something no one else is ever granted as one most surely knows. If his young friend would submit this draft of an agreement–

But his young friend was all apologies: poor Étienne, all that work, if only Nick had been more timely with his news! Financial assistance is not needed. All materials will arrive prepaid (Gérard and Proudhon grin knowingly). Labor will be contracted independently or will be paid from a fully funded payroll account he had intended to open last week (Gérard and Proudhon are more impressed by that). Of course, the bank could waive its fees on that if it wishes but everyone knows these are modest and one had not expected special consideration.

Nick was only warming up but already he was feeling pretty good. He was aiming for something he'd only just come to believe in, a manner of speaking he'd decided, provisionally, to call *vicious pomposity*, until he could think of a better term that also suggested the essential appearance of bland innocence. That last clause was just about there: *one had not expected special consideration!* It was left to Délibes to somehow show relief at the unexpected lightening of his responsibilities.

It was not going well for Proudhon. On the subject of security for the property, this was clearly a police matter, no? Though of course the regular police might be supplemented by a newly created band of auxiliaries under the–

Ah non, Délibes injected with some heat. If the entrepreneurs who choose to rent and purchase these establishments feel the need for more than usual–

Exactly. Gérard's daily civics lesson couldn't wait. That a simple commercial development should be the cause of a parallel expansion to the infrastructure of the state itself—

Nick said, "Let's table that till someone actually detects a need, shall we?" Since that was clearly a better deal than Proudhon would get from the other two, he seconded.

It was not going well for Gérard. In the matter of the difficult and time-consuming rental and furnishing of the shops, one is prepared to serve as agent for the venture, charging one's partners nothing but, instead, recouping one's costs directly from—

But Délibes was shouting, "Nonsense! Anything they pay you diminishes what's left for the venture! If—"

And Proudhon was waving him down patiently, shaking his head and finally being allowed to say, "No, Gérard. How do you expect me to put a stop to shakedowns if we begin with what looks like one of our own? How—"

But Nick was tapping the table with his spoon and everybody stopped again. "*I* think Gérard's had a helpful idea but, you see, we don't need it. It's already rented, all of it. My fault again. I'd have brought a list of the tenants if I'd known you'd be interested."

It was going very well for Nick. He walked over and topped up his coffee and added a little of the thick, fresh cream that Gérard always fetched from the hotel these days for their Saturday mornings. He stirred and took a delicious sip and briefly closed his eyes while he mimed an orgasm of the tongue, then nodded to Gérard to acknowledge the source of his pleasure. He wasn't sure *why* this gesture was a hopelessly vulgar affront to Gérard's hospitality; it was enough to know that it was, and that nobody present would ever find a way to retaliate for it, and he jumped on them with everything he had just as that was once more sinking in all around.

"I'm instructed," he began slowly, thinking, *remember pompous!* "To report," he said, thinking, *remember vicious!* "On the recruitment of casual labor, both for the construction phase and afterwards. It is felt that this is a matter that can naturally raise local apprehensions and so you should be given reassurances, both for your sakes and so you can pass them along."

Délibes said, "Apprehensions?"

Proudhon said, "About barge loads of migrants from Haiti, for example," and Délibes almost choked.

Nick said, "Nothing like that will be permitted to happen. One is alive to the potential delicacies. All casual labor will be recruited locally—"

Délibes said, *"Recruited locally?"* Gérard and Proudhon looked grim.

"—to the extent of the supply. Thereafter relatives of local residents, identified by people known personally to me, will be given preference and offered passage and contracts, provided only that their sponsors agree to see them housed."

On a roll yet?

Getting there, anyway. Délibes opened his mouth again but Proudhon said, "Shut up."

"To prevent a disruption of the local economy, wages will be set at eighty percent of the net that the poorest third of fishermen average. On the basis of experience elsewhere, it is felt that this is sufficient to inspire diligence without luring useful people away from their current trades."

On a roll for sure.

Délibes said, "Who do your friends think they are? What do they think—"

Gérard said, "He's telling us that, isn't he?"

Proudhon said, "I said, shut up. Did it sound like an invitation to debate?"

"Once construction is complete and the need for casual labor declines, it is to be hoped that the more apt employees can be worked into the operation of the casino and its supporting facilities. As dishwashers and waiters, for instance, and other positions for which aptitude is shown and wages are insignificant. In order to ensure that this happens smoothly and without the kind of disruptive and destabilizing corruption that often results from large scale hiring in places like this, I'm to take charge of personnel myself."

On such a roll that he was close to scaring himself. But only close.

Délibes folded his arms and glared at each of the others in turn.

Proudhon said, "There will be a lot of black faces where no one is used to them."

Nick said, "There will be a casino where one is used to a trash heap. Is that what you mean?"

Proudhon said, "By *where,* of course, I meant in intimate proximity to oneself."

Nick said, "This is not felt to be a problem. It is not we nor the other current residents of this place who will supply the bulk of the clientele. That will come from the population of tourists that throughout the Caribbean has shown itself comfortable and even gratified to be waited on hand and foot by blacks."

Proudhon said, "One sees this. One is merely coming to grips with it."

Nick said, "In any case, there isn't a single alternative that isn't a disaster. Recruit blacks from elsewhere and our control disappears entirely. Try to get whites who'll work for equivalent wages and we'd wind up with a handful of useless dregs. We'd have to build them a new slum just to get them off the streets at night."

Gérard said, "Look, Petrov, all that makes good sense. What one finds shocking is to have it presented so peremptorily. What one especially regrets is that such an important matter as all future personnel decisions has been withdrawn from our collective purview."

Nick chose to treat that as a question that lacked an ending. He looked expectantly at Gérard for several seconds until Proudhon said, "How did you come up with this?"

"I didn't. I was instructed. I'm sorry, I thought I'd said that."

Délibes said, "By whom?"

Suddenly on the spot for once, Nick was spared from answering by Proudhon, who said, "Who do you think?"

Gérard said, "How extensive were your discussions?"

"Brief in the extreme. You see, nothing I was told to do conflicts with my own appraisal."

Délibes said, "So you did not protest."

"No, I didn't."

Délibes said, "So they don't know there may be other points of view."

"I don't know what they know about that. I could always ask them."

"Yes," Gérard said. "Why don't you?"

Why wait any longer? "Quite apart from the minor inconvenience, you mean. Because that I could always suffer, I suppose."

Délibes blanched and Proudhon suddenly looked a little ill. Only Gérard seemed to find this turn of the meeting even tolerably commonplace. Indeed, his eyes popped comically open and he even smiled a little, as though he'd unexpectedly run into someone he'd once known rather well.

"Indeed," he said, "we'd expect that much, if only as a courtesy. So what is the deeper misunderstanding that must be clarified?"

"Oh, well put," Nick said. "In fact there are two of them. The first and, I suppose, the more significant from your point of view, is that they have decided. And once they decide, the only question for them is how soon the rest of us understand. But the part that matters most to me is that they expect me to be the instrument of their will, and I can't imagine why I'd even think of disappointing them."

"Well," Gérard said, "as to your own position, one can only welcome that."

Suddenly realizing how he learned this new way of speaking French, Nick allowed himself the peculiar sensation that Gérard was now speaking to a much larger room, a somewhat elegant room well stocked with emphatically not khaki-clad public servants who awaited his words just a bit apprehensively and weighed each of them very carefully when it finally arrived.

"Thank you. I of course see it that way but agreement is always gratifying."

"But as to their, ah, assumption of prerogatives – perhaps in respect to certain particulars but as a general condition of one's existence?"

"Insupportable!" Délibes punctuated this opinion with a fist on the table. China rattled and three patient men sighed.

"In need of serious discussion," Proudhon corrected. "At least, clarification."

Proudhon, also, seemed to be back on some larger stage that Nick had never seen before; it would not have the elegance of Gérard's old haunts and almost everyone would wear some kind of uniform, but easily, as if they'd been wearing them forever. Whatever it was, it suited him well; probably, Nick thought, he sometimes thinks he's been unwise to leave it. Nick offered him the kindest look he had in him and thought, You understand now, don't you?

Proudhon shrugged back. As Nick would come to see it, all of Proudhon's various worlds had probably been distinguished by a refusal to quarrel with even the least pleasant of facts. But that would be later, after there was no more to be said, and it hadn't all been said quite yet, had it? He took the last deep breath.

"Then I must clarify, mustn't I? The basis of this most supportable consortium is the predetermined and guaranteed sharing of profits. No one here has disputed his allotted share and now it is far too late to start. But if anyone wishes to anyway? Étienne? You also? You're still content with everything that seemed to matter when we made this arrangement?

"Good. Then what is needful now is to be sure that profits stay profits and don't slip down to the expense line. When it comes to making clarity obscure there isn't a novice among us. We all know how murky expenses can be anyway but we also know how to make them still murkier. No one disputes this either? This interpretation is supportable, Étienne? Better still.

"It is in no one's interest to let his partners imagine that some of these expenses are profits in a parallel endeavor. *I* don't wish to believe that of anyone but it would be really insupportable for our absent partners to suspect us of such abuses. Least of all will I tolerate them suspecting me. Therefore I will do exactly what they say, even in the most trivial matters, and therefore so will you.

"Even so, the appearance of innocence will be tricky to maintain. No undertaking of this kind has ever been without its mistakes and errors of judgment. I intend that every one of them will be unambiguously theirs."

Délibes said, "You intend."

Gérard said, "From time to time we've successfully encouraged such cautious views with respect to ourselves. You're not perhaps overly impressed by their renown?"

Proudhon said, "Of course he may be. The question is, do we care to find out?"

Délibes said, "I for one—"

Proudhon said, "Precisely. Are one, and they are anything but.

Think about it."

Nick looked Délibes up and down and no longer bothered to hide his deliberation or the insolence it announced; but his frankest scrutiny failed to reveal any changes to the petty martinet he'd grown accustomed to. *Nous sommes arrivés, donc.* Two down hard. Last one still needs a shove.

He said, "Étienne? You spilled my coffee. Would you mind getting me another?"

Délibes sat.

Gérard sighed.

Proudhon said, "Délibes? Go get it. Next time, don't wait to be asked."

Chapter 28

They stopped to eat. Curtis said, "With him she's looking for a way out."

Gonzales said, "But does she know it?"

Curtis said, "She's a long way from an idiot."

Gonzales said, "When has that ever had anything to do with it?"

They ate. Curtis said, "African diplomats! Our country is not rich, honored sir, and neither are we!"

Gonzales said, "Jamaicans. There's bad, bad bugs in the sugar, mon, and the sugar bowl is empty."

They laughed and laughed. They were the laughing black FBI agents and a very short old man twisted in his grave.

They ordered dessert, then got serious again. They didn't exactly give up the idea of an outrageous disguise, the more thoroughly to trump Alois Schrenk, just let it pass because, really, you can't do things like that if you truly hope to see your victim in a courtroom.

Gonzales asked, "What does *nimmer* mean?"

"Never. Why?"

Gonzales nodded. "Thought it was something like that. In the john that time she went away a minute. She just stood at the mirror and said *nimmer* over and over."

"She's a citizen. She knows we can't deport her."

"Sure but maybe he thinks he still can."

Chapter 29

The Regional Manager
June 27, 2001

Olga said, "Sugar Lips, sir, does he even know about the part he just skipped?"

Nicky said, "What part's that?"

Olga said, "Oh, the part where Johnny's boss promoted you from assistant office boy to regional manager?"

Johnny said, "See, I know about that part 'cause it was supposed to be me out there, doing what he did. Mr. D'Annunzio figured your cousin was through after getting us the land and rounding up the players. But Nicky just kept asking for more and more work and reminding Mr. D about what he'd said about loyalty and being a part of things forever. And we kept waiting for him to screw up somehow but he never did on anything big and the main thing was, he was always *there*. It almost seemed like he knew what we'd want done before we figured it out ourselves."

Olga said, "Amazing. And you never asked how it was possible? You never wondered who might be behind it?"

Johnny said, "Of course we wondered and of course we asked."

Olga said, "Good. Then you learned."

Johnny said, "Well, only kind of. We learned it wasn't anybody we had a problem with. We even learned more or less who it was. Who they were. But we never learned exactly what they had on him and we never learned exactly how deep he was into them."

Olga said, "You couldn't make him tell?"

Johnny said, "Sure we could. The truth is you can't *keep* him from telling it. But what you can't do is make it come out in any way that makes sense. Business sense I mean: it makes all kinds of other sense, just nothing that would answer your question. And then there was this other side to it. When Mr. P did these things we wouldn't have done ourselves, first they surprised us. But then we saw how they were really better than what we'd been thinking. I mean the results were better than we were going to settle for. And maybe I can guess why and maybe you could too but he sure as hell can't explain it. Show her, Mr. P. Tell her why you did what you did. Tell her what you were up to and make somebody understand it just this once."

Anne Marie Marçeau
March 27, 1983

Hurricanes have destroyed the beach between the *quai* and the little headland east of Belle Vièrge uncounted times since the *Fleur de Lis* first rose on Saint Sulpice. They have done so a dozen times in living memory and each time the *quai* has stood, much of Belle Vièrge has not, and the beach itself has become a debris-strewn, muck-shrouded reproach to the very idea of habitation. *Beach,* in any case, is not the word. On beaches there is sand, elsewhere on Saint Sulpice there are sandy beaches so lovely that tourists who see them are ruined for Florida and the Côte d'Azur, but this one, poised to catch the very worst of the waves, is swept so thoroughly by each year's storms that in the best of times it never has been more than silt, heaps of shattered shells and jagged, seaweed covered rocks broken from the island's foundation.

Anne Marie, in moments of immense duress and weariness, can be made to admit as much, but she never has lost sight of how, when one admits an especially banal truth (especially to Nicholas), all one may be doing is supporting some far more significant lie. These days she is corrupted, not lobotomized, and she can still resist the pretense that this particular truth in these particular circumstances could ever be more than a lie of unusual convenience and toxicity. *These particular circumstances* are this new invasion in which she is again *collaboratrice* but residues of honesty can linger even here. Sometimes, even, she pretends to rally (though only God knows why, or would if he existed). Today she is doing it again.

"True," she says, "it was without appeal for most. Now it looks, perhaps, like a sidewalk from *High Noon*, does it not?"

Because the deck is on pilings, several meters above the rocks so that a small tsunami could pass beneath – such, anyway, is the theory and, who knows, it may even work. There is a seductive scent of sawdust, almost fully masking the slimy decay below, and Anne Marie resents even that for resembling an improvement to the prior state of rot. Tools and fittings lie in orderly piles and grinning young men of Belle Vièrge stand around in orange armbands and pretend to guard them from Nick and Anne Marie.

"It looks," says Nick, "exactly like what it is – an arcade of expensive shops by the sea, where formerly struggling artists take revenge on the tourists they despise."

Inside these shops there is plaster dust over everything. Anne Marie's new walls are already plastered by a Dutchman from the Antilles and the floor, all whitish tiles from Greece, has been laid by a Portuguese out of who knows where. These and other foreigners will work their way down the arcade, until they meet others working their way out of the casino, and then they will all disappear. But at least the rightful owners of this land have been allowed to fetch and carry, and at least they've been well tipped for it – one must not deny that Nick has seen to that. And, certainly before it is finished and becomes the *Gallerie Marçeau,* there will be more fetching and more tips and, after that, more so-called jobs for sweepers and fawners and the demeaned of many other kinds as well.

"Tell me again. Why will there not be hot dogs?" Calling them *oat doges* and not for an instant imagining what Nick might trade for a real one.

"Because, my dear, this is far more than the exercise in merely crass vulgarity that dazzles you into a state of commercial imbecility. This is aggressive, predatory vulgarity of a most highly refined type, designed to separate one precisely differentiated tribe of fools from the merest fraction of its wealth."

"How one has always aspired to that!"

"*You* shall satisfy the longing to demonstrate culture while acquiring expensive proof of one's dangerous time among the heathen."

"How one has longed to be a substitute for culture!"

"Other shops will provide other things to brag about, for instance, things that might seem to you like simple and overpriced articles of clothing, but that, to really discerning explorers, will stand as potent talismans of the exotic. Forever, or at least until they're washed a time or two."

"Art and corsets too! Can even the Louvre say as much?"

"Above all, the casino will turn men into buccaneers and make women faint from savage temptation, and thus my masters are served."

"What a noble purpose! And what a long journey you've had, just to find your masters! Above all, how generous to share them!"

"But all this good depends on preserving the spell of collective wishful thinking, and all it takes to break that spell is one trifling glimpse of the everyday – one tee shirt, one magazine stand, one *oat doge*."

"One sees this now."

"One may have fish and chips."

"No, one may not."

"One may have paella where no Spaniard ever came except to be locked up under the fort until the next truce."

"Real paella? Surely not real paella?"

"One may have Italian ice in the Caribbean but one must not hear of ice cream sandwiches. One may drink ginger beer from England and gassy orange drink from Spain but one must be made to search for Coke, and then it must come in dusty little bottles left behind by long-dead rumrunners."

"Even rumrunners mix it with *Coca?*"

"But, maybe, you understand all this, and your point is that it's somehow *wrong*."

And, with that, a sweeping gesture that manages to take in the schoolhouse a kilometer away and the new pier stretching the length of Belle Vièrge with the cooperative's icehouse and shed at the end. It is a gesture that says, *indulge your snobbery, my sweet, and look what flies away with the cretins!* It is, in other words, a gesture of the most banal sophistry, calculated to enrage and executed to perfection.

"*Merde!*"

"What is?" Now that he's winded he's the sly little innocent.

"Just admit it once for me. Admit you know what a travesty this is."

"*Tu veux un* Ripley's? I'm almost sure we could get a Ripley's, and maybe a Madame Toussaud's."

"I, Duke of This and That, refrain from murdering *all* the peasants – surely, then, I can rape the ones that please me!"

"Rape, Anne Marie? I've raped somebody, and you got wind of it?"

"Even you know a metaphor when it pleases you to listen. *On explique.* You justify your petty evils with the great ones you disdain."

"Anne Marie, you're confusing us. I'm a criminal. You paint and I break laws. At least I've found a place where the laws need to be broken."

"Oh *Liebchen*, my *Liebchen*, why won't you understand? If I don't accept this job in yonder death camp, *Der Führer* will appoint some real bastard to the post!"

"I'm a Nazi now? I think I could name a few of those here, actually, but I didn't realize I'd sunk that far myself."

"All right, Nicholas. We'll pretend we're speaking literally, in the fairyland of simple truth. You are not a Nazi. You have never fallen for that and it has never appealed to you in the slightest. I grant this freely, in good conscience, with all my simple heart."

"But I'm something, aren't I? It probably won't help but, just once, why don't you say what I am instead of what I'm not?"

But Anne Marie won't do that, not for years and years. It isn't that she can't. It is that the truth would gratify him as much as it would disgust anyone with half a sense of history.

Nicholas the empire builder, taking a pious few minutes each day to consider how the natives might be saved.

The Nicholas of manifest destiny, rallying the lesser colonialists, cutting through the ancient lethargy and waving the plans for his Panama Canal.

Nicholas the Victorian point man of commerce, his homely and bulletproof moral tautologies plugging every cranny where uncertainty might root, now dressing for high tea in the jungle, now drinking gin fizzes on the terrace as his clipper takes on teak in the harbor below.

Well, surely, those pictures have never been without their

attractions, their tingling, panting resonances in the repressed prehistoric id: who but she would forget that, and who could forget it with less excuse? And who – what Marx, what Lenin, what Malraux – has failed to grant such fossils their time, their place, and which of these would fail to see in Saint Sulpice a time and place that has yet to evolve even so far?

And, to be sure, beneath all that there *is* something in him, and it is lonely here, and though she is utterly ruined in every way that matters, that is only because she has had a state of grace to fall from. Nicholas is not the same as his ignorance and this vicious world she chose for herself is not something he has made. Remember, at least, what this very moment could be like in Belle Vièrge if his self-respect came as dearly as hers once did – remember that this much is true, even though he sinks to bragging of it himself. Remember, at least, holding one's breath in the dark and waiting for another pompous, married vice-minister of who knows what to tire of knocking and trudge off to find a whore on the *quai*.

Beauty is a difficult matter. It is a difficult matter even for her and as for those like– Grant, then, that beauty is difficult even to approach, and most must simply use its name from time to time and leave the pain of beauty to those who are willing to work for it. It is yet another Sunday, *oh, là*, it is spring, the breeze is mild, *etcetera*: grant, at least, that to the simple eye the world is once more a beautiful place.

"Someday, Nicholas. Someday when I'm established as Pirate Queen of the Arts and there are better lovers at my door and I can afford to offend you as you deserve. Then I'll tell you everything, I promise."

And so, nothing of consequence for at least another day; no advances of art or philosophy and not even any noticeable retreats; just this heartbreaking island and the tawdry consolations of privilege.

Chapter 30

Koutousoff, Kutuzov – or World Literature Class
June 27, 2001

He came back slowly because Anne Marie wasn't letting go. Sometimes when she was at her clingiest he had to be downright rude to her. Now she pouted on but Olga wasn't having any: even with his eyes shut she broke through, saying, "You know, it does make a screwy kind of sense while you're hearing it. But I see what you mean."

That *you* wasn't him, was it?

Go home, Anne Marie. I'll be back soon enough.

He opened his eyes and watched Olga tell Johnny, "You tell him to tell me why he did what he did and who he did it for and instead he brags about being a bottled up sadist who lived to rub his girlfriend's nose in sleaze. There's nothing to get you from *that* to the man who can make us do all *this*, is there?"

This being a wave around the car that included the truckload of pigs they were passing but Nicky understood all right. He also thought he saw the problem: so much can come unglued when, you know, you turn your fate over to a punchy, addled fantasist in the middle of a complicated felony. But damn, allowances aside, that bottled up sadist crack *hurt*. He found Johnny in the mirror and saw him grow hugely amused about some development to Olga's immediate right. He squirmed some more and Johnny's mirror showed the eyes of a sensitive nine year old who has just been told that Grandma doesn't love him anymore.

Is that me? Oh, Jesus…

Olga said, "I'm sorry, Cousin, but it's just not good enough."

Nick said, "All of it or just the bottled up sadist part?"

"When I look at you that's not what I see, and it's not how I've come to think of you. But it's a fair description of how you say you acted to someone you call your lover."

Relief washed over Nicky. "Oh," he said. "That's okay then. I see what you mean now. Sorry."

Olga said a word that a real Nikolai Petrov surely would have understood, but the phony one pretty much got it too.

"What?" he said.

Now a delighted guffaw from Johnny, and Olga drew an ominous breath. "The *reason*," she said, "that you're explaining about this time to us is so I can understand it. Me. Not you. If you're not going to explain it to me, you may as well keep it to yourself. But if you do that, stop pretending that I should somehow get it anyway."

Nodding and smirking in the mirror, Johnny said, "Pretty much says it for me too."

Olga said, "So if you don't want to be an ex-sadist for me which by the way is a concept I do *not* believe in, why don't you try telling me what you were really up to?"

"I thought I just—"

"Why not start with why you told it as you did? With you as the villain. The way you don't like me believing, I mean."

"Oh. Sure. Because that's how Anne Marie saw it." Had he really not made it plain?

"Excuse me?"

"At the time. That's how it seemed to Anne Marie. I know because she told me. Later I mean. We're still friends, you know."

Olga opened her mouth and shut it again.

Nicky said, "Really, it's true. You can ask—"

"*By all that's holy I don't care if those were the last words of Jesus himself!*"

Nicky was too shocked to speak and Johnny had to spell it out. "What's bothering her is she *asked* you for the story of your career in international crime. And you said you'd tell her but then you gave her your girlfriend's head games instead. So if I were you I'd work on telling her why you'd go and do that."

Olga said, "Yes, Nicky, why? Why oh why did you *go and do that?* Please. It should be such a simple question."

Nicky considered and shrugged. "Well. It just never occurred to me to tell it any other way. There are only two ways to look at that story and mine just isn't as interesting as Anne Marie's."

Olga said – well, actually, she once again just opened her mouth and shut it without saying anything at all.

Johnny said, "I *knew* he'd say that. I should've made you bet me on it."

"You *expected* that?"

"Yep. He's been telling me the story of his life on and off for months. No matter what he does or who he does it to, when he tells it everybody else is always more important than he ever is."

"I see. You had him to yourself for several months, failed to get any straight answers, and that makes you the capable interrogator here."

"Cousin Nicky? I see I need to get back to my driving, but you got a tricky stretch coming up here. Be strong."

Olga leaned in and began to purr. "Nicky? Listen to me, Cousin. Don't look at Sugar Lips, Nicky, *stop it*, look at *me*. There, that's right. We'll just forget about that dumb old Sugar Lips. Big dumb man who can waste my poor cousin's time for months and months and never ask a question that tells us anything."

She patted his cheek, tenderly, then began to fondle an earlobe. "See?" she said. "This doesn't *have* to hurt. But it can."

She twisted.

Nick yelped.

Olga said, "What did you think you were up to, Nicky? Were you really trying as hard as you could to be a jerk?"

"I just had the idea that Anne Marie liked me better as that kind of jerk than as a, I don't know, do-gooder. It was just an idea I picked up out of a book."

"Oh, just an idea from a book. Nicky, where do you think Anne Marie's ideas came from? Or mine or most of Einstein's for that matter?"

"It wasn't a book I read that way, for its ideas. It was a scrap of something I picked up by accident from a famous old book we used at the school. On Saint Sulpice. For the stories in it, to get the kids interested in reading."

"Did this accidental story book have a name, cousin?"

"Sure, it's called *Guerre et Paix* by *le Compte* Léon—"

But at last he had every bit of Olga's attention. She had the earlobe again in one hand and now a fistful of hair in the other that she used for leverage as she hauled her face up to his with an inch at most between their noses.

"*You? You? War and Peace?*"

"Why not?" he said, but very weakly, because there just had to be a really good reason for so much violent incredulity.

"Because it's just not possible."

"Maybe it's a different—"

"If you're playing with me I swear—"

Johnny said, "Don't make me come back there, cousins."

Olga let go of the hair but held on to the ear. "If you've been playing with me you will regret it." And gave a little twist to advertise that proposition.

"Ow!"

"Make this good, Nicky. Make this your best one yet if you know what's good for you."

It was, of course, entirely the fault of Lucienne Bonnard, who, to show him how mistaken he'd been to believe that Hugo is the summit of literature, had required him to lead his boys in the conquest of that Everest of books, the *Guerre et Paix* of Léon Tolstoï. To his surprise, this famous book that he'd heard people make fun of forever turned out to be mostly stories – varied and exciting stories about, well, what happens to people in *war* and in *peace*, plus a dozen or so essays that on the one hand seemed *sensible* and *clear* and surprisingly *interesting* (since we're really into interesting today) but also somewhat like Anne Marie at her most emphatic: what she was aiming for anyway, which maybe we could agree to respect. Nicky Petrov, well instructed in his deficiencies, was fully aware that he had no concept of culture or history and lacked all understanding of art. Still, he allowed himself to fancy that for proletarian types like him and his boys, *Guerre et Paix* is nothing more or less than the richest and most satisfying storybook anyone has written yet. Using it as such, he led his boys on the most amazing adventures, and on Thursday afternoons the combined forces of Belle Vièrge and Petrov's Russia repeatedly ground Napoleon to dust, spat on the corpse, and married the prettiest girls. And though he's learned quite a bit since then, it is mostly as that storybook that he still takes it out and reads from it from time to time. But, in addition to the stories and some really interesting ideas about, oh, war and…but Olga is getting ready to twist again and Nicky gets to the point: apart from the *important parts*, this Tolstoï has incidentally quoted or pretended to quote someone who Nicky still calls *Stairn* – and whose own books, if they even exist, are not to be found on Saint Sulpice – quoted him to the effect that we love others not for the good they've done us but for the good we've done them.

This notion stuck from the start. It is the scrap Nicky alluded to. When he confessed to harboring scraps.

When it was clear that he thought he had finished, Olga said, "And so? You're still going to have to spell it out for us." But she let go of his ear and patted his cheek as she said it.

Well, on that particular Sunday… the one he'd been–

"We remember."

Well, then, on that perfect, lazy Sunday afternoon, where the only hint of a cloud had been Anne Marie's – irritation? – at everyone else's happiness, Nicky recalled this scrap which he sometimes thought about in those days (but hardly ever does anymore) and it occurred to him to wonder if she hadn't managed to hate him just a bit for all the little ways she'd failed to change him. For all the good he hadn't let her do him, if you will.

What? Well, it took a load off his mind, was all.

Because it let him think that much better of her, didn't it?

Because it made her *right*, for one thing, and it's about the only thing that could have done that back then. It made everything Nicky's fault, the way it was still supposed to be in those days, and thus *tout le monde* was once again exonerated. Of course, of the two of them, he supposed that as usual he had been the more content, but in those early days he couldn't see any practical way to repent it, and even then he didn't think any fair-minded person would ever blame him for it very much.

"And–"

But Olga patted his hand, said, "Hush," and flicked the back of Johnny's neck with a lazy slap. "Sugar Lips, you unobservant dolt, this romantic sophomore really did try to manage his love life according to an Augustan aphorism."

Johnny said, "Wow. Is that serious?"

Olga said, "It can be fatal but this one seems to have barely grown out of it in time."

Nicky said, "Does whatever you just said mean I'm off the hook?"

Olga said, "You're off the last one you hung yourself on. You still owe me the history you owed before you impaled yourself. You remember – what the hell you thought you were doing back then, in *business?* Unless Sugar Lips can tell it for you."

Nicky said, "So I guess you've read–"

Olga said, "No, Nicky. Don't climb back on that hook, I beg you."

"It's just, I got some other ideas from it too. About Himmelskirch. It cleared up something that had always bothered me about the place."

"Very well, Nicky, you win again. A five minute break to discuss what literature brings to our daily lives. Go ahead, make me feel like I'm thirteen once again."

"Back then I felt like I was fighting with the Germans except they didn't notice. Felt like it was really important for me to be kept in my place. But we were also supposed to love each other. Especially I was supposed to feel they were my friends while I shut up and did exactly what they told me to do for the rest of my life."

Johnny said, "Cousin Olga? I can't wait anymore, I've got to know – does this amazing book also teach young minds how to think about Germans?"

Olga said, "Well, it has been known to confirm any number of jejune prejudices."

Johnny said, "And?"

Olga said, "And, yes, there are Germans in the book. May I,

Sugar Lips? Certain peoples attract certain caricatures, Nicky. That of the obedient German recurs for a reason. It's a good reason too but it doesn't explain Beethoven."

She was trying her best but she was almost rolling her eyes.

Nicky said, "But then all those years later on Saint Sulpice, after all of that was over, *le Compte* Tolstoï has *le Generale* Koutousoff nail, just nail *l'Allemand scrupuleux*... And the Russian officers couldn't agree about anything but they agreed about that, even though the Germans were supposed to be on their side."

"That was enough? That explained working for modern Germans in Chicago?"

"I just felt like, I don't know, if Koutousoff himself agrees with me, maybe it wasn't such a big– hadn't really been personal with me after all. And *scrupuleux* just says it all, doesn't it? It was the first time I came across that word and I had to look it up and man it was just *perfect*."

"Yes, Nicky, it is very *apt*. Tolstoy is often very *apt*, isn't he? But I have to tell you something – you'll bear with me, won't you? You still want to talk about this, don't you, even if we don't exactly agree?"

"Sure." But with trepidation.

"Well, Nicky, I remember *l'Allemand scrupuleux* myself – I remembered it as soon as you reminded me. And I have to tell you that, to me, that means Kutuzov didn't attach much importance to it, not nearly as much as you have. Because when something *mattered* to him, he always said it in Russian, didn't he? He only used French for proverbs and pleasantries and– Nicky, is something *wrong*?"

Oh, yes. Something was wrong.

He only *used French for...?*

But it's all *in French!*

And Olga had *not* said Tolstoï. She said that other name that was close to Tolstoï but–

And Olga *had* put that Z in Koutousoff. Which made it sound like–

A monstrous suspicion began to descend.

Within no measurable span of mental time, it gave way to the absolute certainty of self-inflicted doom.

As Olga began to pull up lame, he turned away from her not-yet-undeceived eyes.

Which cowardly flinch caused him, through no further fault of his own, to look out beyond the car. Where, solely because God hates the wicked, over her divinely perfect shoulder grazed four or five horses behind a long white fence: beautiful horses, *magnificent* horses, as Olga herself was a magnificent...er...

Horses to tempt the likes of Dolokhof himself! Back when there had been Dolokhofs, of course... Dolokhofs to populate an irreplaceable world now vanished forever, thrown away in an instant like the rest of Nick's worlds, while he sat and watched another pretty woman and babbled nonsense at her for as long as she'd let him.

"Oh no. Nothing's wrong. But you're right, we should get on with it, I've been evading the subject, haven't I? What was that last question again?"

Chapter 31

The Divisional Controller
May 25, 2001

When Diego Fuentes finally picked Roddy John Hall out of the gaggle of emerging passengers, he fingered the little roll of fat around his waist and told his driver to forget about the five hours of roaming nightlife. "Get us early reservations at El Tajìn or El Marisquito. A good table…"

Grasping Roddy's hand he said, "Roddy, you've never looked better. Different but not better. Prosperity suits you."

Roddy said, "Diego, does it ever happen, you have to tell people the truth? Because I really don't think you could do that anymore." But they were both smiling as he said it and Fuentes' smile was as genuine as Roddy's: once he'd been the delicious scent of sin in Roddy's life, and it seemed that no rival had supplanted him in all this time. Walking through the airport Roddy wondered whether Spanish would seem as loud if he understood a word of it. He saw himself being meekly towed along and remembered Fuentes joyously pulling him through O'Hare and then up Rush Street; there was no parallel, was there? Here Fuentes was at home, and there they both had been.

"Your first visit?"

"I went to Cancun once."

"I meant to Mexico proper. To the city."

Then they were in the car. Roddy was torn between watching the beautiful strangeness crawl by and shutting his eyes to the suicide drivers who gave it all they had but, in the end, miraculously failed to ram them. Fuentes kept up his gracious-host patter. He pointed out this sight and that and eventually Roddy took pity.

"It's in my pocket, Diego. Relax."

"We don't get to negotiate?"

"Maybe who pays for dinner. As far as business goes I'm Schrenk's errand boy."

"There will be no negotiating dinner. You visit me for the first time ever and I would dream of letting you pay? If you insult me again you can walk home."

"After I give you the check."

"Of course. I am a gentleman but not an idiot."

On the one hand, it was way too early for cultured people to eat. On the other, it was well past six and Roddy had eaten nothing but airline fodder all day, and he would be flying home again while civilized diners were considering their deserts. Fuentes started them off with scallops in limejuice while Roddy searched the menu for burritos. Roddy didn't think he liked scallops but he tasted one and closed the menu and thereafter ordered only Dos Equis for himself, which did not impress the waiter as he'd hoped. Fuentes called for shrimps in garlic, only calling them *praw-ness,* which didn't sound at all like Spanish to Roddy. Roddy wanted at least two more helpings of that but Fuentes ordered *escabeche.* Roddy had never tasted anything like it and could have gone on eating it all night but Fuentes ordered *Huachinango á la Veracruz* and *Mojarra al Mojo del Ajo* and made the waiter split them so Roddy could have half of each. Then they had coffee – why had Roddy thought he knew what coffee tastes like?

It was over this coffee (and a little *flan* and – as Fuentes' eyebrows shot up – a couple of Kahluas) that Fuentes must have decided that he'd left it long enough and now it was time to become a millionaire.

"Tell me about life at Himmelskirch these days, if it's not too distressing."

"Remember when Schrenk was smart and all I had to worry about was you getting to the Moron?"

"All too well. Your interference was often far too effective."

"Not even the Moron would have fallen for this. I don't know why they didn't just mail it and save the airfare."

"Surely there is the note–"

"I don't know the first thing about Mexican law–"

"After all my hours of instruction?"

"I mean, how it's supposed to work, not how to get around it. But it can't be all that different. In the US, this thing isn't a note, it's a Christmas card. Here's twelve million, don't spend it all in one place. What do you have on him, dirty pictures?"

"My friend–"

"Hey, I didn't mean I want to know. I can figure out a couple of things. One is I'm here to make this a simple, regular deal between two reliable old partners. Another is that I'm doing that because it's anything but. The last is that I'd be better off if I didn't even know that, and I sure don't want to know anything more."

Fuentes shrugged but was grinning as he did it.

"Still," he said, "one is curious to hear how you're supposed to put it."

"Here's your money. Here's your note. You solemnly undertake to pay HAGUS ten million US sometime when you feel like it and then another five not more than one second after the undescribed transaction called Fuentes Agricola SA order number thirty-two sixteen is completed, so help you God. No collateral, no interest, no time frame, no attachments or references. Collectable maybe in Albania but nowhere else for sure and happy birthday to you from Alois."

And passed Fuentes both copies and held out his pen. But Fuentes had brought a pen of his own, an elderly Mont Blanc that glimmered dully in the candlelight, and with it, very promptly because reading the thing at all would have been an insult to Roddy's word, he drew the elaborate and stately arabesque of his name directly across from Schrenk's angular scrawl. Taking his copy back, Roddy again saw the remembered arches and minarets, and he thought how here, only here, amid the dim, foreign elegance and the music and the alcoholic satiety, it might almost be possible, even without trying very hard, to forget what a mockery of business he had just helped to make.

He drained his glass and put it down again. "You know something, Diego?"

"Very little. Enlighten me."

"You really are paying for dinner. I don't know how you planned to get out of it but it isn't working this time, so get us another drink while you get used to losing just that much."

Roddy had a bumpy flight back to Dallas and he was absolutely stuffed. His flight to Louisville didn't leave until dawn and he sat up reading three days' worth of *Wall Street Journals* because he was too uncomfortable to doze.

Still, he remembered the evening so fondly that he'd described each dish for Curtis and Gonzales, and they listened, though what they really wanted to hear were things about Fuentes that, as Roddy told them frankly, he would not allow himself to know. He even asked Gonzales if she ever cooked those things at home but, strange to report, she never had; but maybe that was something she had to say, because of her cover and all.

Chapter 32

Mr. P
June 27, 2001

Sugar Lips said, "Let me tell this one, Mr. P, how about that? You butt in and correct me when I get it wrong. Because maybe it'll keep us out of world literature class for a while and maybe there's parts to this one you even forgot. Maybe you'll be impressed. Maybe I can get some of your cousin's confidence back, show her, sometimes we even watched what you were doing instead of just wound you up and let you go."

Nikolai Petrov
May 27, 1989

Nick came in from the little door on *quai* side that pretended to have been sealed since Louis XIV. He stopped in his office long enough to put on the ice cream suit from way back when in Kingston, with the lapels that Mme. Bousson had narrowed for him, and then, still in sandals but also now in beige silk socks, he went straight in through the back of the *vingt et un* salon. He walked through that, past the roulette on his left and the craps on his right and headed for the bar outside *Les Écrevisses*. A *kir* appeared on the bar before him and

Antoine left his pulpit to report.

"A greedy crowd tonight. There was mutton and I saved you a chop."

"Spring lamb, perhaps? You'll say mutton once too often."

"I'll eat it once too often, that's for sure. The so-called lobsters are going like *frites*. The South Africans don't know what they owe us."

"No problems, though."

"Problems aren't allowed, *Patron*. You want to eat out here? I could sell your table any time I want."

"Sell it then. Maybe I'll work a while anyway."

Feldman was already on his way, his half grin in place to demonstrate what a waste of time it was for Nick even to show up.

"Nick."

"Mike."

"One drunk doctor who tried to crash in shorts. Nobody saw except a party of Germans who thoroughly approved. They tried to tip Henri's guys after they hauled him out and now they can't lose enough."

"That's it?"

"That's it. Hardly seems like a Saturday."

Then Feldman did the trick that showed why he was there – he vanished, and reappeared across the room to help a happy, blackjack-minded woman pick the very luckiest table. Beyond them came cheering and a more insistent than normal ding, ding, ding, as someone got half her losses back from a five dollar slot. That would happen a hundred times tonight, and then a hundred more, and though every such incident would be minutely observed, nobody would tell Nick a thing about them because they were really none of his business. Neither would anyone tell him about the play at the tables or the take from the bar, and Henri's men would escort fourteen more people out but Feldman had already told him about one of them, so everyone was covered if anything got back to Nick. Knowing these things would have upset some people but they were more than all right with him. He would speak to this waiter and that waitress and just possibly to an idle dealer or two, and what they discussed would never seem to be about work. He would have his drink and if he got around to it he would eat his dinner, or else he would have mussels or fish soup at the Café des Artistes, in his jeans, on his way back home. In here he didn't need to pretend to be anything but the occasional ear at the end of some frightening people's telephone, and if that should bother anyone, then so much the better by him.

"Nobody pinching your girls, Nikolai?"

It was Délibes with a buzz on, turning to gaze wistfully at his favorite beauty of the moment as she waited for her tray of drinks in a hooker's stockings and Marie Antoinette's *décolleté* and wig.

"It's not fair, you know. By rights she should be pretending to dust the parlor and going to bed with one for ten *sous*."

"You know, Étienne, all that used to happen is not what happened *by rights*."

The bar faced west and the wall between it and Belle Vièrge was glass from floor to ceiling. Beyond that wall the bay had turned violet; the hovering gulls were deep purple and gold. Behind the moored fishing boats the setting sun was huge and red and even the most snobbish yachtsman would look out on that scene and remind himself to buy a postcard. If one knew where to look one could make out the spot where Old Rosambert used to mend his nets. What one could no longer imagine was why in those days one had always looked away.

"My God, Nikolai, do you deny the laws of nature? You display them like that and then you forbid the world to touch. It's inhuman, and I don't care what you say, it can't possibly be the most profitable use for them."

Délibes was often almost drunk these days and Gérard had grown sour-faced and elaborately sarcastic and one hardly ever saw him. Proudhon, though, had developed a sense of humor; when he came in he reminded Nick of the jolly old beat cop dropping by his old man's bar for the weekly donation. Hard to think of them as monsters anymore. Hard to think of oneself as having beaten the monsters they had been.

"*Mon vieux*, you exaggerate my influence. One has made promises, to people who expect to see them kept. Others may not understand how simple that is but not you, Délibes."

"Indeed, there are those one's partner is strangely reluctant to cross, though one hardly expected them to be such puritans." He nodded sadly and wisely and turned back to admire the interior view, and for perhaps the thousandth time he or one of his brethren misunderstood the nature of Nick's promises and to whom they had been made. But that, after all, was perfectly all right. That alone, in fact, was mostly what Nick was getting by on, circa 1989 and thereabouts.

Chapter 33

Fish

The executive chef of *Les Écrevisses* is a Tuscan from Pittsburgh once named Mark Pirillo. The day he arrived on Saint Sulpice he became Chef Marc Pareille from Marseilles (to put one in mind of fashionably chic fishes, fishes redolent with cachet, fishes that when you name them in a postcard turn Aunt Myra into an envious toad). Chef Marc looked around at the ingredients he could always count on getting and concluded that fish was it. Thereafter there was fish garnished with fish in fish sauce. Also there was almost always some kind of meat or poultry or even both and sometimes the local *langoustines* were rock lobsters from as far away as Australia but Chef Marc did not depend on them. He depended on what he knew he could depend on and what he knew he could depend on was fish, fresh, unspecified. Around the clock thirty stockpots reduced fish to various shades and viscosities of liquid. If Chef Marc's concoctions were often pure microcosms of the day's take off Belle Vièrge, on the menu they were famous luxuries enhanced by centuries of local tinkering: *Bouillabaisse à la Caribe, Ciopinno al Belle Vièrge, Zupa di Pesce al Caribe, Caribbean Chowder, Island Gumbo* and even *Seafood Sukiyaki Caribbean Style.*

Chef Marc was a genius.

The things he made from fish were very good indeed.

Even so.

Professor Olga
June 27, 2001

Late in the afternoon they had the HoJo's almost to themselves. Hunger has never crushed the life of the mind so thoroughly, and with Borodino forgotten for an hour or more, Nick had a BLT club *and* a full order of Tendersweet® Fried Clams with extra tartar sauce. Olga watched in appalled fascination but Johnny was used to seeing men eat like pigs.

"A shake," Nick gasped. "Must find room for a chocolate shake."

Their waitress overheard but Olga shooed her away. She opened her laptop and made Nick touch the keys. "On the big computer you always use the mouse. Left button only, always, and you keep it on the pad to help it roll."

"The pad."

"The rubber thing with the picture of the smiling beanstalk and the upside-down bug. First *Start*, with the flag, then *Settings*, then *Control Panel*, then *Add/remove programs*. Then you give it the name."

"Jesus. What the hell do you call this junk?"

"It's the most virulent strain of something called Windows. The KGB invented it to destroy American business but it got loose and killed them first."

"The fools. The bloody fools." He leaned closer. He caught a whiff of something elusive through the grease-filled air, *Fleures de Rocaille* perhaps, and said, "Better run me through that again."

Johnny rolled his eyes but of course Johnny wasn't really there.

Chapter 34

Entre Acte
June 27, 2001

She missed him at the office but caught him on the cell phone on his way home.

"Sell the house?" They had dinner out when she sold a house.

"I missed the appointment. I spent the day with the FBI. They said they wondered about a hundred and forty thousand dollars but I think they knew all about it. They really wanted to hear about you and Fuentes and especially the Cubans, which I don't believe you ever mentioned."

"But this is very serious!"

"They said that too."

"I'll go back and call for instructions. Doktor–"

"You'll get your instructions here, as soon as I've thought them through. They're almost finished, as is my patience. Try to be here in ten minutes. Break another silly law if you must."

Chapter 35

At a Hyatt in Louisville Olga Kopeikin unpacked very carefully
and said, "It's just as well I'm not a mother. If I had one maternal
instinct I'd never let you do this thing."

Nick had thrown his heap in a drawer and set his Martel on the
table and was admiring her taste in lingerie. "I don't see you as the
maternal type either but that was pretty good."

"That?"

"Calling me a child that way. I almost didn't notice."

"Oh, no, Cousin. You are not a child."

It was still early evening but in a little while the lights went out
anyway. A while after that they came back on.

Olga said, "Evidently we talk." She poured herself a drink and the
lights went out again. "In Sverdlovsk I was a privileged child. I, of
course, didn't think so. It has been explained to me that I'm incapable
of gratitude and now I see this."

"You think in Russian, don't you? When you're relaxing."

"I don't know what I think in. I am *speaking* as an educated Soviet
woman, a species that no longer exists. Now there are only Russians
again and I'm no longer one of those. But unlike you I speak as I was

taught. Always, no matter what I say, or who I am when I say it."

"I'm sorry. I can listen."

"Oh, yes. You see only what you want but you listen very well."

"And I'd like to."

"Then do. In Sverdlovsk my privileges were uncountable but my ingratitude was equal to them. There was, first, the privilege of culture. From my earliest years I was given serious opportunities to learn but my frivolous leanings sabotaged them all. I even mocked my teachers. I was often caught and my parents were shamed as a result. Other children may imagine such things but I had it explained to me, so I know. But one day when I was fourteen our French teacher played us a record of two silly teenagers walking to school. I was genuinely shocked. 'They don't talk like you at all,' I told him. He asked me what I meant and the rest of the class prepared to enjoy another of Olga's trips down the hall. 'You say *bonjour*,' I said, 'and they say *bonjour*.' The class began to laugh but the teacher's ear wasn't completely hopeless. He shouted, 'How did you learn to say that?' and I said, 'You just played it for us!' You see, I really couldn't imagine what he meant.

"Soon I repeated this performance for half a dozen strangers. Six weeks later I went away to boarding school. My mother was hysterical. My father kept saying, 'You have the chance to make us all so proud.' I didn't have the faintest idea what he was talking about. I spent perhaps two weeks with him in all the years that followed and I still don't know how much he really understood. In any case I was no longer an antisocial failure and for a long time the amazement of that sustained me. There were in all perhaps a hundred of us, some as young as twelve, some as old as twenty. There seemed to be many parallel curricula but some classes we had together. These were the conversational language courses. No one learned them all but what you did learn had to be perfect. They only taught me Italian from about seven regions, French from perhaps twelve, German but only Hamburg and Frankfurt, let's see, haughty upper class Spanish from Mexico City, Buenos Aries and Havana, a precise, academic Castilian, nine or so varieties of English plus a very useful BBC and at least twenty kinds of American, many of which I've forgotten because America has.

"To learn American you had to study movies and for the most part we loved this. You can understand why. Usually we had ten hours of class a day and perhaps six hours of homework, but as long as we could learn to imitate one more actor's lines we could always watch another movie."

"Old movies," Nick said.

"A few newer ones but they had quite a library that I'm told came from a wartime merchant seamen's club and USO in Archangel. Mostly we watched those, over and over. But for you to notice, I would seem to have been very careless."

"Only after Johnny said you could be."

"And you do everything Johnny says?"

"You're damn right I do."

"Good. I only wondered. I suppose many countries have such schools, or could afford to have them once. One is given endless tests. One has long conversations with many people. Some of them are obviously medical types, and some of these pretend a great interest in one's deepest aspirations. Some are distracted academics of two classes – the intriguing and the very hateful. The rest seem to be impenetrable dullards, either military robots out of Chekov or simply clerks with a boring hour or two to kill. One sees some of one's inquisitors once and others hang around for weeks. The worst pretend to be one's friend.

"It was seen that I was easily bored and lacked any wish for fortitude to overcome it. It had long been known that I was selfish and elevated myself above others in my private estimation. It was explained quite frankly that these defects of personality could be useful in extraordinary situations abroad, and that at the cost of a little discipline now I might indulge them for a very long time. So others went off to physics class. I had less advanced lessons, though for me they were very demanding.

"I came here as a senior returning to UCLA after spring break in Acapulco. Those movies almost did me in. On the plane I merged with a dozen other girls and took the plunge. 'Mexico wasn't at all what I expected,' I said, and one of them replied, 'For sure!' I had an hour to learn the whole dialect but by then I'd had to do that a few times. I had never been more to the University than some files in their computer, though one or two boys pretended to recognize me. Anyway I'd been getting straight A's for three and a half years. I was a language major of course. The only difficulty was to remember not to know very much about languages. By the time I graduated I felt I was barely literate but at least there was one place in the country where I really fit. And that's where they started me out, with little jobs to build all our confidence before I moved on to my life's work."

"What, marry a rocket scientist? Sleep with the Joint Chiefs?"

"In fairness I was not even asked how I'd like to be a whore. I suppose their tests had been good for that much. In any case such things are far less productive than is imagined. One scientist among a thousand or more has anything useful to steal and then the thief needs to be almost his scientific equal to steal it. What are we to do, breed a generation of brilliant Bardots and introduce one to each promising grad student? As for generals, there are never so many that one can sleep with more than a few without meeting one's past, and almost all are of the type that can copulate for a month and never say anything worth repeating."

"So what, then?"

"Oh, a hewer of wood and a drawer of water. Espionage is as complicated as any modern undertaking and there is always a need for good help, as in the kind you can't get anymore. Especially one can need it quickly and in diverse circumstances. If you can get a person with an ear for idiom and accent, a vain woman who notices how other women look and why they look like it, the little touches you know... Then if she's the kind that likes to get over on people anyway, and all the while look smugly beautiful and self-absorbed – well, that person can come and go almost anywhere on a moment's notice, can be noticed but not remembered beyond a surface that she changes at will. There are so many little jobs crying out for someone like that. They were quite truthful when they said that I wouldn't be bored for years. Of course it would have been moronic to lie to me about that."

And another drink, and a shifting of covers and then a process of getting comfortable again. The windows had heavy curtains to allow the weary salesman his afternoon nap, his Sunday morning lie-in. In the middle of the night nothing got through them at all.

Nick said, "My old man ran a bar–"

Olga said, "I think when you're relaxed you converse with yourself in Bulgarian."

"Excuse me?"

"In French you would say, 'my father was proprietor of a bistro' and 'I beg your pardon.' Now you say your old man ran a bar and *so what* and excuse you all to hell."

"For my old man, who talks a whole lot worse than this, opening his bar would have been an adventure. Later on, having it would be a comfort – whatever else happens, I've got this. What I saw was something else. I saw myself working in the same damn room for forty years and all that really happens is you get old. And I didn't think of myself as being better than that but I never imagined I could stand it. Well, that's ingratitude too. He'd have told me so except I don't think he knew the word."

"What words did he know?"

"Simple and effective ones. If you think I'm leaving this to you, you're full of shit. That kind."

"Did he understand you didn't want it?"

"Oh sure. Why else would it hurt enough to get like that?"

"There is usually more to it, I think. Boys leave home, their parents aren't always bitter and devastated."

"If I'd left soon enough, maybe. If I'd said I longed to go into business for myself, if becoming a computer programmer like I did had been my dream, even if I met a girl who wanted to get out of the neighborhood and shack up by the lake. But I hung around home and never complained about it. I snuck off to night school every so often but I never talked about what I did there, except whether she was a blonde or a redhead. It never interfered with my shift at the bar. I let him think I wanted to inherit his life. He'd come to take it for granted and one day I just said, screw this, I've had it up to here and I'm getting out."

"You should perhaps record this. Then you could hear yourself say, I left home, which was wrong because I refrained too long from doing it."

"How it seems, anyway."

"You had a mother?"

"Maybe I still do. She moved out long before I did."

"But your father wanted you at home."

"I suppose so. To be fair I have to suppose so, because he never said he didn't. He made assumptions that we didn't discuss."

"Can you imagine wishing you had a father who made assumptions of that kind?"

"Maybe. Also I think I may have missed my chance to ever eat another bowl of chili."

Right there, in the dark and for the first time ever with her, the imp she'd begged and begged him to show all afternoon. But neither of them recognized it yet. It was so familiar to Nick that he didn't even notice it and Olga, who did, took it for a clumsy joke and didn't punish it more than she had to.

"Ah, yes. I see. I see, now, that my deepest feelings about my own family are precisely equivalent to yours toward a common kind of commercially processed stew."

"Not equivalent. Instead of. When people want something they can't have, exactly what they want is the least important part."

"The last man to say something like that to me tried to sell me Jesus very soon thereafter."

"What you get for being a chameleon. How was he supposed to know you're the last test tube atheist?"

"I don't know you so well that I can be sure you don't mean these things."

"And it's not my fault if you made me think you're psychic."

And got a pillow in the face, knees on the chest and a devastating job of tickling in the ribs.

"Oh, Nicky," some movie star sighed.

"Oh, God. What?"

"Admit that it's such a banal, maudlin little story. Admit that there's nothing in it to explain your grand career."

"Not to you maybe. We can't all be—"

"I like the truth so much better."

"There's a truth?"

"There's always a truth, someday I'll tell you how they taught me that. You remember yours, don't you? How you stole the money for the GRU? To spread commercial dissention between allies and generally cock things up?"

"Oh. That's the truth now?"

"Well, it's what happened, isn't it? Anyway, it's been the truth for months."

"I seem to have blocked it out completely. Remind me why I'd go and do that."

"Because of the blackmail of course. Because I made you. Which I could do because you'd slept with that woman whose husband turned out to be in Johnny's business and who'd have killed you very slowly if he'd learned."

"Oh. That woman. Which one was she, by the way?"

"Oh, I don't remember exactly, but she existed and so did her husband and so did a few men I didn't make up who got to know her and then went away forever, *very* unexpectedly. The FBI had to be able to check, didn't they?"

"That's sort of reasonable. I think if you moved just one knee I could probably breathe. This is supposed to make them love me?"

"Well, since you've been working for me, and I've been working for them, it sort of makes them your accomplices, doesn't it? You've more than paid your debt and you know, cuckolding one of the boys is the kind of thing that can even start them giggling."

"How have I paid my debt?"

"Many things too boring to discuss but if they ever ask again I think I'll tell them you've been extending the Monroe Doctrine by destabilizing French spheres of influence in the Caribbean. I wish I'd known about that before, it would have made so many little inventions unnecessary. But the important part you forgot to ask about is why you paid it."

"All right. Why did I pay it?"

"You paid it so they won't get greedy tomorrow. Otherwise you could be such a temptation."

"I'm such an amateur and so lucky to be cared for by experts."

"Well, you are and you are."

"We'll let that be the truth then. You want to slide down here while I try to fit this truth into my boring cover story I've been working on for twenty-five years?"

"Perhaps I'd better slide back over here. It may help you concentrate, since you must tell me all these homely little lies."

Chapter 36

Mr. and Mrs. Schrenk
June 27, 2001

"Twelve million dollars," she repeated. That wasn't all he'd said but it was the part that struck her.

"He took certain minor risks that he characterized as appalling. He broke a few laws that have never been enforced there, that exist in fact only to be violated for the profit of privileged specialists. I don't imagine you know how that's done."

"No, I don't. And to think I could have known any time I cared to ask you."

"There is still a profit, you see. Not a great one but a profit nonetheless. Compared to that is the probable write-off of six million in product that no one else needs and that is approaching its shelf life."

"My God. What came over me? A profit for Himmelskirch and I'm worried about the FBI?"

"We control only our own actions. Our responsibility ends with them. The FBI is far beyond all that."

"Perhaps it was, Alois. Now it is closer than the trash at the end of the driveway and it is your responsibilities I find inconceivably remote. I freely grant that they may be very near to you."

"If they are near to me…"

"Don't waste our time. Mysticism doesn't suit you and it's far too late to make me an obedient little helpmate. Solve this or I will."

"How could you?"

"Oh, I didn't mean your problem. I meant solve mine."

"They are different?"

"I would not have thought so, I would have sworn up and down that our problems would always be one and the same, but that is what you are now insisting. So be it. Solve my problem or I will. Solve it soon."

And having said it as well as she ever would, she stood and walked to the stairs before he could once again compose any elegies to duty like the ones she'd memorized so many years before.

Chapter 37

Strolling toward the stairway in search of the pool, he and Olga wrapped up in fluffy hotel bathrobes and carrying fluffy hotel towels, Nick was reliving an old complaint and trying to make it come out *smart*, somewhat like Olga's own story.

"If you grow up around a bar, you grow up in the middle of a business, but working for the Germans was different. Not even my old man came out and *said* I had to work there for life. The Germans had no problem with it – oh, you want a job, good, sign here, and when you retire in forty years we'll tell you what town you want to move to. One guy they sent over quit. He got a better offer and grabbed it. *We* saw nothing wrong with that, we took him out to dinner to celebrate, and two days later Schrenk drives up from Kentucky. We're all crammed into a little auditorium they had, half of us standing. Schrenk stood at the podium and cried. 'We had no right to do that to you. I can only swear that it was not the least intentional.' After a while I got it. He was ashamed for inflicting a traitor like Wolf on us. He thought we'd blame the company because of the disrespect it implied."

They entered the stairwell. Olga waited until the door closed behind them, then turned to face him. "*Scrupuleux*, Nicky. Remember? That's all. Kutuzov *noticed* it but it didn't make him *do* anything." Then she trotted on up before Nicky could argue.

There were three or four young people in the pool – not in the actual *water*, you understand, just close enough that they had an excuse for standing around mostly undressed; they watched the approaching oldness with dawning horror.

Olga took one look, turned to Nicky and demanded: "Swim or talk?"

Ready to walk back outside into the corridor if talking was his choice. Ready to dive in without another word if it wasn't. *Not* ready to take off her fluffy robe and stand there chatting, which was clearly what the moment called for.

Holding the door for her as they slipped back out, he said, "People think it's about obedience with people like Schrenk but that isn't quite right." Obedient had been her word, he thought, it must be safe to say obedience, *that* can't be why she's rolling her eyes at him... "It's more like everybody has to hurry up and find their place while they're young and then just stick to it forever. Unless somebody tells you to think about something, not only do you not need to but it's very wrong to try." Heading back toward the stairs because the children at the pool are looking their way and laughing, and he will *not* let himself come unglued just to teach them some manners... "A couple of times Schrenk asked me questions and he seemed to like my ideas. After that I'd try to suggest something about work and Schrenk wouldn't even listen. He'd just say, 'We can't *all* be running the company you know, Mr. Petraki.'" Now turning around and heading back to the pool: damn it, he will *not* crawl back to his room just to please a handful of spoiled rich kids. "I took it wrong at first. I figured he'd used me up and didn't have a reason to be civil anymore. But then I realized that he *was* still civil, he was nice as ever in fact. It concerned him *as a friend* that I wasted my time playing with ideas above my station."

"I'm quite sure Kutuzov never said that scrupulous Germans can't be *nice*, Nicky. I'm quite sure that wasn't his point at all."

He could almost hear perfectly stifled yawns between every word.

"Now, Cousin, I have been dragged up the hall and down the hall and have decided not to be dragged much further. I really do propose to get wet. You may watch or participate. If you're easily intimidated I'd suggest watching. If any of that sensitive ego is invested in memories of your lost athletic prowess, I'd very much suggest watching."

This time it was she who held the door for him.

Nick got halfway through it, turned and stopped. "*Ce soir pour ta plaisir,*" he announced, changing both language and subject, "I'll be demonstrating an authentic Australian crawl, learned over the course of an entire summer from probably the finest teenaged swimming instructor the Chicago Park District ever employed. *Nous verrons* how it stacks up against the best the Soviets could teach their so-called 'amateurs' at the Sverdlovsk Academy of Exportable Subversives. At least during the immediate pre-Glasnost era."

Olga snorted, possibly also in French.

"This, *tu comprends*, will be the authentic Australian crawl that has been wowing the ladies at the *Piscine Jean-Jacques Olier* forever. Since M. D'Annunzio *lui meme* stood on the rubble of *L'Épicerie Pichet* and waved the plans and gave it all to the people of Saint Sulpice. *Tu rappelles M. D'Annunzio, oui?*"

"*Oui, j'avais pensé.* But until now I had not associated him with famous episodes of athletic prowess."

"*Et diailleurs* it's the same stroke that knocked the girls dead off *La Plage des Sulpiciens* even before he showed up. So the haughty foreigner would do well to remember–"

But the haughty foreigner had pushed right past him, her robe and her load of towels fluttered down at the edge of the pool, and she was flashing across the water in what looked to him like Olympic freestyle form. Maybe it looked that way to the lounging children too, because they were no longer talking and had turned to stare at her: *foreign* people *swimming* in the *hotel pool?* And better than *they* could do it?

Nick, also, was now in the water, determined to give the kiddies even more of a show, but she wasn't going to make it easy, was she? As he sprinted through one length and then back the other way, she stayed right with him and even seemed to dart ahead a little every now and then, almost as if she was showing him that she *could,* before dropping back into formation. Well, after all, he did have a few years on her, and one of the very first things he'd noticed about her was her outstanding, ah, physical condition; maybe he should just take his lumps and be thankful they weren't worse. It was as he was almost resigned to seeking consolation in that thought that they turned again for yet another lap and he realized that ever since he dove in she had been doing the backstroke and patiently waiting for him to notice.

Re-cocooned inside their fluffy robes, they slopped back to the room while Olga tried to stop laughing – or, perhaps, tried to wish to stop would explain it better. "Oh, my poor Nicky!" she somehow wailed while whispering, "You really have no idea whom to believe when everyone around you is bragging, do you?"

Chapter 38

A La Casa Ruiz
June 27, 2001

Sal Ruiz asked his old man, "So what you going to do with yours?"

Hector Ruiz, who did not think of himself as Sal's old man, said, "Do you know why you're talking like that now? Speaking that lazy broken English to me? Because if you don't know, I'll be happy to explain it."

Sal Ruiz said, "Maybe you'd better. 'Cause, you know, you bring it up like you think it means something, and I always respect your opinion."

Hector Ruiz said, "You know, I think I believe that. I think you do respect my *opinions*. But sometimes I think you respect them so much that you don't have any respect left over for anything else. Those are the times when you have to talk like you are tonight. Are you sure you don't know why?"

"No Papa, you really going to have to tell me I think."

"It's simple. It's because nobody ever taught you how to speak Spanish without respect, and *that's* because your mother would have made me kill anyone stupid enough to try. So when I saw this vulgar country's disrespectful nature begin like the polluted air itself to emerge from the corrupted soil and subvert your character bit by bit, I had to let you learn this ignorant *barrio* way of speaking English. So your mother could keep her illusions about what you were becoming, or at least pretend to, and I, in turn, could remain at liberty to earn a living for us all. And that's why, still today, when you want to mouth off, you have to do it like this. Simple, as I said."

"Okay Papa. So what did I *mean* to ask you that I *forgot* to ask you because I carelessly happened to be speaking English and could only make these ignorant noises instead?"

"No doubt, my son, it was on the tip of your tongue to request my advice and ask, in grave and solicitous tones, Papa, should I put my share of our coming good fortune in the bank, or buy a second car and hire my nephew to drive it for me? Because that *is* an excellent question, one which I am sure would have occurred to you if only you'd not been distracted by the barbarous cacophony that unfortunately has been emerging from your lips all evening. Now that you've had time to hear it, don't *you* think it's an excellent question?"

"My nephew? No sh– I mean, *really*, Papa? Must I?"

Chapter 39

Joke Time
June 27, 2001

It was not even close to midnight yet. Olga, still dripping, called down for *(bloody red)* steak *(please für uns, for us)*, asparagus *(auch too)* and a *(grosser)* bottle of red — *much red vine, Fraulein, to rebuild my obedient liebchen from zo much goot Cherman sex vee joost haffing, mach schnell bitte please for us!*

The last two glasses of all that wine poured and Olga long since safely back in her lavender peignoir, she offered Cousin Nicky a particularly promising and tender little glance and reached across the debris of the dinner service, perhaps to pat his cheek or let him kiss her adorable knuckles... Instead, she grabbed her favorite earlobe and twisted, *hard*.

"One more time, Cousin. The password."

Not once more but a dozen, and not just the password but the whole impossible procedure.

"I call it up. I type what I type. After that it takes over and sings me lullabies. I just look at the screen and wait for it to happen, then I make my call and run. I remember all this. If I screw up like you seem to think I will, it won't be because I can't remember this part. I just haven't touched a computer since 1976."

"Touch this one right and you'll never have to again. Walk me to my office."

"Left just inside the building." He surveyed the table. A saucer marched *left*. "*In* the second *side* door, right, two lefts." The saucer zigged and zagged. "*In* the second *office* door which says 'Plant Protection, Market Research, Simpson.' And why just those words? What's changed? Why not also *Pflanzenschutz* and *Marktanalyse* in brass? Christ, I still remember them, don't I? Why don't they still have to pretend they're all learning the only proper words anybody has ever come up with for anything?"

"What's changed, Cousin?" Calling him on it this time. "Maybe Mr. Schrenk has changed a little, Cousin. Maybe he thinks *somebody* ought to try changing, so why not him?"

Misunderstood *again*, and again it was his own damn incoherent fault!

Maybe, just maybe, you can't go fifty years without ever trying to explain yourself to anybody at all, and then expect, one night in a very strange country and a half-forgotten language...

Every trace of his faux *Chermin liebchen* vanished, she had put the dishes on the tray, replaced the cover and carried them to the door.

Addressing her disciplined lavender derrière, he said, "I'm not *mad* about it. I was never *mad* about it. It didn't turn me into a thief. I just found it frustrating. We all did. Hall understood, he'd try to explain it for us."

Now she was on her way back but at this she stopped. "*Hall* tried to tell you how *you* felt?"

"How we *all* felt, that's what I'm trying to say. He'd joke about it, crack the whole office up sometimes."

This had her moving again.

"*Hall* used to tell jokes, and they were *funny*? Can you remember one?"

She was interested again: this was *good*. She was almost right on top of him and leaning in expectantly.

"Sure. He said that the real story of World War II was how the Germans drove to the gates of Moscow and ran out of forms to fill out. We just—"

He didn't think anything was broken. No ribs felt cracked. He wasn't even in any great pain. The fact was that he had no idea how or where he'd been hit. In a moment he tried tipping the chair forward again but that did no good, so he rolled off it and crawled to his feet.

She stood, very still, on his side of the table, with her back to him. Then she picked up his wine glass and slowly emptied it into hers, which was then exactly, perfectly, full. Picking it up anyway, quite quickly in fact, she drank it all in one swallow without spilling anything. But she didn't put it down again. She held on to both glasses as though she had simply forgotten what one does with them after they're empty.

Chapter 40

A La Casa Fuentes
June 27, 2001

Diego Fuentes stayed out on the patio after dinner. After half an hour his wife came back out and said, "Just tell me this – is it going to be good or bad?"

He thought it through quickly one last time and said, "Good, then. If it has to be one or the other, it's good."

"But not all the way through."

"Yes, all the way through. But sometimes, even the best of changes take getting used to. I think this will be one of them."

"For both of us?"

"At least for me. Not only will I not have to work again after tomorrow, I won't even be able to pretend that I have any work to do."

"Will you be expecting lunch every day then?"

"Do you think I would do that to you?"

"I merely asked. Some men get strange ideas at times like this. You should have a club, you know."

"Yes, I've been thinking so myself."

"Don't be hasty. I'll start enquiring in the morning. Will you be out here much longer?"

"I don't think so, no. I think this would be an excellent time to come in."

Chapter 41

Captain Kopeikin
June 27, 2001

When her whisper finally came, it was surely the original voice of Olga at last.

"You're such a naturally charming people but I'm sure you've always known that. Because of the introspective habits you just can't help confessing to."

"I'm..." The knowledge that he had just done a perfectly horrible thing was now spreading through him, a little like he'd imagined a seizure might feel.

"Sorry?"

"No. Not yet, anyway."

"What, then? What are you?"

"Mostly scared I think. Not of you but..."

"Not of me? You're sure?"

"I don't think so, no."

"Of what, then?"

"I'm not sure. Of how I could do that, I think." He had been sharing beds with women for more than thirty years and had never guessed that this could happen.

"If you aren't scared of me now then fear is not for you. If a *real*

Russian ever heard you tell that joke, there'd be no end to what she'd do to make you pay for it."

"That's right, you're not a real Russian anymore, I keep forgetting."

"I almost was again though. I almost was. I think it might be passing just a little."

She put one glass carefully down in the middle of the table, then seemed to notice the other one and put it down too.

"For what it's worth I think I'm finally sorry. How does that work again? You not being a real Russian anymore?"

"Much as you're no longer the real Nicholas Petraki, though I doubt that you can see this."

Nick started in and scared himself badly: as if he would know how to just jump in and *talk!* He bit it off and heard himself laugh a little bitterly. Seeing no point in holding back after that, he said, "In many ways I think I am."

"Yes, in many ways, of course."

She picked up both glasses and walked back toward the door. She didn't turn her head to talk but somehow her whisper was perfectly clear.

"And in all the many ways that you still are what you once were in spite of everything I've learned about you today, I still have in me many original pieces of a real Russian woman. But pieces only, and now mixed with so much else that no real place has ever given me, that I have made for myself out of hot air and bad dreams." She set the glasses on the tray by the door and turned back toward him. "Real people of any kind at all do not spend their lives pretending to be others, and especially they do not pretend it the better to wage war on still others. A lifetime of that has spoiled both of us for all the things that people mean by real. This is why we find ourselves together here for a little while tonight, because there are no real places for us to go to anymore."

Slipping off the pegnoir, she rolled it up as his mother once rolled dough for pastry: lazily, because his mother was a lousy cook. She tossed it onto a chair as if it were a sack of socks, as if she couldn't remember why she'd ever bothered to put it on, and in the slip-like thing he'd known would be beneath it she slithered back into bed. She waited as if for something to happen before continuing. She waited, he would have said, more than somewhat haughtily. He picked up his chair and set it straight in front of the table. She didn't quite nod.

"After Russia became a country again many Russians returned from where they'd been sent, but Russia understood me very well by then and wanted no part of me. Not even in handcuffs, as you fancy you're still wanted back where you were real."

Nick had turned off all the lamps except for the one on his side of the bed and he too was back in bed. "What happened?"

She showed no sign of answering. He reached out and turned off the lamp.

"I think you're going to live until morning. You don't have to hear this."

"I want to hear it." To save himself from silence. "Otherwise I might forget to shut up." To prove that things could still be said? "What happened?"

She took a long, deep breath, and when she spoke again Olga's whisper was gone, its place taken by that familiar soft, cold purr. "Very little at first. At first there was simply no work for me to do. I was told to get a job and remain plausible."

Think of it: all it had taken to reveal that purr for the artifice it had surely always been was a halfway funny joke he hadn't even made up himself.

"For over a year I heard nothing but no one cared to come and fire me. Then I received an utterly improper message. I was to prepare for a special assignment. Someone who knew my real name would make contact with me and I was to do what he said. There are elaborate protocols in my kind of work and they cover every conceivable eventuality. That kind of message has no place in them and the man who delivered it must have known better. I moved out at once and called an emergency number and reported that I was compromised and the messenger was taken – at best. The next day I left my new place for much less than an hour and returned to find that my bed had been set afire, then doused. I moved again and no mere three or four professionals could possibly have followed me. This time I did not report, but three days after that I received a phone call in Russian from a thug I didn't recognize. 'Olga Nikolaiova,' he said, 'I've wanted to meet you for a very long time.' Over a regular telephone you understand. At first I thought it was the FBI calling to say I was surrounded but it turned out to be something else. I had been sold as a commercial resource to some countrymen in New York. It was the first time I was sold but not the last."

Nick peered toward her voice but there was nothing to see anywhere. He saw that there never would be anything there for him, and he wondered if the pain of hurting himself in his shallowest spot would be the hardest remorse of all. "You couldn't just run?"

"Of course, if I wished to die or spend my life in prison. It was not just I that was sold, Nicky. It was the network I worked for and all the files that went with it. Perhaps sale is the wrong word. Perhaps someone in Moscow had merely changed jobs and taken a few things with him when he went. How could I know who was safe and who was not? Nevertheless I'd have found a way if Johnny hadn't bought me from them."

"You must think you owe him a lot."

"Must I? Then I suppose I do, and never mind what any woman

would feel when she looks at Johnny, and to hell with how you explain that to yourself. We may not be real anymore, Nicky, but we are *something* and my life has made me very different from you. I look at you and I see you lose your place five times a minute and then you tell me your old man made you do it, grasping Frenchmen made you do it, the only woman you couldn't have made you do it again and again and again. When I think I'm as annoyed with that as I can possibly become, you reach back and toss out a dozen words that don't even mean anything to you, and before I know it I'm back in the deepest part of the Army again, holding my breath in the dark and wondering how many of you I can kill before the rest of you find me. But then you say you're sorry, so once again you're just my dimwitted cousin and I'm merely here to help you find your destiny tomorrow. Everything about this scares me almost to death and I think you almost understand it and would like to help, and that scares me even more."

"You really think I think other people make me do everything?"

"Not completely or I couldn't stand to talk to you. Don't imagine that makes us close. If you really were one of those wretched people, I couldn't even stand to spit on you."

"And incompletely I'm like that."

"I think you try to talk yourself into it as a kind of game. And if you keep trying, then someday you'll finally convince yourself that you really didn't make the choice that put you here. I don't want to be around when you do."

Nick tried to see the justice in that and failed. "That's not quite right. I was going to say *fair* but we don't believe in fair, do we? I remember lots of choices. I remember lots of choices on Saint Sulpice. But the big ones, the one that got me there and the one that got me back, I didn't notice at all. Both times I was doing something else and I realized they'd already been made."

"They'd been made."

"Oh, I know who made them all right."

"Cousin, I doubt that very much. I think all you really know is what everyone else would say. But it's gallant of you to pretend."

Neither could see the other, they weren't nearly close enough to touch, and he was stiff and ready to roll over. She had just announced a truce, but he couldn't bring himself to turn away. It was silly and it annoyed him very much that he could be this silly just then. Of course he'd always known that he could be endlessly silly around pretty women but it annoyed him still more to learn at his age just how annoying this silliness could be. It occurred to him that he was almost as mad at himself as she was. He snapped on the light and bounced over to the glasses and the Martel. He poured himself an inch and turned, offered the bottle but saw her look and said, "What?"

"It's a little late to keep you from drinking, but you're not touching that if you think you really need it."

"It's all I have to offer and I want to babble at you again."

"Your self-confidence is delusional. After what your babbling has already accomplished?"

"Yes. Because it has just hit me how to answer your question."

"My *question?*"

"From earlier. What I was thinking way back then."

"Okay, Cousin. Let's find a way to really say it. Pour me one more and put out the light and talk to me for a just a little while."

He walked over, took her glass, poured, put the bottle back, but he was slow to put out the light because they were almost friends again and he liked looking at her so much. She seemed to see that and grinned and shook her head, and it was somebody he'd never met before who winked and said, "Douse it, Binky, if you don't want to kill the mood." Whoever she was, he had to admit that she fit right in.

"Damn, you do look good, Cousin." But he knew she wouldn't answer and then the light was out again and he was back where he belonged. "You know how sometimes, you're not paying attention to what you're thinking and one thought just follows another one that seems to have nothing to do with it? And sometimes you notice and ask yourself, now what did those two things just have in common?"

"You should perhaps not assume that our mental processes have a great deal in common, Nicky."

"Don't worry, I think I'll remember not to for a while. But I was thinking about a couple of things we won't discuss when I figured out what I should have told you this afternoon.

"Every day for the people like me on Saint Sulpice is the same, every day they're unhappy, but to them it's all about something that's over, that was over years ago. You see that and two things stand out. First is it can't possibly be true – here they are, walking around, money to burn and living like kings, how can it be that they can't change whatever bothers them? But you also catch yourself thinking just like them. O Lord I did it and now I'm here and now I have to put up with this forever."

"But what makes you special is you see this and they don't."

In a tone so casual he would probably have agreed with it once.

"What makes me special is I just can't stand to be like anybody else."

"You were meant for better things and lost your way, poor lamb."

In a tone so sad he knew he'd have bought it almost any other time.

"See, we can talk because you see how much crap that is. Almost everybody's meant for better things but almost everybody's somewhere else, doing them. But I'm *not* meant for them because no matter how good I ought to be having it I will never stand for fitting in. Put me where what you'd call real people act like they should, and I've always been trouble and I always will be. But kick me out of there, stick me with some bastards who are just rotten enough and suddenly I'm exactly what's needed. Can you–"

"Oh yes I *can!*"

She had jumped to her knees again and incidentally thrown the covers to the floor. If only he could *see*...

"Bravo, Cousin, I *know* that feeling, I know it better than any name I've ever had..."

The bed was *pitching*. That lavender slip-thing had to be *oscillating*.

"Cousin, there is *nothing* you can tell me about a vocation for foiling the bastards where they live! And you had to find yours for yourself, imagine..."

The bed was *quaking*. It was a *bed-quake!*

"No one showed you the way and took care of your troublesome family while you learned. You had no training, no guidance, no dialectical process to order your thoughts when it's three in the morning and you're on the run again..."

Face it – the bed was doing what beds are supposed to *do* sometimes, even if it had cruelly left him out of it for once...

"I *do* understand, I do, I'm really not laughing at *you* Cousin, it's just the idea..."

Oh yes she was – her and the bed both...

"No comrades appearing with sentimental messages and tiny stale seedcakes... No one to call for help, no major from the General Staff to personally review your plans... Oh my... No years in the gymnasium to show you how we cope when we find the secret fascist stealing our wine in his boxers... No my dear Nicky, don't speak, don't speak, Nicky, please, I want to remember you like this always... Oh my... No greetings transcribed onto fly specs, telling of secret promotions and ceremonies *in camera*, what a way to...no medals, even if one never sees them…oh my brave Nicky! Nothing to look forward to…not even a post at the College of Senior Conspirators when your time among the bastards is finished… Oh Nicky forgive me, it really isn't you but I cannot…" And she really couldn't, so she just gave in to it until it seemed that she and the bed had succumbed to their last convulsion. In a while they got it back under control, took a few breaths, and she said, "Oh, that felt good, Nicky, you can't imagine. That felt better than what I think you've been imagining for hours…"

The bed was more or less horizontal again, though it should have been reaching for a cigarette…

"So, in a little while people will say what a wonderful thing you've done but basically you'll have done it for spite. To spite the bastards one last time. Is it so bad, then, that I'm helping you do this wonderful thing accidentally, as yet another man's creature? For the very worst reasons in the world I do it, but suddenly the saints are real after all and they *do* see everything after all and they don't care about anything but what we do tomorrow and so they're finally smiling down on me. If you can have it your way, Cousin, why can't I have it like that?"

Nick thought, Damn, at least I amused her again. Then he thought that in the blackness she could allow herself to look any way she wanted to. She might be smiling broadly, trying not to giggle any more, or her teeth might be clenched in fury at his meandering folly, or maybe she'd even meant a little of what she'd said at the end and was getting over being a tiny bit weepy. He decided that since he must have a picture to take home with him, she would be wearing her tricky little grin, with just enough of the mockery showing to remind him how much they both needed it.

Then she said, "And also–," and then some more beside, but this time Cousin Nicky really had gone to sleep.

Chapter 42

Margarite geboren *Altmeyer*
June 27, 2001

Just dialing felt like the worst thing she'd ever done and that was enough to tell her she needed a grip. By the time Curtis answered she thought she had most of one, but right away he said, "How'd it go?" and for a second she couldn't imagine what he meant.

"He's here, I said what we agreed I'd say and I'm alone now. I have no idea how it went."

"Good, good. Good."

And then some more reassuring mumbling on both their parts until she thought she would scream. But just before she did Curtis finally started in on their script and for a while she could have got by on grunts if she'd had to.

"Remember to keep thinking this way: what would he do if he was really innocent here? You know because you told us, right? He'd throw himself away and he'd throw you away and he'd try to save the company's money. Keep him thinking like that, because tomorrow's no time for him to suddenly grow up. Keep him thinking he's innocent and he'll walk in the end because then he'll be a *nobody*. Innocent guys who remember to act strong for their wives, follow the company's orders and send all the money back home are *nobodies*, and nobodies end up walking when all is said and done."

And then she must have started really babbling because Gonzales was talking her down. "We'd tell you if we could," Gonzales said, "but really it's better for all of us if you don't know yet. But you'll recognize it when it comes, I promise you that. When that happens just remember that we're all in this together."

Sometime well after midnight she woke up and realized that she'd fallen asleep with the bedroom door still locked. She started to jump up and open it before it struck her that that had been a very realistic touch, and maybe she had a future at this kind of thing.

.

Chapter 43

Diego Fuentes
June 28, 2001

The banker signed the order for the transfer, passed it to the waiting underling, leaned back and grew luxuriously conspiratorial. "A nice vacation for a lot of currency," he said. "Twelve million in, a quiet rest in the vault, then ten million on its way back home again. I wonder. What will become of what is left?"

"What is left," Diego Fuentes said, "is the best commission I've ever earned."

"That," the banker agreed, "is the best commission one has ever heard of."

"Alas," Diego Fuentes said, "after such a coup, one must accept that certain avenues are now closed. I've been thinking about real estate but I'm frightfully ignorant. Do you suppose the bank might see its way clear to advise me in confidence?"

They agreed that such matters are best discussed over an appropriately serious lunch. Before they left, Diego Fuentes asked if he could borrow the phone. As the banker considerately went off to arrange for a car, Diego Fuentes called an old friend at the Ministry of the Interior. "Ernesto," he said, "it is my somber duty to reveal a shockingly flagrant violation of a very important law. I suspect that the public servant who discovers it will be appropriately rewarded. When I tell you who's to blame, you'll understand the seriousness of my own position. It is no exaggeration to say that I may never earn another peso at my trade."

Chapter 44

Johnny Wonders
June 28, 2001

Room service came at six, Johnny at seven. He picked up the bottle of Martel, held it up to the light and put it down again.

"He didn't have any," Olga said, and for a moment Nick himself believed her.

The wine bottle and its two evil glasses were long since gone, and he and Olga were mostly packed. They took the armchairs, Johnny sat at the foot of a bed, and they talked it through one last time for an hour and a half. At the end of that time Nick poured them the last of the coffee while Johnny pulled out a cell phone and called time and temperature. He wasn't satisfied with the reception and went to the window and opened it. He called time and temperature again, almost leaning through the screen.

"It's okay here," he said, and dialed again. "Mr. Hall, please. Please tell him I'm a friend of Curtis and Gonzales." Then he handed the phone to Nick.

"Roddy? It's Nick. Think you could make it home for a little while this morning? How about ten on the button?" And flipped it shut as he'd seen Johnny do it, just in time to smother the leading edge of a mighty bellow.

Then Johnny called his dear Aunt Maggie in Lexington, who said she had seven prime steaks so don't be late for dinner. After that they sat and talked for another half-hour, this time about anything that struck them. What struck Nick was: "Roddy used to be quite a hunter. Back in Chicago he had a cabinet full of rifles."

Olga said, "Alas, in this country it's to be expected."

Nick said, "You tell me he's as crazy as ever. I was wondering if he'll be tempted to produce one. Once Johnny gets assertive."

Olga said, "Well, then I'll have to hurt him, won't I?"

"*You'll* have to hurt him?"

"Of course, it's what I'm for, isn't it?"

Both she and Johnny grew quite interested in Nick's face.

"Why, Sugar Lips, you never told him! How sweet!" Olga blew Johnny a kiss, then turned an arch and quizzical look on Nick that slipped a little as the full depth of his ignorance seemed to sink in.

Nick blinked a few times and said, "Damn. Would that be hewing wood or drawing water?" In the car, Johnny had said, *You were right there with him, weren't you?*

He excused himself vaguely. Once in the bathroom, it came to him that she had also said, *No one cared to come and fire me.* He heard, *I had less advanced lessons, though for me they were very demanding.* He recalled that she was mostly what she had *made for myself out of hot air and bad dreams* and she was still around because *Russia understood me very well by then and wanted no part of me.* Just now he had heard what he had managed not to hear last night, but somehow last night it had all been talk, an expression of her mood, the kind of thing he might say himself if the moment seemed to call for it. He turned to go and had barely a second's warning before he began to throw up. When he figured that was over he straightened up, washed his face and tried to breathe again. He decided that at last he'd heard enough and maybe the saints do see everything after all. He brushed his teeth with her toothpaste and a finger and used some of her mouthwash because he'd already packed his own.

Nick walked back out and kissed the top of her head. She let out a breath that she seemed to have been holding. He took that to mean he should kiss her again, so he did – somehow he owed it to her, although neither of them was real anymore. Looking up, she said, "Thank you, Petraki. For once you got it just right." Then she turned her face so he couldn't see it at all and pointed it at Johnny.

Johnny stared back at her for a second or two, utterly blank, utterly dead. Then he stood and said, "Let's go drive around Roddy's block a lot."

The packing was finished in no time at all. Olga used the TV to check out and they headed downstairs. Olga seemed a little miffed at Johnny at first but she came out of it soon enough.

By the time they reached the car Nick's lips had stopped their tingling.

Chapter 45

Roddy's Reunion
June 28, 2001

They were parked with the sun behind them, two houses down from Roddy's Bauhaus Tudor, when a beige Lincoln peeled around the corner, roared straight at them with its tires smoking, locked its brakes and fishtailed into Roddy's driveway. Roddy left the car door open, made the front porch in three strides, and hurtled inside, leaving the memory of his jiggling to shimmer in the bright morning sunshine.

Nick said, "Jesus. That's Roddy?"

Johnny said, "I think we should give him a minute. Or just call the paramedics from here."

Olga said, "I'll do it," and was out of the car before anyone could argue. Johnny hauled Nick out and they were ten steps behind her when she knocked. The door opened right away.

There was a moment's silence before Roddy blurted out, "Mrs. Simpson!"

Olga said, "Mr. Hall, we really have to talk."

Roddy said, "It's just, I was expecting someone else."

Nick said, "Me, I'll bet."

Then he was inside and Roddy had him in a bear hug. It knocked most of his wind out and a couple of ribs hurt alarmingly; maybe Olga had connected better than he'd thought last night, and Roddy was going to finish the job.

"Mr. Hall," Mrs. Simpson said, "you have to let him breathe."

Roddy backed off. He held a large half-empty bowl of chips, the missing half now scattered across twenty feet of foyer.

Behind Nick, Johnny said, "I think we're clear." Nick looked over his shoulder and saw him in the doorway, looking back, left and right, with his left hand on Nick's back and his right inside his jacket.

Roddy said, "Nick…" but that seemed to be all he could manage.

Nick said, "I guess you know Mrs. Simpson."

Roddy's face was a war between at least two separate panics. "I thought you were in Tuscaloosa. I didn't know you knew where I live. I'd have cleaned up…"

Mrs. Simpson looked in at the empty, spotless, gleaming room. "Such a disgusting mess!"

Nick said, "Roddy, you look great. A hundred percent different – but great."

Roddy giggled delightedly and sat them down. He took the middle of the couch, which put Nick on the downslope of a medium-deep crater. Johnny Wonders took the chair on the right and Mrs. Simpson took the other one and said, "You know, Mr. Hall, I've almost come to think of him as my cousin. But what it really is, we look out for him. It's what we do, JW and I."

"JW?" Roddy asked and Johnny Wonders reached a hand over and said, "Pleased to meet you."

"Somebody has to do it," Mrs. Simpson said. "It's a full time job, believe me."

On its way back home, Johnny's hand had stopped for a potato chip. Now he stared hard at the fluorescent fuzzy green spots, then glanced furtively around as if wondering where he could stash it.

"So, Mrs. Simpson. You don't really work for Schrenk?" It seemed that Roddy had finally caught up.

"Well, yes I do. I even cash my paycheck. But basically I keep an eye on him, for Nick."

Johnny said, "See, Mr. Hall, there's people took an interest in your friend. Maybe we don't make it any clearer than that, okay?"

Nick said, "Believe me, I'd never be here without them."

Mrs. Simpson said, "And that's why we've come to see you."

Roddy said, "I think I can guess already. You're working with the FBI too, then?"

Nick said, "Too, Roddy?"

Mrs. Simpson said, "FBI, Mr. Hall?"

Roddy said, "Sure. Curtis and Gonzales. They're after Schrenk for the Cubans and they know all about Nick." As if, *that explains it,* and Nick thought, Okay, Johnny, break a leg. And sat back to watch the show.

Johnny Wonders sat as though flash frozen and stared at Roddy with impossible disbelief and outrage. The eyes Johnny Wonders wore now were not the eyes he'd walked in with. They *had* to have been a disguise because now Nick was really seeing the eyes of Johnny Wonders. *Eyes that make contact:* you hear that and it always seems like such a *good* thing to say about someone, but no other eyes had ever reached out like the eyes of Johnny Wonders, no other eyes had ever made the contact these eyes seemed to promise.

Nick thought, Cue the second murderer, and Mrs. Simpson's voice dutifully emerged in Olga's best demented whisper.

"Don't whine, don't stall, don't even think. Are you talking to the FBI, is that what this is?"

Roddy also might have been watching a play. He seemed to be agreeing with himself about something rather important.

Mrs. Simpson hissed, "Stop it, there you go thinking again. Who did you talk to about this man?"

Roddy said, "You don't understand." But he didn't appear all that upset about it.

"Nothing," Mrs. Simpson whispered, "ever mattered like making us believe that."

Roddy said, "Sure, I can do that," even though Mrs. Simpson clearly didn't believe it.

Johnny said, "Pretend a little like it matters." At least he was breathing again.

Roddy said, "I tried to tell them everything, you see. About Nick. Everything I knew, but they wouldn't talk about him. They said they already knew it and they wouldn't tell me anything about him no matter how hard I tried."

Mrs. Simpson whispered, "What's *everything*?"

Johnny said, "What couldn't you tell them no matter how hard you tried?"

"How he was innocent. How he never did it. But see, they knew. That's what you don't understand. They already know that."

Nick tried not to show any of his relief. It was one thing to hear from others that Roddy had stayed faithful, but quite something else for him to come out and say it. He decided to get a little pissed off. He turned to Johnny. "Stop it. He's my friend."

Johnny stared at him.

Nick said, "I *left* him there. He had to take it all himself."

Johnny Wonders stood up. His jacket was unbuttoned now but his hands were safely on his hips. He twisted one way and then back again without moving his feet, like he was a batter trying to get loose in the on-deck circle. He kept his face toward the ceiling, pointing it at first one corner, then the next. Then his entire body shrugged violently, and he sat back down again, calmly, as if nothing had happened. Roddy stared.

Mrs. Simpson said, "Staying behind doesn't have to make him a friend, Nicky."

Nick said, "He was already my friend. He still is."

Johnny said, "It's your call, Mr. P. You know that. But you'd better be pretty fucking sure."

It was Mrs. Simpson's turn to stare at Nick.

He said, "I've never been so sure about anything."

Mrs. Simpson said, "Roddy – can I call you that, I think I need to, and you can call me Olga. Because to be honest Nicky's making us closer than I'd ever hoped we'd be. One knows everything about friends as close as he'd have us be. Tell me all about your life. Tell me about the FBI. Tell me especially how you love Alois Schrenk and all his works."

It took Roddy a few minutes to catch his stride. What he told was not exactly one single story end to end, but Mrs. Simpson seemed to follow it perfectly and nodded him helpfully along.

Johnny was somewhere else, somewhere nobody wants to be.

Nick didn't have the faintest idea what he was showing but whatever it was, it seemed to please Roddy very much.

When Roddy petered out, Johnny said, "You can feel this way about a man and do nothing for twenty-five years?"

Roddy said, "That's true. I can't explain it."

Nick almost missed his cue, but remembered and said, "Back off, JW, okay?"

Mrs. Simpson said, "Roddy, it's never too late. How'd you like to do something now?"

Nick said, "Roddy, remember Zuckerland? Remember Schrenk's bundle of twixes and Fuentes' little games?"

Mrs. Simpson said, "They're still at it, Roddy. The law's still the law, the embargo's still the embargo and they're merrily selling your product to Cuba."

Johnny said, "Bet you don't know nothing about that, do you?"

Roddy said, "Yes and no. What I see is stuff going to Mexico. What I know is what anybody could figure."

Mrs. Simpson said, "Who do you think the FBI will get, Roddy? If Schrenk tells it his way. Him or you? His people or yours? Why should this time be any different than the last?"

Johnny Wonders said, "They shipped fifteen million worth down a couple of weeks ago." Sweat still showing through his shirt but not even bitter now; but if Roddy won't notice, why should anyone else?

Roddy said, "Sure. I know that."

Mrs. Simpson said, "Fuentes paid today."

Roddy said, "No he didn't. The bank sends me an email. I'd have known as soon as it was transferred."

Johnny said, "That's right, you would have. That's why you had to come here." Like, maybe, the TV science man telling the kids why ice is hard and not so wet. And just as the TV science man would have, they let Roddy think about that for a second.

"You knew what time he was going to send it?" he asked. "Because if you were already here…"

Nick said, "Fuentes isn't such a bad guy, Roddy. He remembers his friends when it doesn't cost too much."

Mrs. Simpson said, "So we know and Fuentes knows and soon the FBI will know, I'm sure. But Schrenk doesn't know, does he?"

Roddy said, very slowly, "No, he doesn't. I'd have emailed him but I'm here. I'd have written up the deposit and entered it and he'd have seen it when he checked the cash for the day but I didn't do that either."

Johnny said, "Maybe you should be busy and forget to do that till a whole lot later."

Nick said, "Sure but he's got to tell him sometime. What if Schrenk walks off with the money when he does?"

Roddy said, "He wouldn't dare. Not twice. Not even him."

Johnny said, "Maybe you're right. But what if somebody else took it this time and made it look like him?"

"How?"

Mrs. Simpson said, "The FBI are closing in, aren't they?"

Johnny said, "They got to you and word is they got to his wife."

Nick said, "They're after Himmelskirch's precious cash. They want it desperately. He'll have to send it to Berlin, won't he? If he thinks they're going to take it."

"Sure. He learns it's here and he hears about them and first chance he gets, it's gone."

Nick said, "He'll transfer it himself, won't he?"

"You think he'd let me do it?"

"You suppose he'll check the account number?"

In a while Roddy's laughter seemed to turn into some other kind of fit and Nick considered getting seriously worried. But Roddy came out of it eventually and then, though it was still a long time before noon, they had to have a beer for old time's sake, even Johnny, Johnny most of all. Johnny seemed to have made a great and favorable impression. Nick wondered how on earth that could have been. He got another bear hug from Roddy and had to promise to write or call. He and Johnny made it through the door while Mrs. Simpson covered their retreat.

Alone with Roddy, she said, "Your office, maybe fifteen minutes? Then you can show me around again and take me to lunch and flirt all you want because I'm not Mrs. Simpson anymore, am I?"

"You think I'll ever see Nick again?"

"I can tell him to write and he'll listen, believe me."

Roddy giggled and nodded.

Mrs. Simpson said, "What?"

Roddy said, "Still do anything for the girls. Same old Nick."

Chapter 46

Mrs. Schrenk's Reunion
June 28, 2001

Nick said, "You were pretty convincing there for a minute."

"Sometimes things remind me of my life. It shows up when nobody's even looking for it."

"Jesus."

"I don't try to do it, you know. I start playing and then I convince myself it's real again."

"Again?" Nick said, and then he thought, Why the hell don't I just shut up for once?

"See," Johnny said, "I'm okay now. I'm back to being broadminded and I understand how that was your business and all. So now you can tell me something that's just as fucking personal."

"What?"

"You can tell me you knew you were lying when you called that man your friend."

Johnny walked around the left side of the car, Nick around the right. They got in the back. Olga Kopeikin climbed in front and looked from one to the other. "Oh, dear God," she said. "Not you two."

Johnny said, "The shit you got to put up with."

Olga said, "Know what I think?"

Johnny said, "If I did, what would I need you for?"

Olga said, "I think you'd better meet somebody you don't like pretty damn soon, or else we'd better stop and let you mug somebody."

Nick said, "We're going to Lexington now, aren't we?"

Olga and Johnny just looked at him.

Nick said, "Because if we are, nobody needs to be mugged on my account."

Twelve minutes from Roddy's Olga pulled into the yard of a gravel-hauling outfit. A small red helicopter was idling at the back, its blades twitching impatiently. A youngish man in khakis ran up and said he was Armstrong, the pilot. "Known Mr. Giannotti long?" he screamed.

"Years and years," Johnny screamed back but they were already close enough to the infernal machine that no one could hear a word. Nick let himself be strapped in and wondered when it would quiet down. Then Armstrong twisted the throttle and he realized what a foolish idea that had been. As they brayed and shuddered off toward Lexington, he let himself think he just could see Olga driving, back the way they'd come.

About this time Margarite Schrenk got a call at work and hurried home. There she sat and pretended to wonder why on earth Gonzales thought she should sit there for at least three hours. She sat for over an hour while Nick shook and swayed as they followed the highway and he saw many things that didn't seem to go together at all. What stuck in the end was a Cossack-flavored sense of roads as invaders bearing other invaders onward while the most powerful invaders roar overhead toward the front – that, and objective proof that horses just can't stand helicopters.

At eleven forty-four Curtis's cell phone rang while he had a mouth full of cheeseburger. He chewed seven times, swallowed, said, "Thank you," flipped the phone shut. "Long day, I think."

Gonzales was chewing only a small piece of lettuce, so she could ask "Why?" right away.

"The money came home an hour ago. Ten million."

"Schrenk know yet?"

"If he does, we got lots of people to be disappointed in, don't we?"

About that time Roddy opened an email and showed it to Mrs. Simpson. "Ten in," he said. "Net minus two from Fuentes for the month but why should your customers actually make you money?"

"Minus two?"

"Sure. Twelve out a couple of weeks ago, short term note okayed by Schrenk."

Mrs. Simpson smiled. "Twelve even? One transaction? Not eleven plus something else?"

"No. Why?"

"Do you know, I am suddenly so much more comfortable about Señor Diego Fuentes. Someday I really must let him buy me a wonderful dinner."

At twelve-forty eight, about when Margarite Schrenk had mostly figured out what she'd have imagined was going on if she hadn't been sure she knew, Mrs. Simpson took the last bite of a huge chicken Caesar, dry, and said, "We should get the check. We don't want to be rushed."

Roddy sighed at the dessert cart. "You're not coming back when you go, are you?"

"I doubt it very much. In a little while it would be pretty hard to leave."

"Kind of been my luck. Get to really know somebody on the last day I'll ever see them."

"I think things might change now, Roddy. Once Schrenk is finally gone I think it will all be much simpler again."

"Give me time, you mean. Go out and meet people like you every day."

"I'm hiding around every corner, Roddy. You have only to look."

The helicopter settled itself at the edge of a quarry. Johnny tipped the pilot a couple hundred and told him he was great. Armstrong figured they'd want to hear about how he flew Apaches in the reserves and Johnny had a hell of a time turning him off. Johnny led Nick to a dusty black car in the parking lot and somehow knew where to find the key.

In a neighborhood of fine old houses, he knocked on a carved oak door and it opened right away.

"You must be Mrs. Schrenk," Johnny said. "You can keep the hundred and forty."

It was supposed to drop her in her tracks but Margarite Schrenk had turned to look at Nick. "Nicholas Petraki," she said. "The savior of my dreams. You've aged well. Welcome to you and your highly respectable friend. Agent Somebody, would it be?"

"Not really," Johnny admitted.

"Perhaps you have a name anyway?"

"How about Nick's highly respectable but mostly handsome friend? Think that might do? I didn't know you two ever met."

"We used to meet at very dull parties. It hurt him very badly not to make a pass at me."

"He's over that now."

"Really? Somehow he doesn't look it."

"He meant, I'm over my scruples."

Margarite Schrenk's eyes got quite large and for just a second she was a delighted schoolgirl. "Why Nicholas Petraki! Your scruples! And just when I thought I might never laugh again. I can keep the Cubans' money? Or Fuentes'?"

Johnny said, "You really think your husband takes kickbacks?"

"You sent it?"

Johnny nodded.

"Why?"

"You spend a day with the FBI and you can't figure that out?"

"Does this approach often work for you? Spontaneous confessions to strangers whose lives you've almost destroyed?"

Johnny said, "It has its points. Like, now, we get to talk a while. Twenty minutes ought to be enough."

To prove his point, they were definitely inside, well within the Schrenks' living room, both men looking at Margarite Schrenk and she turning from one to the other.

"This is ridiculous," she said. "Come in the kitchen and sit."

Nick had ten seconds to take in the ground floor but that is enough time to steal many impressions. Silk wallpaper in subtle stripes. Good Chippendale imitations throughout and one or two pieces that might have been real. A very old or very well faked silver silk rug with tiny peacocks scattered across it. Faded etchings of old timey Southern scenes, possibly Lexington, certainly hers. Three dull Dresden cups and saucers, each under its own glass dome on a sidebar, and next to it, even more jarringly out of place, a small cracked and faded black and white photograph in a plain black frame. And suddenly Nick had come up short and was staring at the eyes of Alois Schrenk burning from the emaciated face of a young *Feldwebble*, bent, with a wrench in each hand, over the breech of a mobile eighty-eight MM flak gun with at least one bald tire, surprised by the photographer but desperately grinning for the last picture ever going home, coming to attention while almost squatting and failing to fill the uniform issued long before to a much heavier man. There is a little smoke in the background and maybe some of the specks in the sky are airplanes; other than that, just a few glum, bareheaded men in *feldgrau* and what seem like miles and miles of wheat. So. Not winter yet. But '44, definitely. Schrenk will be born in '45 and these men are not going to see another spring.

"His father, of course. He used to live in Alois' office but I made him move out here. They spent entirely too much time alone in there. You have no business with him." Still, Nick hung back just a second so the picture could finish its speech. *Do what you're told*, it said. *Do what everyone must. If you do it till it kills you, it just might be enough.*

Then they were seated but that was all. Margarite Schrenk offered no coffee, no tea, nothing. She glanced at the coffee pot so they would notice that it was full and asked, "So what is your part in this? What do you bring to the FBI's table?"

Nick said, "We rang the dinner bell. We said, here it is, come and get it."

Johnny asked, "You know what entrapment is?"

"Yes. I used to think I knew but now I'm sure of it."

Johnny said, "Well, because we've been sneaking around and really breaking laws, entrapment's exactly what nobody can make stick anymore. That's what we do for them. In return Nick becomes a useful citizen again."

Margarite Schrenk said, "How perfectly revolting."

Johnny said, "Still, from your point of view, right now we're a better source of information. Than the FBI, I mean. We're more trustworthy 'cause all our wants and needs are out here in plain sight. Plus they know everything about the law but this is about crime and we're the experts on that."

Margarite Schrenk said, "Really? Do you know as much about crime as Nicholas?"

Nick said, "You know, I didn't make Alois decide that the law is putty for really superior executives like him."

Margarite Schrenk said, "Oh no, Nicholas. Nobody could get any ideas from you."

Johnny said, "Had to fall apart someday, Mrs. Schrenk. Would have come down with us or without us but at least this way you've got some rule-benders you can deal with."

Nick said, "Maybe you'll decide to tell them we came here and told you this. It won't matter to us but you do want to think it through for your own sake."

Margarite Schrenk said, "Oh, yes, for *my* sake. Of course. And here I am, suspicious and ungrateful."

Nick said, "You probably think the FBI can imagine it's obliged to you. For being cooperative, and a good citizen perhaps."

Johnny said, "Look, Mrs. Schrenk. There's something you need to understand about people like the FBI. They like to look good. They don't mind not being noticed. But they just can't stand looking bad."

"Not so different from me, really," Margarite Schrenk said. "There are really very few like you, you know, who must be hateful to be satisfied."

"See," Johnny said, "there you go, I didn't think you'd get it. They're all real, real different from you, unless you basically go around lying all day so you can look good walking on people."

"I'd remind you that not everyone walks on others but you'd never believe me. I don't have the impression they're lying to me. You are, of course."

"The ones you're talking to, sure. Most of them like to be straight when they can. The trouble is, they always answer to somebody else, and so on up the line. And nobody ever, ever took orders like your basic FBI drone, and nobody ever forgot about it quicker afterwards. Go ahead and trust them up to a point; that's the point where they get to keep their own promises. Just understand that sometimes they're not allowed to do that. Sometimes they have to break every single one of them and then it eats at them for hours."

"What are you saying? Get it in writing? Lie to them on principle?"

"Nothing like that. See, there you're separating yourself. You're backing away, which is natural but it's the last thing you really want to do. What you really want is to get closer. You want to get so close that when they tell it their way, they have to tell it your way too."

Margarite Schrenk went to the refrigerator and poured herself a glass of mineral water. She drank it, went to the sink, washed it out, then stared hard at Johnny for a second and shook her head. It seemed that she might be crying just a little. She dabbed at her eyes with a dishtowel. Walking quickly over to Nick she slapped him hard in the face.

"Maybe this is good for me," she said. "Maybe when it's done it will be as good as anything I could ask for. But don't you even dream of taking credit for that."

Nick said nothing and somehow managed not to rub his cheek.

Johnny said, "It'd be good if you were over that."

"I'm over it, unless I change my mind. I just told them things and then came home. Therefore I am not close enough, is this what you wish to tell me?"

"How many ways could somebody twist what's happened so far? And there'd be nothing you could do?"

"I don't know. Maybe Nicholas could tell me."

Nick said, "What do you think will happen to those chemicals in

Mexico?"

"How would I know? Surely the FBI will have them seized."

Johnny said, "They could have asked the Mexicans. They haven't."

Margarite Schrenk stared. She went to the sink and got her glass.

Johnny said, "They're going to let it go through."

She turned around and stared some more.

Nick said, "It's by far the more serious crime."

Johnny spread his hands and shook his head. "What I was saying. It's the way they come off best. Not much of a trial the other way. Maybe no trial at all. Your husband has a good lawyer, he could walk. Not the company of course. Company pays through the nose, but see, it's all in the financial pages. But that stuff goes to Cuba, you get headlines. You get hours and hours of talk shows about really greedy foreigners with sexy wives, and then you get a trial that lasts forever."

"But we'll stop it," Nick said. "It'll never leave Mexico."

Margarite Schrenk poured another glass of mineral water. "You'll stop it," she said.

"No strings," Nick said. "No quid pro quo. Because we're truly rotten bastards but we're far, far better for you than the FBI."

Johnny said, "Uh, Mr. P? Something you don't know. We already stopped it, this morning."

Nick said, "Really."

Johnny said, "Fuentes made a call. I didn't get around to telling you."

Margarite Schrenk said, "Fuentes saved Alois."

Johnny said, "Who'd have believed it, huh?"

Margarite Schrenk said, "Diego Fuentes has already saved my husband, and you're telling me he did, and I haven't agreed to anything yet. Perhaps I'm in shock."

Nick said, "There's really nothing to agree to."

Margarite Schrenk said. "No?"

Johnny said, "Mr. P, you know, that's not strictly true. There's plenty of wrong ways left to play it."

Margarite Schrenk said, "But you'll help me be smart. You'll help me get closer to the FBI."

Johnny said, "You could be worried. You could call Mr. Hall for advice."

He picked up her phone and dialed it. He gave the phone to Mrs. Schrenk, who said, "Hello? Mr. Hall?"

She said, "Ten million dollars!"

She said, "To Cuba? Why, who could have imagined!"

She said, "Alois's loyal Mrs. Simpson? Of course. What a fantastic surprise. I must tell Alois and make him stop it, mustn't I?"

She said, "Nick Petraki? There?"

She said, "Then he made unbelievable time. He's here right now. Was there something you forgot to say to him?"

Then she hung up.

Chapter 47

Mrs. Schrenk's Right Arm
June 28, 2001

In Louisville Roddy cradled the phone and turned to Mrs. Simpson.

"See?" she said. "We're going to get him, aren't we?"

Roddy rubbed his hands together and couldn't stop grinning.

Mrs. Simpson pulled a CD ROM from its case and said, "Here. Let me borrow your computer a minute."

In Lexington Margarite Schrenk told Johnny and Nick, "Get the hell out of my house."

Nick grimaced and sighed.

Margarite Schrenk said, "I think I will tell the FBI you were here."

Johnny nodded as though she'd wished him well. "It's about a hundred to one you just did. You know, when it doesn't get to Cuba, the Cubans won't pay."

Margarite Schrenk said, "Then you are badly informed. The Cubans paid today."

Johnny said, "You already know better. Fuentes paid today, two-thirds what he owes, no vig. With Berlin's money that your husband lent him to prime the deal."

Margarite Schrenk said, "Do I have to beg? Go. Just go."

But Nick was puzzled. "What you have to ask yourself is, why did Alois have to lend Diego that money? When he could pay in a couple of days anyway, and they give terms to anyone else who asks? And why the early partial payment, which nobody expects?"

Johnny said, "Cubans pay on delivery, wouldn't they? Pretty much like everybody else."

Nick was even more puzzled. "So?"

"So if you waited for that, for the whole thing, then you sold your goods to Cuba, didn't you? You couldn't say you sold them to Mexico, not if nobody in Mexico ever paid for them. I mean if you were Mr. Schrenk. Be hard to explain, wouldn't it? But this way—"

Margarite Schrenk threw her glass across the room. She still hit a dozen or more service aces every time she played and most of the water was still in the glass when it hit the wall. It was amazing how much of that water landed everywhere and how small the little pieces of glass and ice were that skittered across the floor. She looked hungrily at Johnny and said, "I haven't slapped you yet. I really want to very much."

Johnny said, "Mrs. Schrenk? Don't do that. I'm not like him. I'm not like him at all. Get close to them, Mrs. Schrenk. Take what we brought you, put a ribbon on it and shove it down their chimney."

Margarite Schrenk said, "Everything's very simple for you, isn't it?"

Johnny said, "What we all need here is focus. I understand you got a personal problem too but you don't have to decide about him now. You can go or stay when the rest of this is over."

Margarite Schrenk opened her mouth to scream at him and Johnny waited for it. When it didn't come he finally wiped the mineral water off his face and said, "Go ahead, yell all you want. I'll go when

I've said this." He said it quietly and a bit resignedly, as though he was always hoping people would be sensible though they hardly ever are.

Margarite Schrenk said, "You know you're a monster, don't you?"

Johnny nodded. "I know why you got to believe that but it doesn't make me want to add to your trouble. It might help, you don't think about anything except we're getting you out of this crime you married into back when nobody but the government could say you knew any better. You got to know it's up to you to fix it. Your husband won't do nothing but play it out and then you both go down. Our way you keep your life or you take it with you somewhere but it's still your call. Give us an hour, okay? Two-fifteen, two-twenty'd be perfect. Nothing till then or nobody can control it, but don't wait any longer."

Then he went. Nick would have liked it explained it a little more but Johnny just turned and walked back out through the house. Nick followed, filling his head with Corporal Schrenk and the Dresden cups as he went.

It took Margarite Schrenk about five minutes to think it through every way there was. She went back over it for the ten it took to clean up the broken glass and mop the floor, but she hadn't missed anything and at last admitted that she really would have to get closer. She thought she might cry over that but in the end she didn't. She decided she should take some time to think about what that meant, when the opportunity for thinking arose once more. She hoped it would be soon.

In the car Nick suddenly wanted to talk a lot of nonsense but Johnny made him recite the script three times and they got past it. They pulled into HAGUS's lot with Nick in blue coveralls and cap.

Johnny got an armload of fluorescent tubes out of the back and loaded Nick up. Then he walked up three concrete steps and held the door for him and started to say something but Nick said, "I know. In the second side door, right, two lefts, second door marked 'Plant Protection, Market Research, Simpson.'"

Johnny said, "Key?"

Nick said, "In my hand," and walked into the building.

Forty minutes later Alois Schrenk got a call from home. He had something on the tip of his tongue but before he could say it his wife told him, "I've just spoken to Mr. Hall. I thought I'd let you deny receiving the ten million dollars before I called the FBI. But if you deny lending it to Fuentes yourself, I don't think I'll even listen."

By some odd coincidence, they got cut off just at that moment. As he was bellowing into his phone for Louisville she made one last call herself.

Chapter 48

Old Home Week – or The Lavender Box
June 28, 2001

At 2:18 the phone on Gonzales' borrowed desk rang and she listened to it for a moment. "You stay where you are," she told it. "We'll call you later."

Curtis looked up from his borrowed keyboard.

"Mrs. Schrenk," Gonzales said. "Schrenk knows the money's back and the idiot's really going to move it."

Nick had his cap off, his coveralls thrown over the back of a chair and his light bulbs stacked in a corner. His face was covered with sweat but at least his hands didn't shake. It was the same old Himmelskirch – Mrs. Simpson's office was about six feet square. He struggled with the mouse thing and eventually typed "n:\public\petraki." In all it seemed to take quite a while because he'd forgotten how a keyboard is laid out, he kept pressing "enter" instead of "tab," the n: drive was in Louisville and T1 lines aren't all they're cracked up to be. But in the end a lavender box, exactly the shade she wore to bed, appeared on Mrs. Simpson's screen. It said, "Auntie is here. Be at peace." After that he thought he almost was but continued to sweat anyway.

At 2:25 Roddy got a frantic call from Schrenk. He listened for several seconds and said, "I really haven't had time to look today." Then he hung up and pressed the do not disturb button on his phone. Mrs. Simpson shut his door. Soon they could see people taking calls and turning toward Roddy's office with doubtful looks. One worried woman walked to up to Roddy's window and mouthed *Schrenk* a half dozen times but he gaily waved her off and Mrs. Simpson merely beamed at her and after a moment she went away. Mrs. Simpson lowered the blinds.

At 2:35 Mrs. Simpson called the local FBI. She gave the phone to Roddy and he asked if Agent Curtis was there. Then he asked if Agent Gonzales was there. Then he asked if he could leave a message for either of them and, when pressed, decided on Curtis because his swagger reminded him of his new friend JW. Could they tell him please that Mr. Hall had called and that thing they were waiting for had happened and the other thing they wanted him to hold off on when it did, he hadn't done that yet? Could they tell him that, and it's spelled Hall, plain old Hall like you walk down? And oh yes the guy they didn't want to talk about was in town today – maybe they should tell him that too.

Curtis and Gonzales had had one script each for Roddy John Hall and Margarite Schrenk and they had had to junk them both. Not entirely believing that the third time is the charm, for Alois Schrenk they settled on a pose of excessive professional courtesy from which they could branch off into many other parts from their repertoire. They got to Schrenk's office ten minutes after he got through to Roddy John Hall. It was a smart, low, red brick building with no sign and the minimum of landscaping, though what it had cost money. The parking was all in front and one car was a silver Mercedes, license well memorized. The front door to the building was open.

Gonzales said, "Front door open," and Curtis agreed that it was.

Then his cell phone went off. He listened a second and said, "Thank you." To Gonzales he said, "Hall is heard from."

"Damn," Gonzales said, "they can cover their asses, can't they?"

HAGUS had most of the place and directly in front of them HAGUS was spelled out in big brass letters over wide-open double doors.

"Office door open," Gonzales said and this time Curtis repeated that and the time into a small recorder that he pulled from his jacket pocket. Inside there was a counter and a perky young woman in a headset who was saying, "...they confirm it, Mr. Schrenk." Gonzales stopped but Curtis told her, "No time," and they were around the corner bellowing, "Mr. Schrenk!" After that, the act they'd brought was as useless as the other two.

In the lavender box on the screen in Mrs. Simpson's office a shimmering hammer and sickle had appeared, and under it the legend, "On the whole, I'd rather be nuking Philadelphia..." Nick giggled insanely.

Schrenk was out of his chair and advancing. He thought about asking for a warrant but refrained because he might not make it back to his keyboard if they had one. He settled for demanding ID, though his wife had described them well enough.

Gonzales said, "Mexico has impounded fifteen million dollars' worth of Nematotal. It seems it was imported for domestic use and certain fees were waived. Then somebody tried to turn it around."

"Send it back here?" Schrenk asked.

"Send it to Cuba, of course," Curtis said

Schrenk was not impressed. "Then what does the government of

Cuba say? Do they not protest the loss of their goods?"

Curtis said, "They say nothing, of course. We could wait a long time before they announce they have worms in their tobacco."

"If we had time I could explain supply and demand to you. Then you might see how foolish that is."

"If we had even more time I could tell you about lines of credit to distressed third world countries run by crazy old men. The Bureau prefers accounting or law but my degree was in economics."

Schrenk said, "Then perhaps over coffee or cocktails sometime we could discuss this interesting hypothesis."

Gonzales said, "There's nothing hypothetical about it, Mr. Schrenk. The Mexicans say it was going to Cuba and your wife says you knew it too."

In Louisville Mrs. Simpson picked up Roddy's mouse, clicked on the file called \public\petraki, and deleted it. Then she dialed the phone. "Urgent for Aunt Marsha," she said. "Petraki's been to see Big Bird. Big Bird thinks he's headed for the bunker."

In Lexington Curtis said, "Mr. Schrenk. We don't have a warrant. This is your office. You can do what you want but don't begin to imagine that the testimony we give could be impeached."

Schrenk said, "You are certainly correct. What is that to me?"

Gonzales said, "So the ten million dollars you got from Mexico today is evidence of a crime and as soon as we find a judge we *will* seize it, sir."

Schrenk sat back down.

Curtis said, "If you do anything to prevent that there will be grave consequences for you personally."

"Mr. Curtis," Schrenk said, "Miss Gonzales. I know my duty as well as you know yours."

In Louisville Mrs. Simpson said, "I have to go now, Roddy. Remember the time because they do know how to check." But Roddy was already far, far away. He just grinned and grinned and when she slipped out she saw no reason to raise the blinds.

Schrenk swiveled the monitor a bit to shield it from Curtis and Gonzales and typed his password. For years his passwords had been his birthday, his mother's birthday, her anniversary, then his, then their telephone number in 1959 when, at last, they'd finally got one. Then Berlin had sent a memo on computer security, requiring random passwords, regularly changed. The memo was in English because it had been translated for distribution in the US and the choice of *regular* where *frequent* was meant was an incalculable blunder. You do not say regular to Alois Schrenk unless you mean it. Nobody would have been in that room if Berlin had not said regular. He changed his password every second Monday and on that basis even Nicholas Pope's air travel had been arranged. In truth, Schrenk's passwords were never entirely random but they were legal within the parameters set down by corporate security. They were legal because they were utter solipsisms. This was the second week for P_b_D_b, which had succeeded S_p_B_d and would itself give way to b_D_b_D on Monday. All three strung together stood for Sächsische, Pariser, Bayerische, Dorfer, Bergische and Darmstädter, but only Alois Schrenk would ever know that. Like all of his passwords, these were the names of streets in the Charlottenburg section of Berlin that the boy Alois once walked in the same order. No one who stood on any of those streets today would think to walk them that way but at one time that was how you went for bread. First you walked through several dozen expired passwords to arrive at Sächsische. You avoided the crater that entirely blocked Dorfer between Sächsische and

Bergische. You avoided the heaps of rubble that made parts of Bergische and Darmstädter impassible. You especially hurried past the place on Bayerische where Erika would take the Negro GI's into the alley. Then you wandered through many, many future passwords, and finally you got to stand in line at Frau Wilhelm's tiny bakery. Alois Schrenk changed his password every two weeks and never repeated one because it was forbidden. In a few months he would have to turn around and pick his way back home; he would pretend it was one of those days when he managed to buy a loaf, or even two. In a year or two he'd finally get back home and then he'd have to start walking to school, but by then he would be old enough. He feared that in about two thousand and six he might run out of walks entirely. He clicked his mouse twice, moved it around and then clicked it again. He began to type.

The lavender box said, "Berlin plots and seethes but Zhukov is relentless."

"Mr. Schrenk," Gonzales said, "you're on notice."

Schrenk stopped typing and stared at the clock. It was not a happy stare. The clock said two forty-four and the wire closed at three.

Curtis pulled out his cell phone and pushed a button. "I need a wire block, fast."

Shrenk clicked his mouse again and slumped.

The lavender box said, "Liftoff." Nick stood up and started running in place.

Gonzales said, "What did you just do?"

The lavender box said, "Request for confirmation intercepted. Turning it around."

Schrenk stood up and turned off his monitor.
Curtis said, "You sorry son of a bitch."

Nick stopped running and picked up the phone. The lavender box said, "Acknowledged. Vanishing now. Run on home." Mrs. Simpson's screen turned solid blue.

Schrenk's intercom buzzed and everybody jumped.

"It's gone," Nick told them. "Me too, Alois. I switched it all back, okay?"

A door slammed on the other side of the wall. Curtis ran though aisles of cubicles to a window, Schrenk following, Gonzales heading for the front door. At the window Schrenk froze. He boggled. He turned scarlet and screamed, "Petraki!"

Curtis took off, ranting into his phone while he ran. Gonzales had several steps on him but a dusty black car was peeling out of the lot before she was through the front door. The car took two fast lefts and she didn't even get the plate. Curtis was now beside her, still yelling at his phone. He ran to the first corner, saw nothing and finished his call. "That's it. Left on Magnolia Trace, then anywhere." He hung up just as Gonzales' phone rang. "Anastasia reports the trickster in your area," it said.

"Not anymore," she told it, and turned to Curtis. "What the hell's a wire block?"

"I just invented it. It helps idiots make up their minds."

Then Schrenk was there, demanding, "Why didn't you shoot him? Don't you realize what he's done?"

"*You*," Curtis said, "have the right to remain silent. Since it's one of the few rights you'll ever see again, I suggest you exercise it to the full."

"You have the right," Gonzales continued, "to…"

Johnny turned down an alley, then slid to a stop ten feet from a silver convertible with its top up. "Get your bag," he told Nick, then got out, knelt behind the convertible, pulled a key out of the tailpipe. Unlocking the driver's door, he waved Nick into the seat. "Touch the wheel, the door, the shift, I want prints all over the dash and seat. There, some more there." Nick touched and grabbed for a minute or more before Johnny pulled on a pair of pigskin gloves, wiped the key and said, "In the back now. You get to ride in your own car at last, sir."

In the back Nick found a shopping bag full of clothes. He pulled them out and sorted them on the seat.

"Get dressed," Johnny said. "Try to stay down, Mr. P. Just this once the ladies need to miss the thrill."

Mr. P again – see, everything really was all right.

After Nick changed Johnny pulled into a drive-in and made Nick get in the front. Then he rolled to the window and bought them each a cheeseburger. Eating, to Nick, was like swallowing lead but he was managing it when Johnny's phone rang. Aunt Maggie told him that Amy just had a baby boy and there in the waiting room she was sure she'd seen what's his name, number forty-four for the Falcons. Johnny told Nick, "You're on the four-forty for Atlanta. We need to make it in fifty-one minutes, which I got a hundred says is thirteen more than we need." Twenty minutes later Aunt Maggie called to say that a woman at the hospital just had triplets but she couldn't see them because she wasn't family. Johnny said, "Three of them just showed but they're waiting for the wrong guy." With a bet on the line Johnny timed the drive so well that he could park exactly thirteen minutes before pulling up and dropping Nick at departures. While they waited Nick felt an urgent need to gush and chatter but Johnny spent the whole time arguing with Aunt Maggie about the menu for the picnic.

At the terminal Nick gave him his hundred and said, "Tell me this isn't the best part for you."

Johnny kissed the bill and said, "Have a nice flight, Mr. P. You did good. See you around."

The metal detectors were sensitive this time and Nick's belt buckle set them off. He had to stand with his arms up while a jovial young woman ran a wand up and down him.

"If that isn't working," he offered, "I have just about enough time for a strip search."

"That's the kind of talk," she said, winking, "people say supposed to offend you. Go on now, get on back to your wife."

Nick was still grinning over it when he heard a not loud but thoroughly penetrating contralto.

"*Je*sus, sugar, think you could have cut it any closer? I was beg*inn*ing to *think* you fell *in*."

Chapter 49

Hölle and Teufel
July 4, 2001

Hölle said, "You're comfortable, I suppose?"

Schrenk said, "I should go home. This is undignified."

Teufel said, "Journalists at your door are undignified. Police cars in your driveway are undignified. Better class motels are at worst a trifle boring."

Hölle said, "When I type this up I'll say you were quite content and grateful for the company's solicitude. Surely that's what you'd want me to report."

"Of course it is. What could I have been thinking?"

"And what," Teufel asked, "could you have been thinking at your office that day? That it is suddenly illegal to sell pesticides to Mexico? That even politically appointed judges could possibly think so? And why on earth did you send the whole forty-six million? They told you they only wanted Fuentes's ten."

"I was imagining this interview but somewhat differently. I was imagining you asking why I'd left them anything to seize, and not having an answer, and then your usual pleasantries."

Hölle asked, "Do you think the FBI knew you'd send it all?"

"How should I know? I didn't know myself until the last second.

But they said they were going to impound ten million, not which ten million. They said–"

"Oh, we know what they said. They even *admit* it, you see. Extraordinary, isn't it?"

"No," Hölle said, "it's unprecedented. No one can remember anything like it."

"You mean saying they did it," Teufel protested. "Not doing it, surely."

"Yes, saying it, of course."

"But still, it may have got them their crime – if they insist upon it. Impeding their investigation is such an anticlimax after all they've been leaking, though."

Hölle told Schrenk, "There might even be sympathy for you, you see. Admitting they browbeat you. Bragging how diligently you were harassed. Perhaps enough sympathy to make prosecution a problem. It's almost as if they'd arranged it, in fact. You do see that, don't you?"

Schrenk said, "Oh, that would make sense. Go to such elaborate lengths to be left with nothing. What a useful way for police to spend their time."

"Nothing," Hölle said.

"*Verzeihung?*"

"You said nothing. What an interesting way to describe forty-six million dollars."

Teufel said, "Ninety-eight column centimeters in the *Wall Street Journal.*"

Hölle said, "Another grand blow against Castro. Half the Congressmen in Florida are claiming credit. Those are the friends you've left us. The other half want war."

Teufel said, "Did you know that their anonymous source tried to tell the *New York Times* that the figure was *sixty-one* million? He included the price of the product you see. The *Times'* man was enthralled by the sophistry but he printed their snide little sound bite anyway."

"All right," Schrenk sighed, "tell me."

Hölle said, "You really haven't heard it? I must say, you might follow this more closely."

Teufel said, "Let me be sure I remember. Yes, I have it. *Whatever the courts eventually decide, at least they fined themselves pretty good.*"

Hölle said, "Do you still think that is nothing, Mr. Schrenk?"

Schrenk said, "And Petraki? What do they say about him?"

Teufel said, "Now there's your nothing, Mr. Schrenk. Isn't that peculiar? Except to us and the police, they have nothing at all to say about him."

Hölle said, "Of course, in some ways you can understand it. For a desperate criminal, Petraki behaved most unusually."

Teufel said, "He seemed more a spectator than a participant, in fact. You hear the story and think at once of guardian angels."

"And here, of course, I ask, 'What story?'"

"Oh," Teufel said, "not really a story, I suppose. Just little bits of this and that, that couldn't possibly be true. He visited Hall and said nothing at all. He visited your wife and said even less. At your house he even brought a featureless friend who was silence itself."

Hölle said, "He turned in his rental car seventy-five minutes after he left you."

Teufel said, "But an hour and a half before, while according to all the best people he must still have been enjoying your hospitality, he checked into his flight."

"Which took off," Hölle said, "a quarter hour before he returned the car."

"The FBI are ever so sure," Teufel added, "that he wasn't on that plane. But, do you know, I have the distinct impression that not many people believe them.”

“For instance,” Hölle said, “there are the police. They manage to imply a great many doubts. Then, of course, there are us.”

Schrenk looked at Hölle and then at Teufel and, just as Hölle had said, he saw no signs of belief in either of them. “But I saw him. He was there. They saw him too, those government agents.”

At last Teufel’s smile turned pensive. “Yes, so you say. You saw him and so did both of your wife’s new friends. They still say so too. I must say everyone is sticking to the story but, then, it’s early yet.”

“They go everywhere together,” Hölle said. “Did you know that? Last night they took her to dinner and when they parted, she gave the black woman a kiss. She’ll get you off, I think, but only with them of course.”

“It’s all so *unusual,* isn’t it?” Teufel remarked and shook his head like he’d never believe appearances again.

Then Alois Schrenk saw the rest of his life quite clearly. Whether he saw all of it or not, the next few days were easy. What he lacked was anything to say, because he’d been explaining it for forty years and nobody who didn’t know it already had yet to get it from him.

But, anyway, Teufel had only paused for effect. “The Cubans then. Do you know, it’s almost unbelievable. Of course Berlin made inquiries. We are innocent after all, we can’t have them blaming us. But they say the most amazing thing. They say they haven’t ordered a liter of product and have no foreseeable need for any.”

“Petraki,” Schrenk said, “and Fuentes…” but no one seemed to hear.

“But what’s most unusual of all is that the authorities in Zurich think they’ve identified the man that opened the account. They’ll never prosecute of course but they traced him because he was already on their books. As a suspected courier for the GRU.”

Schrenk said, “My God.”

"Indeed," Teufel agreed. "Then we have Mrs. Simpson. Could she have seen you type your password?"

"Mrs. Simpson? Certainly not. She is a model employee in every respect and she has never stood within five meters of my desk while I type it."

"Only she's nowhere to be found, you see, and the FBI don't seem the least concerned. Binoculars, perhaps? Little opera glasses she could hide in her purse?"

Schrenk said, "My God."

"Indeed," Teufel agreed.

"What you must understand," Hölle said, "is that you'll never spend a penny of it. However much they said they'd let you keep. However much they pay as a reward for services like this. Even if a hundred and forty thousand is all there is, though I'd hate to think so little would suffice."

"Your wife could have it, though," Teufel said. "There's not much we could do about that. If I were you, I'd call her right now, before I had time to get my hopes up again. Tell her to just take it and go."

"Tell her," Hölle said, "to run all the way to your friend Fuentes. Tell her we've grown old and lazy. Tell her that if she runs far enough, we may give up on her."

"But," Schrenk said, "you can't really believe—"

He bit it off and thought, *so this is how people turn into groveling dolts.* "Excuse me," he said. "Of course you believe that. Of course you always will." Choosing the message he'd prefer them to misunderstand next, he resolved to be silent for quite some time. With kind of a bow and a sweep of his hand, he invited them onward, then silently left for Prussia while Teufel tried four different smiles and Hölle glared incredulously. Then, just as though Schrenk was still protesting, Hölle gathered himself up to finish his speech. He'd been working on it for a very long time and by now it was much too good to skip just because no one was listening.

Chapter 50

Nicholas Petraki
July 14, 2001

The seaplane plopped down and waddled up to its buoy and Anne Marie yelled to Dr. Bondieu to start the charcoal. Two cruise ships were anchored outside the harbor, six dozen yachts were scattered where they wished and so the harbor was alive with small craft shuttling to and fro and tenders running tourists to the *quai*. The little speedboat with its rooster tail way up did its best to upset them, zooming out to the plane to pick up its passenger, then, instead of heading in toward the *quai* as usual, zooming off to one of the new private docks at the far end of Belle Vièrge. As the man hauled himself up the steps the doctor approached. Most of his extended family stayed behind to watch the kids but the three eldest women went with him.

"*M'sieu Johnny. Ca va?*"

"It do indeed. How you doing, Doc?"

"Passably. You think you can satisfy us with millions? Next time bring me nurses. All but one must be competent and that one must be exceptionally pretty and kind hearted."

"You truly are your father's son," Claudine said.

"And you'd have it some other way?" Dr. Bondieu asked.

"Indeed no, but it is not for the pretty ones to complain."

"Where's it going exactly?" Johnny asked the doctor.

"Right there, at the end of your property, of course. *L'Hôpital Belle Vièrge* sounds innocent enough for a tourist with a timorous digestion I think. Respectful. Reassuring. Redolent of religious consolation. *We* have always found it so and we value all our visitors very highly, M'sieu Johnny, not just you."

"And of course," Colette said, "the most important visitors will have their own clinic, right next door."

"The *Clinique Philippe Bondieu*," Anne Marie said, and started to cry. Anne Marie had taken to crying in her forties, about the time she began to get wealthy by local standards, and neither she nor her friends took much notice of it anymore.

"Where prices will be absurdly high," young Dr. Bondieu agreed, "and even the most trivial symptoms will be subjected to searching tests."

"Leave them with pocket change, okay?" Johnny said. "Let them spend their dying hours at my tables."

"You're a bad man, M'sieu Johnny," Dr. Bondieu said.

"A very bad man," his mother agreed.

"A man of surpassing cunning and evil," *her* mother said. "So like my husband."

"We do not deserve you," Anne Marie said, and began to cry again.

"Will you stop it?" Johnny demanded. "You know we raked off half for bogus expenses you can't question and I took half what was left as profit? You have any idea how much that was?"

"Yes," Claudine said, "enough to build three more hospitals and three more clinics and make three islands we'll never see very happy. To hell with them."

"They can flatter me all they want but Doc, you'd better

remember where to get your light bulbs and linens."

"Oh, you are a terrible man," Anne Marie wailed. "Please tell us more stories of your wickedness, that we may despise you more completely."

"And carpet. How do you say indoor/outdoor? I got a shitload. How do you say that? I need to dump it. *J'ai besoin de vous emmerder en tapis volé.*"

"Thank you, beast. Don't stop. If only Nicholas could hear."

"Where *is* he?"

"He'll be along," Claudine said. "He *says* he had to get his sparkplug changed again but I think he's down at the bank, visiting the money. They have a new redhead. He is almost as bad a man as you."

"Oh, he is far worse," Dr. Bondieu said. "He tries to steal one's mother, merely because she is beautiful. Then he goes out and brings back millions for our hospital but only because she makes him. It's well known what an evil man will do when a beautiful woman makes unconditional demands. Just think where we'd be if she'd ever given in to him!"

"And who's to say that she has not?" his grandmother demanded with considerable indignation. "This is your mother you're speaking of as if she were some feebleminded nun!"

"Yes, as beautiful as us, Grandmother, but, alas, without our brains."

"You hear that, *Maman*?" Claudine said. "His brains, his beauty?"

"Well," Colette said, "it is true that I may be at fault. He didn't get either of them from his grandfather."

"My grandfather was not as intelligent and beautiful as we?"

"Ask that one," Colette said. "She's been painting him for thirty years and he grows uglier each season."

"Sure," said Johnny, "but he's up to eight hundred dollars a head.

Where the *hell* is Nicky?"

Claudine said, "He'll be along."

Anne Marie said, "True, he always does appear."

Dr. Bondieu said, "Yes but not necessarily before all the fish burn up."

Colette said, "He's had cold dinners before. Thank God he has never tried to fish. He would sail off one day without his boat."

Claudine said, "The tide would bring him back, *Maman*. He'd float back on his oar and wonder why he was wet."

Dr. Bondieu said, "Even he knows drowned fishermen never come home again."

But for no reason he could name, Johnny felt himself blush, and Claudine, who knew a lifeguard when she saw one, winked at him. She said, "Yes, but he would never notice that it was *he* who is drowning. He's drowned so many times before, you see. Or we see, if you don't."

Sound and smell of sizzling snapper, garlic, oil, thyme and oregano wafting past on driftwood smoke. Pop and hiss of beer bottles shedding their tops. Crescendo of many children playing many different games at once. Sun plunging into the bay.

Johnny said, "Let's eat. I'll take care of his cut. Some weeks it's almost all I get to do."

About the Author

Many years ago the author, strictly obeying the most proper of instructions, found himself presented with the opportunity to commit the very theft that is the root of this story. All of the people involved and all but three of the circumstances were utterly different from those described here, but those three circumstances were the bare beginnings of this book.

The first of these is the trivial fact that, like the story's irredeemably bent hero, the author was charged with teaching a computer how to pretend to be an accountant.

The second concerns the actual method of the crime itself, which would have gone just as set down here, had the author found the... *courage* will do, I suppose... to actually attempt it.

The third, which is the true inspiration of the story, is that in preparation for a routine audit, the author's boss ordered him to "think like a thief" in search of vulnerabilities. The author had never heard these magical words before and found them thrilling. To be *ordered*, amid all the usual frantic drudgery of business, to daydream about daring crimes, to imagine himself the daring rogue who dares to do them! It would have been churlish not to have spent every available hour at the task.

When the author revealed the exciting possibilities to his boss, they retired to the bar downstairs to discuss it over a beer (things really were different in those days). They tried to poke holes in every part of it and finally concluded that the first stage, the theft itself, would almost certainly work, but that the next bit – surviving the ensuing years – was simply too scary to think about. The boss said something like, *You know, I've always thought that everyone has his price, but now I see that mine's a whole lot higher than I thought.* The author concurred in no little wonder, and to this day believes that his complete absence of temptation revealed things about his character that are far less pleasant to contemplate than the banal, instinctive honesty everyone credited him with at the time.

I'd like to thank my proofreader R. B., my editor R. Berenbaum and, especially, my long suffering agent, Robbie.

www.ingramcontent.com/pod-product-compliance
Lightning Source LLC
Chambersburg PA
CBHW051517260626
47170CB00003B/656